"...well-written, with excellent details that create a sharp picture of each time period and location...Johnson maintains suspense throughout, and the story is always engaging ...A well-crafted book that weaves together historical facts and fiction to explore conspiracies behind Lincoln's assassination."
— *Kirkus Reviews*

"Rich in authentic details, populated with real and fictional characters whose humanity and passion ring true, thick with biting suspense and enthralling intrigue, and brims with originality and fresh perspectives on a heroic era that never ceases to fascinate devotees of historical fiction. Highly recommended!"
— *The Columbia Review of Books & Film*

"This outstanding historical novel follows one man's quest to clear his father's name after Lincoln's assassination."
— *Foreword Clarion Reviews*

"...historical fiction at its best...a top recommendation for any enthusiast of historical fiction who like their characters to match settings through realistic portraits and insights from the past."
— *Midwest Book Review*

"...fans of historical conspiracies will enjoy reading *In Search of Tom Candy*..."
— *Reader Reviews*

"...a passionate story of mystery and history...a great read."
— *Portland Book Review*

Book design by:
Arbor Books, Inc.
www.arborbooks.com

Printed in the United States of America

First Edition Printing

In Search of Tom Candy
Dairl M. Johnson

1. Title   2. Author   3. Fiction

ISBN: 978-0-9891359-1-7
LCCN: 2015908835

IN SEARCH OF
TOM
CANDY

Dairl M. Johnson

To my sons and daughter, Jeff, Glenn and Jill,
and to my granddaughter Mia

ONE

The Search Begins

1904, New York City

John Stanton was ready.

"Keys, wallet, watch," he muttered, patting his hands down his body, ensuring he had everything he needed. Opening his brown leather briefcase one more time, he checked that all his papers were in place. Although he'd reviewed them a thousand times and could recite the information they contained by heart, it wouldn't hurt to have them as backup should his presentation begin to fall on deaf ears. His fellow reporters could be harsh; they trusted the written word and little else.

Grabbing his black homburg and pushing it onto his head, he went out and locked the door behind him. Once downstairs, he stepped out from the doorway of the boarding house but then stopped short. Bringing his forearm up to his face, he pocketed his nose and mouth in the crook of his elbow as if that would save him from the stench of the streets. He'd been in New York City for six months, and already he hated it. Too crowded, too bustling, too noisy. Too many strangers with perpetual scowls on their faces.

And the smells…dear God, the smells. Urban transportation had grown exponentially in the last decade. Electric trains crisscrossed the city, and gasoline-powered automobiles chugged through the newly christened Times Square. There was even an underground train system getting ready to open toward the end of the year. Still, work animals were the main mode of transportation. More than a hundred thousand horses and mules lived among the million human souls in Manhattan and the outer boroughs, and the evidence was everywhere: Piles of manure littered the streets, infested with flies and making the air very unpleasant to breathe. Add to that the scents of urine, harness oil, and hay constantly wafting from the livery stables on every other block, and any inhalation at all could be downright nauseating.

John headed east on Wall Street at a good clip, his long legs carrying him quickly toward his destination and away, he hoped, from the noxious cloud that enveloped him. Few others were out this early in the morning—five thirty, giving him half an hour to get to the office. Surely it was more than enough time.

Turning north onto Broad Street, his boots—gray lace-ups he'd bought at Macy's with his first paycheck, the most fashionable things he'd ever owned—slipped a bit on the cobblestones. He caught himself and kept going. All those years of rugby in college had made him agile, fast on his feet, and fairly rugged as well, with a strong but lithe body. It also taught him to be aggressive and opportunistic when he had to be. John Stanton was a tough competitor and did not like to play by the rules, a trait that did not go over well with his surly editor-in-chief, T. Burton Blackwood. Picturing the man's face—his heavy, dark mustache framing his eternal frown; the daggers that shot from his eyes—John quickened his pace. He knew the wrath he'd face if he were just a minute late.

After a couple blocks, he decided to hire a horse-drawn carriage to guarantee a prompt arrival. Stopping at a corner, he raised his hand in the air, waving to catch the attention of a coach. As the driver pulled over, his dark, silver-dappled mare huffing and shaking out her blond mane, John backed up a little and nearly landed in a mound of dung at the curb. It was more than one animal could produce, leading him to believe this was the work of an enterprising cottage business he had heard about: Residents of the city's wealthy neighborhoods would pay haulers to collect their horses' waste and dump it in poorer areas in the middle of the night. This made the problem twice as bad and turned the streets into cesspools whenever it rained. John always felt bad for the ladies then, as they suffered the indignity of trailing the hems of their long skirts through it. Those with trains made out even worse; the extra fabric acted like a sponge, pulling clumps of the fetid waste out of the puddles and moats.

He surely suffered from the journalist's curse, as his friend

George had called it—always paying too much attention to details.

"Nassau and Spruce, please," he told the driver as he hopped up into the open cab. The man—older, pot-bellied, a tangle of white hair sticking out from under his tattered, black bowler hat—nodded gruffly in response. His coat was well worn, shiny at the elbows and collar, and his hands bore a thick layer of calluses from handling the reins from sunrise to sunset every day. Quite Dickensian, John mused as he settled back onto the carriage's cracked leather seat and the driver let out a "Hyah!" The horse, with one last snuffling snort, clopped away, bringing them out into the light flow of early morning traffic.

"Bitter Fighting at Democratic State Convention in Albany!"

"Long Island Farmer Runs Off Trespassing Fox Hunters at Gunpoint!"

"Thieves Take Twenty Thousand Dollars in Cash While Harlem Man Sleeps!"

John descended from the carriage and right into a swarm of newsboys peddling the early edition, calling out headlines to entice buyers, each more lurid than the last.

"Three cents, three cents!" one of them cried at him, holding out a folded-up copy of the *Tribune* as John fished a few coins from his pocket to pay the driver, not to purchase a paper.

"Sorry, I don't need one," he said to the boy, who couldn't

have been more than eleven or twelve years old. John recognized him; this block was his regular beat. His and a half
dozen other children who should have been in school, not out
here working. John felt a great deal of pity for them. Hands
and faces smudged with newsprint ink; gaunt bodies; and an
anxious, hungry look in their eyes. Another boy, a regular too,
had one leg and leaned on a feeble wooden crutch, holding a
stack of papers that must have weighed twenty pounds under
his free arm. John's childhood hadn't been ideal—his father
had died soon before he was born, leaving his mother to
struggle with raising John alone—but it was paradise compared to what he saw here. Every morning the scene tugged
at him, but as always he tipped the brim of his hat down over
his eyes and ran the gauntlet to the building where he worked:
154 Printing House Square, headquarters of the *New-York
Tribune.*

Inside, the lobby was quiet and cool. Most of the staff
would not arrive for another couple hours. John went to the
elevator; this building was among the first in the city to have
one. Working on the ninth floor, he was thankful for it. He
opened the wooden door and then the metal gate, stepped
in, and slammed both closed. No operator at this hour, so
he gripped the crank at the side of the car and pushed it forward. The elevator rose shakily, grinding as it climbed up
to the top floor—though it wouldn't be the top for long. A
two-year construction project to add another nine floors and
a clock tower was underway. John had learned to tune out
the constant hammering and clanging of iron beams.

When the elevator neared his stop, John brought the lever

on the crank back, rolling the contraption to a halt. He pulled the doors open and stepped out…into a large and empty newsroom. Had the meeting already started? Was he late? John reached into the pocket of his dark-gray waistcoat and pulled out his watch. Ten minutes to six. He was early. So where had everybody gone?

With long strides he made his way through the maze of desks all strewn with papers, black Remington typewriters with half-written stories in their platens. It looked like his coworkers had all up and left, no time even to take their belongings. Such was the nature when Blackwood called: all those in earshot dropped everything and ran.

The door of the meeting room was shut. John paused just outside, closing his eyes and rubbing them, preparing for the lashing Blackwood would undoubtedly serve him even though he was not late and had no idea what was going on. The man did not tolerate excuses, not even when they were actually the truth.

John smoothed out his black coat and trousers then doffed his hat and raked his fingers through his short, brown hair, giving it a crude part. One deep breath, and he grasped the door handle and pushed it open. Inside, a dozen sets of eyes turned toward him and all speaking ceased.

"Good morning, good morning," he said quietly to each of his colleagues as he scuttled toward the one empty chair. Of course it was right next to Blackwood, undoubtedly because no one wanted to be that close. Once seated, he looked up at his boss, who stood like a monolith at the head of the table, looking down his strong, broad nose in silence.

John waited for him to speak, but nothing came. So he cleared his throat, sat up straight, and said, "Good morning, sir."

The group gaze shifted from John to the editor-in-chief, nervous for his response. Again there was none; he continued staring coolly at John, hands clasped behind his back, lips pursed tight.

When he finally did speak, it was slowly and through clenched teeth. "You are late."

Now the reporters all glanced at one another. They knew that tone of voice. Blackwood was a tyrant, running the newsroom as if it were his own little kingdom. He was rude, sullen, terse, and his criticism stung like a whip.

But he didn't scare John. "Actually, I'm early," he replied with a hint of a smile. He took out his watch again, held it up, and tapped his finger on the face. "See here, five fifty-three." Then he just sat there, looking up at his boss.

The stalemate seemed to last an eternity, neither man willing to avert his eyes first. Then Blackwood blew a puff of air out his nose, a wheeze of contempt and disgust.

"Everyone else was here. So we began without you." He turned back to the table. "As I was saying…"

John stopped listening at that point. Normally, he paid attention to the updates Blackwood gave at the beginning of every reporters meeting, but today he was preoccupied. His leather briefcase sat on his lap, his arms encircling it as if he were afraid someone would snatch it up and run. He looked around at the other men, but none looked back, too enrapt in the tyrant editor's speech. Half were bootlickers; the rest were just plain scared of losing their jobs. John, perhaps, should have fallen into the latter camp. It had taken him years to get this position. He'd applied to all the big papers in the city as well as in Chicago and Boston, where he was from. He'd sent writing samples and pieces he'd done for other publications; he'd written letters professing his journalistic skills and, at times, borderline begging for a chance. The *Tribune* had been the first to agree to take him on. Or to have pity on him; John was never sure.

Either way, he supposed, he had Blackwood to thank for the opportunity, though no one would know the editor-in-chief had ever wanted John there by the way he treated him. Blackwood hated everyone, but from day one he had seemed to hold a special ire for John. He was a miserable old man, self-centered and, in his own mind, superior to all around him. Still, John did not understand it. He was, today notwithstanding, always on time; he was an ace researcher and could get publishable quotes out of even the most stoic witnesses. He was thirty-six, a bit on the older side for this trade, but kept up with and often surpassed his peers who were just out of school. And, truth be told, his writing was much better.

"All right then, Mr. Stanton."

Blackwood's gravelly, basso voice caught John's attention. He stood up abruptly, holding the briefcase to his chest.

"Yes," he stammered, "ah, yes. Well. Mr. Blackwood, I do have a story to propose today. I have been doing a little research—"

He set the case down on the glossy, dark wood table, opened it, and took out its contents: a stack of mismatched papers at least six inches thick, some bent at the corners, some newspaper sheets ripped at the fold, the top page stained with coffee-cup rings. A rubber band splotched with inky finger-prints held the whole thing together. John set it down with a thump, and the other reporters snickered.

He looked up at them and smiled. He'd forgotten they were even there. This presentation and proposal were all he thought about; this was his chance, he knew, to pen an exposé—a big story that could define his career. And, more important, it might answer some very personal questions for him. This was the reason he'd wanted to be a journalist: to find out finally what had happened to his father.

But, first things first.

"It all started with an Englishman named Tom Candy," he began, just as he had practiced so many times in the mirror above the chest of drawers in his room. Unbinding his notes and riffling through them, he pulled out a page and gave it to Blackwood—a story from the *Tribune* fifty years earlier. "As you'll see there, he was a pioneer in the American cattle trade. In fact, he drove a herd of longhorns from Texas to New York, which had never been done before. Afterward he—"

"Not interested," Blackwood replied, dropping the paper and letting it float down onto the tabletop. He did not look at John. "That's all for today, men. Get to work."

And with that the meeting adjourned. As the other reporters filed out, they looked at John, who stood there dumbfounded.

"Sir, you didn't even hear my proposal," he said.

"I don't need to," Blackwood said icily as he collected his

own papers and the write-ups of the other men's ideas, all of which he had accepted. "I know that story. Just like anyone who was alive and breathing in eighteen fifty-four." He glanced at John, one bushy eyebrow raised. "And I guarantee you, no one is interested anymore. It's ancient history. Drop it."

He walked out of the room and slammed the door, the final punctuation on his rejection of John's story.

"He wouldn't even let me speak." John leaned back, and the old, oak office chair in which he sat let out a sharp creak. He pulled his fingers through his hair again, smoothing it and erasing the part he'd made less than half an hour ago.

"Mm," grunted Bill, who sat to John's right, in front of a Linotype—one in a long row of the machines. The *Tribune* had to employ a whole group of typesetters just to get its editions ready to print on time. These men spent hours each day in this poorly lit basement of the building, trying to interpret the reporters' writings as best they could. Bill, at the first machine in the row, held in one hand a paper scribbled over in black ink, and he squinted through his half-moon glasses, trying to make sense of the reporter's scrawl. Finally he got a word, and he turned to the machine to key it in. Once he heard the matrices—small, metal, lettered blocks that, when put in the right order, made up a line of story text—falling into place inside the machine, he turned to John.

"Does that really surprise you?" He peered at his friend over the top of his glasses then pushed them up on his nose.

"Blackwood doesn't listen to anyone. He shoots down everyone's ideas."

"Yes, and then turns around and presents them as his own and expects everyone to applaud his genius." John let out a murmur of discontent as he sat up straight again. Once more the chair echoed his sentiment. Then he laughed. "I suppose I'm fortunate. At least now I know he won't steal my story."

Bill laughed a bit too as he turned back to his work. "See? Always a silver lining, John. Always a silver lining."

He went on with his typing, and John swiveled his chair around so he could survey the room. The *Tribune* had only recently purchased this printing setup: the myriad linotypes, which produced metal slugs with raised letters, each making up one complete line of text; the tables on which to assemble the slugs and, thus, the stories; and then the enormous presses that ultimately turned out the newspaper, ready for distribution. The printing room was cavernous, and all the machines' little pops and clicks swirled around in a constant echo. From where John sat, it sounded like a swarm of mechanical bees.

"Why are you so interested in this old cowpoke, anyway?" Bill asked, leaning over in his chair to retrieve the slug he had just finished as it exited the machine.

John looked at him for a moment, letting the non sequitur sink in. "Oh," he said. "You mean Tom Candy."

Bill glanced back at him, eyebrows raised. "That's the fellow you want to do the story on? Tom Candy?"

"Yes, yes," John said, leaning forward, setting his elbows on his knees and folding his hands. "He's important because he was the first cattle driver to move a herd of longhorns from Texas to New York, fifty years ago. It was quite a feat. And he wasn't even American. He was an Englishman. And his assistants on the drive included a Mexican vaquero and a Cherokee Indian."

"Oh yeah?" Bill smiled. "That does sound interesting. What a crew!" He handed his newly minted slug to an assistant, a young man, who carried it over to one of the tables. Bill threw a few ingots into the Linotype's melting pot and went on to his next line.

"And there's one other thing. You—" John paused, looking down the line of typesetters, all immersed in their work, the artificial insect buzz filling their ears. He leaned in closer behind Bill, until his chin was nearly on his friend's shoulder. "You know about my father," John said, dropping the volume of his voice.

Bill stopped, his hand poised above the keyboard. He didn't face John, just looked at him sideways from the corners of his eyes. Then he nodded once. "I do. You've told me."

John peered into the older man's face for a moment. They hadn't been friends for too long, just since John had begun at the *Tribune*. Bill, his senior by at least a decade, had been bringing journalists' words to life in this basement cave for at least that long. They had met on John's first day, at McMahon's, a pub down the block where the *Tribune* folks went to drink and eat, and found they had some friends in common back in Boston. John had felt a sense of camaraderie with easygoing Bill, enough so that a few weeks later, John confided in him about his father—Edwin Stanton, the secretary of war under President Lincoln—and the strange circumstances under which he had died just weeks before his only son's birth.

"I think," John went on now, "Tom Candy might know something about it."

The hand in which Bill held his paper sunk down to his lap, and he once again turned around in his chair. He took off his glasses, blinked his eyes a few times. "John, how could that be?" He shook his head. "Your father was in office during the Civil War. He even served under Johnson after Lincoln was killed, if I'm not mistaken."

John nodded but remained silent, his hands steepled before his mouth.

"So it sounds like this Candy was in business long before that." Bill paused, doing a little math in his head. "The numbers just don't add up. They shouldn't have even crossed paths."

John sat up quickly. "But they did!" His fingers sought out his hair again. He wished he'd brought his briefcase down from the reporters' floor, but he'd left in such a seething state of fury, he simply hadn't thought of it. He had so many notes about times when Tom Candy and Edwin Stanton might have been in the same place at the same time. "I've done a lot of research, you know. Into my father's death."

Bill smiled kindly. "Yes, I do know." He remembered all those late nights when, as he'd locked up the printing room, he'd found John knee-deep in the newspaper's archives just across the hall, a fiery look in his eyes as he pored over old text. And the times Bill had introduced John to his friends at other papers around the city, men who could grant him access to their employers' annals as well.

"Well, that's what led me to Candy's story. His name has come up over and over again. I can't quite put my finger on the overlap between him and my father, but I know it exists.

That's why I want to do this story for the *Trib*. If I can find Tom Candy, maybe I can—"

"Find out more about your father," Bill finished for him quietly, nodding his head and lowering his eyes. "It was a good idea. I'm sorry Blackwood didn't go for it."

John looked away again, bringing his fist up to his mouth so he wouldn't let loose the string of obscenities that came to his lips. He took a deep breath, then another, trying to calm himself. Digging into his father's past had been his sole motivator for becoming a journalist in the first place. He'd figured that with a reporter's access, he could open doors he'd never have even known existed otherwise. And that had been the case. He knew more now about his father's life and death than ever before. He felt he was on the brink of an enormous discovery, of finding the key that would help him make sense of all Edwin Stanton had gone through.

But Blackwood had thrown this boulder in his path, and John didn't know how to go around it.

"John, I know you'll get your answers," Bill said gently, hooking his glasses around his ears once more. He glanced absently at the paper still sitting in his lap then looked up again. "But not while you're working here. I don't know what sort of bee you put in Blackwood's bonnet, but he doesn't like you. That's clear as day. And he's not going to bankroll some big investigation you've brought to him completely out of the blue. If you want to find Tom Candy, it'll have to be in your own way. You just have to figure out what that is—and what you're willing to do about it."

TWO

They Come to America

1849, New York City

Tom Candy stood on the deck of the *Shenandoah* as the transatlantic freighter cruised into New York Harbor. The day was oppressively humid and hot already at nine o'clock in the morning, but he didn't mind; after six weeks in steerage, with only one visit above deck to empty his chamber pot allowed per day, he was thankful for the reprieve. The spaces below were overcrowded, dark, damp, and gloomy, not to mention the rat and insect infestations. On this trip the captain had crammed 240 passengers onboard in addition to tons of goods for delivery to America. Subsequently, the ship was heavy and slow.

At least the weather had been decent with no serious storms, so the voyage had been mostly smooth. Tom had spent most of the time playing shut the box—an old English pub game that had been a tradition on the high seas for hundreds of years as well—with other men in the bunks, and turning his plan over and over in his head: first, he would arrive in New York, and then he would go to California and find his fortune in gold. The steps in between—well, he wasn't exactly decided on those yet. But he would find a way, he was sure of it. An enormous lode had been uncovered on the West Coast early in the previous year, and already the poor and working class of England were emigrating in droves, each looking and hoping for a windfall that would change his life. Tom had no particular interest in the trade—only the money, which he would use to fund his own cattle-driving business in this new world. Of course, he would have to find some gold first.

Now the sun beat down on his shoulders like a blacksmith's hammer, penetrating his dark frock coat. When he'd heard the ship was nearing the coast, he had doffed his grubby traveling wear—brown pants, a white shirt, leather braces, and a durable if not dirty working coat—now stuffed into the small valise by his feet, a gift from his brother before Tom had left home. It must have cost him nearly a month's pay. He'd put on this new outfit he had purchased just before departure. He had wanted to look presentable and dignified when he arrived, but he hadn't considered the difference in temperature. He was not used to the heat and had dressed too warmly.

It took nearly an hour for the slow-moving ship to navigate into the port at South Street and then another for the seamen to tie her down at the dock. They shouted at one another as if they had never worked together before, or perhaps had done so for too long. Everyone seemed to know best what to do, and no one else would listen. Tom stood on the starboard side observing the whole thing, leaning with forearms on the railing, watching as the crew fussed and fought, some even almost coming to blows.

Finally, a deckhand came by and let him know the captain had given the all clear for the passengers to disembark, and Tom made his way into the flow of people already moving down the gangplank, just one more anonymous visitor from a faraway land. From what he had heard, New York saw its fair share of them, and probably more. Even in the small village where he'd been born, just outside of Bath, England, he'd known a young man who had made the voyage. No one had heard from him again. Tom always wondered what had happened.

Most likely absorbed into the masses, he thought now as he set foot on the ground, his first contact with American soil. This was a momentous occasion, and he stopped to savor it for a moment as swarms of people—other travelers, boatmen, ferry captains, police officers, vendors hawking everything from small cakes to leather goods, even children in tattered clothes with no parents to be seen—bumped and jostled him. Horses clopped along the cobblestones, leaving invisible clouds of stench as they passed. Tom was used to bovine smells from his years of living and working on his father's cattle farm, but this was something else altogether. The air he breathed seemed almost halfway composed of it.

On this first glance, he thought New York was much like London: overcrowded and overbuilt.

He decided to keep moving. Now that he was here, anyway, he had to fill in those missing steps in the middle of his plan—the ones that would get him to California somehow. He had several choices of transportation: horses, obviously, some drawing carriages or even covered wagons; he also knew there was a railroad system. There were more boats, of course, but he was unsure of the country's major waterways or if there were even any that would get him all the way to his destination. And then there were always his two good feet.

"Oh, sorry!"

Someone nudged Tom from behind quite hard, sending him nearly to the ground, but he managed to stop his fall before he went face first into the grimy cobblestones. He righted himself and looked at the woman who had just apologized, and found that he knew her—well, sort of. She and her husband had spent many afternoons reclining on chaises on the *Shenandoah's* deck. Not that he had been ogling her then, but he remembered her mode of dress: mostly white shirtwaists with long walking skirts, quite different from the complicated, flapped-and-gathered frocks of the other ladies he'd seen onboard. Tom was no great arbiter of fashion for women or men, but he liked this one's simple style.

"Oh, yes," he replied, "uh, no problem at all, ma'am. Can I help you there? Do you need some assistance with your—your luggage?"

He gestured to the trolley next to her, loaded with six steamer trunks and as many suitcases. She turned toward it too, seeming as if she hadn't noticed it before.

"This? Oh, no," she replied. "No, that's all right, I'm just waiting for my husband." She half turned and searched the crowd for a moment, then pointed toward a tall, husky man wearing a distinctive, maroon-colored felt derby only a short distance away, though the crowd made him difficult to see and impossible to hear. He was talking to one of the ship's valets and handing him a small amount of paper money. Then he clapped the boy on the shoulder, slid his wallet into his coat pocket, and headed over to his wife.

"Hello, hello," he said as he approached, his voice louder, Tom thought, than it had to be. The man stopped and looked him up and down. "You were on the boat. I've seen you, but we haven't met. I'm Orville. Orville Pritchard." He thrust his hand out to Tom and gave him a gleaming smile as robust as his American accent. "And this is my wife, Sarah."

Tom shook his hand and smiled as well. "Pleasure to meet you," he said, nodding at both Orville and Sarah in turn. "Tom Candy. I take it that you're from here?"

Orville let out a hearty guffaw, turning his face to the skies a bit to let the sound of it escape up above the crowd. "More or less, yes," he replied, glancing at his wife. "Is it that obvious?"

Tom laughed too. He couldn't help it. The man's good-natured demeanor was easy to adopt. "Well, no one speaks like that where I'm from."

"And that is?" Orville asked as Sarah opened and fished around in a silk, tartan-design purse she'd bought in London.

"Bath, England," Tom replied without skipping a beat. "Or near to it. Small village; I'm sure you've never heard of it. No one has. Listen, do you think you could give me some advice? I hate to sound like I don't know what I'm doing, but…well, I don't know what I'm doing."

He smiled sheepishly. Tom was a humble man but always

quite confident in himself. On a normal day, bashfulness didn't come to him easily. In this case, however, it seemed first on his roster of emotions.

"Well, of course," Sarah replied, her voice loud and firm. Tom imagined even a woman had to be a bit brash to be heard over the din of this city. "You've never been to New York before?"

"No, I'm afraid not," he said. "And I'm aiming to get to California."

Sarah smiled and looked at her husband. "Oh, we went there last year." She turned back to Tom. "You'll *love* it. Such wonderful weather—it seems like the sun is always shining. And the people are real pioneers. You'll never meet more ambitious folks in your entire life. Are you going to join in the gold trade?"

"Yes, that is my intention." Tom was a little taken aback by her forthright manner. He'd never had such a conversation with a woman before. What a strange land this was.

"Excellent," Orville declared, reaching around his wife to grip the trolley loaded with their luggage. "Why don't you come with us? We aren't going quite that far ourselves, but we can get you part of the way and probably help you with planning out the rest."

Without waiting for a reply, Orville put one arm around Tom's shoulders to encourage him to join them and gave the trolley a push with his free hand. Impressed by this friendly gesture, Tom decided to go along for a while and helped push the trolley as it bumped along the uneven road, from cobblestones to dirt and then back again. They made their way to

South Street proper and Orville hailed a carriage, then another just to carry all their belongings. On the ride to the Battery, the couple sat on one seat and Tom on the other across from them, and Orville spoke almost the entire way about one thing or another. First was all the traveling he and Sarah did. They had just returned from two months of touring in England; earlier in the year they had spent three months in Africa, which he had found exhilarating, though it was a bit too rustic for her. They had loved California, as she had mentioned, and the Texas coast at Galveston was nice as well, as were most of the Southern states.

"You certainly move around a lot," Tom said at last, his neck a bit tired from nodding his head so much and his cheeks aching from keeping up with a polite smile.

"We do love to travel," Sarah said, her first real contribution to the conversation since they had set out across town. "And we're very, very fortunate that we have the time and the means to do so."

Again Tom noticed her utter lack of coyness. He couldn't help but smile at her, though he directed his question at Orville. "What, might I ask, do you do for a living?"

"I come from a long line of plantation owners down South." Orville sounded quite proud, even boastful. He leaned back in his seat, puffing out his chest though he most likely didn't notice he was doing so. "Tobacco, cotton—the big crops. I've never owned one myself..." He paused, glancing at Sarah, who simply waited for him to go on. "Truth be told, Tom, I could never stomach the thought of having *slaves*." He whispered the word as if afraid that someone might overhear. "I know business is business, but…something about it just never seemed right to me. So when Sarah and I married, we headed north and tried to distance ourselves from that life. I got in on the ground floor with the railroad—importing materials, working with the building companies to obtain rights to land, that sort of thing—and it's treated us very well. Very well indeed."

He looked out at the street, lost in some thought, and the three rode in silence for a while. Tom followed his gaze to the storefronts, brick townhouses, warehouses, churches, and rooming houses with wooden "vacant" signs swaying in the breeze. The throng of people and animals had thinned out. It was so quiet now in comparison to the docks, Tom found it a bit disconcerting.

However, as they neared the Battery, everything came to life again. It was at the tip of Manhattan Island; the area was named as such due to the guns and mortars that had once been positioned there to protect the settlement. Tom glimpsed the sandstone outer walls of what appeared to be a fortress.

"That's the Castle Garden," Sarah told him, noticing the direction of his gaze. "It was used to protect New York from the British forces before the War of 1812. Now it's a concert hall." She laughed a little; Tom had to agree, it was a comical juxtaposition. "We saw Wagner's *Taanhäuser* there just a few years ago, didn't we, Orvy?"

She looked at her husband, who had pulled out his wallet and was preoccupied with seeing how much money he had. "Oh," he said when he realized she was speaking to him. He looked to Tom and smiled. "Yes, it was fantastic. A real spectacle. Do you like opera, Tom?"

He shrugged. "Can't say. I've never been to one."

Orville laughed as he stowed his wallet again. "Well, we'll have to remedy that sometime, won't we?" he asked jovially but absently as the carriage drew up to a curb and stopped. He turned in his seat to peer at the luggage carrier behind him. "Excuse me," he said then hopped down onto the street and went back to talk to the driver.

Springing to his feet, Tom jumped out too, then reached up for Sarah. "Ma'am?"

She smirked. "Please, call me Sarah. I'm not old enough to be a ma'am. At least I hope I'm not."

"All right, Sarah," Tom said as he grasped her hand to help her down from the cab. A few yards away, Orville stood with the carriage driver, his wallet open. This time, Tom could hear him speak; he was haggling over what it would cost for the driver to get all their luggage down to the wharf. Good thing the driver was young and hale, Tom thought while retrieving his valise from the floor of the cab.

"Let's start walking," Sarah suggested. "My husband will take care of everything here and then catch up with us."

Tom nodded and fell into step with her. She walked with purpose, obviously well aware of where they had to go.

"So, may I ask where we're headed?" he asked. He had been holding on to the question for some time; Sarah and Orville were being so kind to him, he did not want to seem ungrateful. Still, he thought, it would be good to know exactly what their destination was and how he might fit in.

"Cleveland, Ohio!" she said cheerily. "Unfortunately, there's no means of transportation that will get us from here to there directly. We've already booked passage on a steamship going up the Hudson to Albany, and from there we'll take a train to Buffalo, and then another ship the rest of the way home. Have you been on a train?" She did not pause to hear Tom's response. "Well, either way you'll love it. Train travel is truly a modern miracle, don't you think?"

She stopped abruptly as, Tom was beginning to understand, she was wont to do. She scanned the lineup of boats along the docks, her eyes finally settling on a bright white ship six slips down. "That's it. The *Golden Mare*. We'll just have to make arrangements for you to board. But don't worry, it won't be a problem. Orville and I are quite good friends with the captain. I'm sure he can help us."

Sarah had been right: Booking passage for Tom on the steamboat was simple. And despite his insistence that he didn't have the money to pay for a room and would be quite fine in steerage once again, the captain waived the difference and put him up in the quarters of a first mate who was ill and would not be making the two-day trip.

Likewise, Orville and Sarah insisted on paying for Tom's hotel room for the night. The boat would not sail until the morning, and the couple had already planned to stay and perhaps see a few sights while they were in town, particularly two new neighborhoods that had cropped up due to the overwhelming amounts of immigrants who had, ironically, gone to California for the Gold Rush and come back to New York empty-handed: Kleines Deutschland, or Little Germany, and Chinatown down by the East River.

Tom, however, wanted nothing more than a warm bath (he would have liked hot water but did not get his hopes up) and to sleep on a bed that did not seem to be made of rocks and dried cow dung, as his bunk on the *Shenandoah* had. He got both—even the hot bath—as well as a meal comprised of small purchases from several street vendors: two ears of roasted corn; a savory pie; cold, fried soft-shell crabs; and some fruits for dessert. With this bounty piled up in his arms, he returned to the hotel so he could feast in his room alone, in perfect peace and quiet.

When he'd had his fill, he lay down on the bed, which was indeed quite soft, at least in comparison to what he'd had for the last month and a half. Best of all it was not swaying with the movement of the churning sea. When Tom closed his eyes, though, he could still feel the motion, and it kept him from sleeping. And when he could not sleep, his mind raced. Thoughts of things past, things he could no longer control or change, flooded his memory. He had sacrificed so much to be here—not just monetarily, but in leaving his family and his love, Clara, behind. He pictured her now as he had last seen her, with her soft, yellow hair tucked under a lavender sun bonnet, tending her family's vegetable garden outside their modest home. She was a passionate young woman, but unfortunately her desire was mostly for the church, not for Tom. Their relationship had started off promising and, he remembered with a flush, quite intimate. Clara had seemed very interested in him and to like his attentions, which he gladly showed her any chance he got.

They had been courting for about a year when Tom's elderly neighbor asked him to drive his cattle down to Smithfield Market in London. It sounded like a great adventure, and Tom easily agreed. It took him and his brother, Joseph, three weeks to go the hundred or so miles of the messy and often difficult trek. Tom would never forget the days of rain and flooding, and the resulting marshes and mud, or walking miles to cross a river only to find the bridge had been washed out, then having to wade and swim the cattle right through the flood waters.

Still, he had loved the challenge. The money he made on the cattle wasn't too bad either. His old neighbor had warned him of the thieves and cheats at Smithfield, but Tom made a good go of it. He sat back and let the buyers come to him, and he heard several offers before he chose the best—no bargaining, no settling for what he could get. He found he had a knack for it.

When he got home, all he could think about was getting out there and driving again. But that was not the business he and his family were in. Preoccupied by this dream, he confided it in Clara and was surprised when she did not mirror his enthusiasm. In fact, she seemed downright put out by it.

"Cattle driving?" she asked, wrinkling her nose. "That's rather a...*dirty* job, don't you think?"

Tom agreed but said he didn't mind it one bit. The money he stood to make would more than make up for a few muddy days here and there. Clara nodded politely and listened to the rest of his story in silence.

But after that day, something about her changed. Sometimes she was friendly toward Tom, others cold and distant. And his emotions were equally mixed. He knew she did not approve of his desire to enter the cattle trade; she had not come out and said it, but the change on her face had been obvious. More and more she found reasons not to be home when he came calling, and, finding her there less and less, he curtailed his visits. Tom had once planned to marry this girl, but that future prospect seemed dim. And without it, he was at a loss. He could become a cattle driver, but what would be the purpose? Why have all that money with no one to spend it on, without a family to support? He spent hours and days just turning the dilemma over and over in his mind. If he would not marry Clara, what would he do with his life?

His answer came one day when he traveled into Bath proper to do some errands for his father. All his duties done, he stopped at a pub for a pint—a rare treat—and as he sat and drank he overheard a conversation between a few young men. One had just received a letter from a cousin who had gone to America.

"'Alive with opportunity,' he says," the young man exclaimed, waving said letter in the others' bored-looking faces. "Full of immigrants, people just like us, and all of them landed. A plot there can be had for a fraction of what we'd pay here. Not to mention all the gold they're findin' out on the West Coast. Can you imagine?"

Tom downed the rest of his pint and left. The wheels in his head turned incessantly the whole way home. By the time he drew his horse up to the stable at his dad's farm, he had a plan to go to America. If there was open land, there were cattle— and settlers who needed them for sustenance and supplies. He could head out west first and find this coast that was full of gold. With that capital in his pocket, he could buy and drive the cattle where they needed to be.

Tom immediately shared the idea with his dad and brother. Of course they didn't want to see him go, but they had always supported each other in whatever they'd wanted to do, and this would be no different. Joseph and their father enthusiastically helped him prepare for the trip over the next few weeks.

Shortly before Tom was to leave, he paid a visit to Clara. Despite their tumultuous relationship, he wouldn't have felt right leaving without seeing her one last time and saying goodbye. When he shared with her what he planned to do and the success he hoped to find in America, she nodded primly then informed him she was now engaged to be married to Andrew Dugan, a schoolteacher with a job that was stable—and, most important, very tidy and clean. He was also a deacon in the church Clara attended, which would help her greatly in her desire to devote all her time and energy to working in God's service.

Tom was of two minds about this news. He was happy that Clara finally might have found some happiness, but he had to admit he was a bit jealous that it was with another man. Even though Tom had already mapped out his future—loosely, but mapped out nonetheless—and was excited about his upcoming trip, he went home that day feeling crestfallen.

And here he was in the new world, still dejected. He rolled over in the hotel bed and closed his eyes. Eventually he drifted out of his stubborn consciousness and into a deep slumber. His dreams were a confusing blur of faces—his father and brother, Sarah and Orville, even his mother, who had departed this world when Tom was just a boy—and his sleep was fitful. When the sun rose, he gave up trying and got out of bed. He put his good suit back on, grabbed his valise, and headed downstairs, aiming to have a cup of strong black coffee—an American drink he had already readily adopted—before meeting his new friends at the *Golden Mare* as planned.

The ride upstate was bearable. Tom felt a bit of seasickness at first, no doubt from the greasy feast he'd consumed the previous night and not enough sleep. The black-as-night coffee he'd practically inhaled on top of an empty stomach right before getting on the steamship wasn't helping either.

But once the vessel got out of the North River and onto the Hudson proper, the construction sites that had lined the shore downtown gave way to the farms and gentle, green slopes of Upper Manhattan, and Tom forgot all about his malady. After the fields and pastures came the private riverside estates, no doubt belonging to wealthy merchants who spent all week in the city then headed out to these palatial retreats on weekends. Tom imagined the grand, lavish parties they hosted, New York's elite meandering, drinks in hand, along the pergolas that led down to the water.

Farther up were the brickyards and iron foundries of Fort Lee, New Jersey, right across the river from New York, where flatboats ferried cattle, sheep, and hogs to hungry, big-city markets. Then came the fishing smacks and oceangoing craft gathering in the Tappan Zee, where the river grew wider.

Tom stood at the prow of the ship for hours, taking note of how the land changed as they moved north, from towns to farms and then back again. The ship made an S-turn at the old Continental War barricade that had stopped the British from sailing upstream to capture the mid-Hudson Valley; it was now, another passenger informed him, a military school called West Point.

When his feet grew tired, Tom retired to the shade of a leeward overhang, where Orville and Sarah relaxed in deck chairs and stayed out of the heat. The three stayed there, it seemed, for most of the two-day trip, leaving only to sleep and eat, though some meals they took right there on the deck, listening to the side wheels of the steamer thrash the water.

When they reached Albany, there was another mad dash, this time to a train station where they would board for the final land leg of the trip. Tom wished they could continue on by boat. Albany was the eastern terminus of the Erie Canal; it ran from there to Buffalo, their next destination, and he would have liked to see better the country the by-then famous waterway passed through. But he knew that traveling by train would be quicker, covering three hundred miles in less than a day, and Orville and Sarah missed their home. They wanted to get there as soon as possible. Since they were his kind hosts and tireless tour guides on this trip, Tom followed whatever they wanted to do. Anyway, his water travel was not done yet. They would take another steamship from Buffalo to Cleveland, Ohio, the Pritchards' destination.

"Oh, home sweet home!" Sarah proclaimed when they finally set foot on land again. She took a deep breath. "You never know how much you miss a place until you leave it for a while." She glanced at Tom with a grin. "But I suppose I don't have to tell *you* that."

"No, no." He laughed as he stretched his arms up over his head, easing the cricks out of his back. "I'm quite in touch with that sentiment."

They stood on the wharf waiting for Orville to arrange to get their luggage moved, as usual. Tom looked around, trying to get the lay of the land. He hadn't quite made up his mind about what he would do once he got here; he'd rather thought he'd wait and let the scenery decide for him. On this voyage so far he'd seen so many different types of land: industrial or rural, filled with close-together housing or one homestead every ten or so miles. So he had no idea what to expect in Ohio.

But he knew what he was looking for. Tom wanted cattle land: large, open expanses of hard-packed dirt and scrub bushes, dotted here and there with lakes and rivers the animals could use as watering holes. Then huge meadows of grass, green and waving in the wind as far as the eye could see, with shade trees that would give them shelter.

Cleveland didn't have any of these. It was a city like New York, with stone streets and smokestacks and ships lined up in the harbor. Not that these were bad things; Sarah and Orville obviously loved the place. But they just weren't what Tom needed.

He broke the news to Sarah and Orville. It wiped their excitement of being home away for just a moment.

"Are you sure?" Orville asked, putting a hand on Tom's shoulder and giving it a strong squeeze. "You know you're welcome to stay with us as long as you need to get your bearings and work out what's next for you. We'd be happy to help—"

Tom held his hands up, a little smile on his face. He appreciated their hospitality and warmth, and in truth could have spent the next year here with the couple, quite happily exploring what to him was an enormous, bustling city—compared to dreary old Bath, anyway.

"I'm grateful for all your assistance," he said, nodding at each of them in turn, hoping they could read the earnest expression on his face. "I'm not sure I would have made it this far without you. For that I'll be forever indebted."

"Oh, no," Sarah said, blushing a little and glancing at her husband, then back at Tom. "We didn't do much. And we do wish you'd stay." She paused and smiled. "But I understand that you can't. Listen to me well, though: You know you can come back to us at any time, yes? For anything at all?"

Tom nodded firmly. "Yes. I know."

The three of them looked at each other for a long moment. Tom was the first to break the silence. He stepped forward, right hand outstretched to Orville.

"Sir, it was my honor to meet you," Tom said as they grasped each other's hands and shook hard. "Thank you."

Orville bowed his head and raised it again. "All the best to you, Tom. Good luck and godspeed."

"And remember us when you're a wealthy gold tycoon," Sarah added with a laugh as she stepped in to give Tom a light, fleeting kiss on the cheek. Then she stood back and took his hand in both of hers. "Most of all, take care of yourself. All right?"

"All right," Tom agreed, and with a tip of his hat, he turned and left. Though he wanted to, he didn't look back, not even to wave one last goodbye. At last he was on his own to find his fortune in America.

Tom began his journey on foot. He'd had enough of boats and trains; he wanted to be out in the air and with his feet on solid ground. He meandered around the state of Ohio, stopping here and there to rest, conserving the small amount of money he'd brought by renting cheap rooms rather than staying in hotels or bartering work for room and board. He loaded ships, unloaded trains—whatever dirty jobs were open to him, he did them gladly. Twice he was hired by butchers to sell their meats in the marketplace, once in Strongville and then again in Medina. The latter had a brisker trade, and Tom peddled pound after pound of mutton and dressed-out beef. But he did not enjoy it in the least. He did not like butchering. He would rather deal with the live animals.

Making his way slowly west, in Cincinnati he loaded cordwood onto a steamboat, this time for pay—only two dollars for a hard day's work, but it was better than nothing for Tom. Perhaps not so much for the men who worked this dock regularly.

"Phillip," one of them grunted at Tom as he came up to the woodpile. Phillip had been working for an hour already, and it showed. Though the autumn air was still and cool, sweat poured from his brow, and splinters and mud stuck to his shirt.

"Tom," he replied a bit warily. Though the Pritchards had been uncommonly kind to him upon his arrival in America, in his solo travels Tom had found they'd been exactly that: *uncommon*. Not many were as nice as they had been. The common person here, it seemed, would lie to his face and spit in his beer for being an outsider. Or maybe he was just mingling with the wrong crowd.

Phillip stopped his work for a moment. Breathing hard, he wiped the back of his wrist across his forehead. He appraised Tom…then smiled at him. "Welcome aboard, Tom. Now get to loading."

They started out in silence and continued working that way for some time. Finally, as they whittled down the mountain of cordwood into a manageable hill, they were able to slow their work, giving them time to get to know one another.

"So I guess you're not from around here," Phillip began.

Tom smirked. Did everyone ask that question here? "No, I'm from England," he replied as he hefted a log into the ship's hold. "You?"

Phillip smirked right back. He liked this one's sense of humor. "Born and raised on the Ohio River." He swept an arm out, indicating the waterway before them. "Might not be as majestic as the Thames, but we like it."

Now Tom let out a laugh. He paused his work too and brushed the stray sawdust from his clothes. "Don't have much to do with the Thames myself. I'm from the north. Place called Bath."

"Really. And what're you doing here, might I ask?" Phillip returned to the logs, picking one up in each hand. Tom saw the muscles of his forearms clench. He must have been doing this work for a while.

Tom picked up some wood as well and shrugged his shoulders as he tossed it. "What is everyone else doing? Looking for my fortune."

Now Phillip let out a hearty laugh. "Sorry," he said when it abated. "It's just—well, you're right, you know? Who isn't looking to get rich these days?" He jerked a thumb at the diminishing pile. "Not gonna happen like this, though. So what's your plan? You got some big business in mind?"

"My plan was to go to California—" Tom began.

"Gold?" Phillip interrupted.

"Gold," Tom agreed. "But I haven't made it there yet. To tell the truth, I'm not sure that's where my heart lies anymore." He thought for a moment. "And I'm not sure where it *does* lie either."

Phillip resumed with the wood. "Well, what do you like to do?"

Tom picked up a log, one of the last few. "Back home I worked with cattle my whole life, tending and raising steers. I guess you could say it's a family business. My people have been herdsmen all around Northern England going back for centuries."

With the wood gone, Phillip picked up two brooms and tossed one over to Tom.

"And you want to stay in that business?" Phillip asked as he began to sweep.

Tom followed suit. "In a way. But I want to drive cattle, not tend them."

Phillip stopped, resting an arm on the tip of his broom's handle. "Driving cattle? And there's money in that?"

"Not so much in the driving but in the selling." Tom continued to sweep, looking down, unaware the other had stopped. "Get them to a market, find the highest bidder—you can earn a pretty penny, to be sure."

Phillip watched Tom's movements, his sweeps of the broom across a long arc, pushing the bits of wood chips and leaves into the river. "You have some experience in it?"

Tom stopped then. He recognized the curiosity in Phillip's voice. Knew it, because he'd felt it too. "Yes, some." He held his broom upright in front of him, clutching it in both hands. "Enough to know what I'm doing."

"But you don't have the money," Phillip said, his body relaxing a little now that the job was over.

Tom, however, straightened up, pushed his chest out a bit. "My finances are—"

"Whoa, whoa," Phillip said, walking toward him slowly. Tom watched him with a wary eye. "No offense meant. I just—" He held his arms out to his sides and looked one way then the other. "Never seen a rich man down at the docks loading cordwood for a buck." He reached into a pants pocket and turned it out, showing it was empty. "We're in the same boat, so to speak. If I had two nickels to rub together, do you think I would be here?"

Tom let his breath out in a gust, releasing his momentary anger with it. He didn't like having to be so on guard. But always being among strangers will tend to do that to a man.

"No, I'm sure you wouldn't," he said. "So, what's *your* plan?"

Phillip reached over, took Tom's broom, and carried it under his arm as they walked. "I have no plan," he said, and

Tom could hear the defeat in his voice. Phillip looked at him with a sad sort of smile. "Nothing like yours, anyway. You sound like a big thinker, Tom. I admire that. Wish I could do a little of it myself."

"Why can't you?" Tom shot back. He stopped and turned to face Phillip. "No, really, why can't you think big? It's free, right? Don't need two nickels to do it."

Phillip laughed. "Okay, you got me on that. So, I can be a dreamer. Great. But what good will it be if it's only a dream?"

Tom started walking again, and this time Phillip strode to catch up. "What do you know about the butchering business?"

Phillip just looked at him, not sure what this change in topic meant. "Uh…not much? Why do you ask?"

Tom was silent for a minute as they walked down the wharf. The ships, now fully loaded, were leaving their dock moorings one by one. He watched one as it pulled away, maneuvering into the main current to ply its way upriver.

"Because I've had this idea," he said, turning his attention back to his newfound friend, "but it's not something I can do alone. This made me think I couldn't do it at all, because I have no one here in America I can work with." He looked Phillip up and down, his eyes critical. "I'll buy that you're a hardworking man. That's obvious. And I can tell you'd be ambitious if you were given the right outlet."

Phillip stood up tall. "Damn right on both counts."

Tom smiled. "Yes, good. So my idea is—if you want to hear it?"

"Of course I want to hear it."

And with that, Tom launched into describing an idea he

had formed in the last few weeks. He still wanted in on the cattle trade; that had never changed. But now that he'd seen more of how it worked—the seemingly endless process of driving, then butchering, then selling—he knew he couldn't do it all by himself. He could be content just to drive the animals to wherever they needed to be, but that would only make him half the money.

"So what I think is that I need to control the other bits as well," he concluded. By then, they had reached the end of the docks and a little hut where Phillip stored his brooms. He stood with a hand on the door, holding it open, but made no move to put the tools inside.

He gazed out over the nearby water, obviously deep in thought. "So you want someone to butcher and sell the cattle you drive." He looked at Tom. "Is that what you're saying?"

Tom nodded. "Yes, yes, that's it. Then we split the profits from the whole operation and invest in another herd to start the process over again."

"Meeting your own demand with your own supply." Phillip grinned wide. "That is an *idea*, my friend. I like it!"

"Then be my partner."

Tom's quick offer hung between them in the chilly air. The two men looked at one another. Tom's eyebrows raised expectantly while Phillip's lowered in concern.

"Your *partner*?" he asked. "Tom, I don't even know your last name."

He smiled and thrust out his hand. "Candy," he said with confidence. "Tom Candy, at your service."

Phillip continued to watch him for a moment then looked

out at the river again. He moved his head back and forth a little, then up and down, as if having an argument with himself. Finally he looked back at Tom, reached out slowly, and shook his hand.

"Phillip Armour," he said. "And I guess I'm your new business partner."

THREE

The Secretary of War

1862, Washington City; The Civil War Rages

President Lincoln entered the Yellow Oval Room through the door in the east wall that led there from his private passageway.

"Edwin," he said. His secretary of war was seated in one of the rocking chairs before the fireplace, unlit on this warm afternoon. The damask drapes were drawn, leaving the room bathed in shadows. "Thank you for taking the time to meet with me."

The man held a book up in his hands, one of the many on the shelves that lined the room, trying to catch a ray through the cracks in the thick curtains by which to read. He lowered it and looked at the president.

"How is the passageway working, sir?"

Lincoln smiled as he crossed the room to where Edwin sat, his long legs carrying him there in just a few strides. Beyond the door through which he'd come lay a private tunnel of sorts by which the president could traverse between his personal quarters and this parlor. He used it sparingly, generally only when the White House hallways were crowded and he did not wish to stop to answer question after question after question. Especially when he was headed for a meeting like this—one he wanted to keep as confidential as possible.

"It's the best idea I've ever had," he replied with a wry grin as he sat down across from Edwin. He'd had the passageway and entrance to this room installed only recently.

The secretary did not react. He stared blankly at Lincoln silently, as if awaiting directions.

The president cleared his throat. "Yes, well. Let's get to it, then. Edwin, we need to discuss your...how shall we call it... your reputation as it stands right now."

This did not elicit a response either. Not because the secretary of war was shocked but because he already knew what his commander-in-chief would say. Edwin Stanton was a hated man, and he was well aware of the fact. In the single year since Lincoln had appointed him to this position, he had uncovered untold amounts of corruption and waste within the federal government, particularly the military—fraud, misconduct, nepotism, and myriad other reprehensible acts that had gone unchecked, or at least overlooked, for many years.

And he had made it his goal to eliminate this tarnish, to do whatever he could to restore these institutions' otherwise gleaming images. He was a man of loyalty and honesty, and he felt it was his duty to his country to call to task those who would undermine its integrity. Not surprising, this had earned him many enemies, some in high places. Fortunately, Lincoln was not among that set.

"Sir, no disrespect," he said, putting the book aside on a table by his chair, "but haven't we had this conversation before?"

Lincoln leaned back in his seat, also a rocker, and pushed against the floor with his feet. The chair creaked a bit as it rolled gently back and forth, back and forth. The president found the rhythm soothing.

"None taken," he replied, keeping his voice on an even keel. He was not angry with Stanton, just exasperated, as they *had* been through this issue already. More than once, in fact. Lincoln had asked Edwin to join his staff specifically because he knew of the man's penchant for righteousness. A lawyer by trade, Edwin had given up his lucrative private practice to serve as attorney general under James Buchanan in the last months before Lincoln took his oath of office. It was a lame duck administration by then, and Buchanan seemed to have given up. He was letting the country drift into chaos, and aggression between the states was on the rise. Edwin was desperate to halt this downward spiral, but his pleas to Buchanan fell on deaf ears. Eventually, Stanton resigned and went back to his practice. If the nation would burn, he would not be an accomplice to it.

Two years later, however, Lincoln called Stanton back to public service. The president's current secretary of war, Simon Cameron, was ineffective and corrupt; he caused more problems than he solved, and Lincoln could not get him under control. He removed Cameron and appointed Stanton to the post.

"But therein lies the problem, Edwin," Lincoln went on, sitting forward now and putting his elbows on his knees, folding his hands out in front of him. "We have discussed this before, and there has been no resolution to the problem."

Edwin looked away. *Problem*, he thought. He did not like that characterization of his work.

"You've made enemies," Lincoln continued. "Do you know how many of my staff have come to me with concerns about you? Everyone from aides to your own generals, Edwin. Your dedication to this cause seems to know no bounds."

Stanton continued gazing out across the room at the yellow wall covering dotted with gilded stars. The pattern was mesmerizing. "I know what they say about me," he said, his voice low and flat. "And I know which ones are looking to have me put out of office."

"That is not going to happen," Lincoln assured him quickly. "You know I need you here. You're doing important work. All I'm saying is…"

He paused, trying to think of how to put it. He scrubbed a hand over his face and through his hair. His eyes burned; he felt like he hadn't slept in weeks. Perhaps he hadn't. Since the War of the Rebellion had started, all the days had begun to blur together.

"All I'm saying is you have to be careful," he offered at last. "Watch who you talk to. Don't share so much information. Tell me, of course, but *only* me. Can we agree on that?"

Edwin turned back to the president. The two men locked eyes for a long moment.

"Yes," Stanton finally said. "Yes, we can agree on that. Consider it done, sir."

Lincoln sat up straight, his mouth once again curling into a soft grin. Stanton knew this meant he was pleased. The president was not one to express strong emotions.

"Good, good," he said, standing and stretching to his full height. He towered over Edwin, who stood up also as a show of respect. "Then you'll let me know when you have information to share."

This was not a question but a statement. Nonetheless, Stanton nodded in assent. The president nodded back, and they shook hands. Then, without a word, Lincoln went and slipped back out through his secret door.

Edwin paced so much in his office, he thought it wondrous that he hadn't worn a groove in the hardwood floor. It wasn't his regular office, which he had left for security reasons. And it wasn't a large space, just enough for a desk, two straight-back chairs, and a shelf of books. He moved now from one end to the other, following his usual route. He found the pattern oddly conducive to thought.

"Watch who you talk to," he muttered, imitating Lincoln's low-pitched voice and unhurried manner of speech. This sentence stuck in Edwin's craw like a bitter pill he could not dislodge. Why had the president issued this warning? And why now?

He thought back to the business he had conducted over the last few days, weeks, and even months, searching his mind for any clue that something was more amiss than normal. Edwin was used to opposition; he had practically made it into a career. But for President Lincoln, whom Edwin respected and considered a strong ally, to come to him with this stern admonition—well, it was unusual to say the least.

The two had always seen eye to eye on most topics, and especially on Edwin's crusade against corruption. Lincoln lauded his efforts not just in private but in public as well. At a recent cabinet meeting, in fact, the president had stood up for Stanton when the secretary of state expressed some dismay about Edwin's recent focus on his own military generals currently out on the battlefields.

"Secretary Stanton has my full faith and permission to act," Lincoln had asserted, his eyes boring into the secretary of state, putting the punctuation on his point. "Think of our nation as beset upon by a tumultuous ocean. Edwin Stanton is the seawall that keeps its crashing, ceaseless waves from engulfing and submerging us. Without him our government and our country would drown. Indeed, I believe even I would be destroyed."

This recollection stopped Edwin in his tracks. Not so much the praise he had received, but the memory of that day as a whole. He had attended the cabinet meeting in the morning then gone to eat with James, an old friend and a fellow attorney, who was in Washington on business. They hadn't seen one another since Stanton had come to head the War Department. They headed for a local lunch room known for its quick service—a real draw since everyone in this city was in a hurry.

Sitting in the corner at a small table, they talked over cold beef sandwiches and flat, warm beer, which still was better than the food in the Confederate capitol. At one point his friend remarked how overly crowded it was.

"You can thank the Confederacy for that," Stanton had said with a dry laugh. "Since the war started, journalists and war correspondents have been swarming here. All looking for that one good quote or to get the politicians' statements before the other fellow does. Real vultures, if you ask me. I can't turn around anymore without running into one. Some of them even travel in packs."

"Well," James had said, "even vultures have to eat, right?"

Stanton felt relaxed as they clinked glasses at his friend's joke. Then they downed their drinks and ordered another round.

"So, what's it like working in the White House?" James had asked while they waited. "Is Lincoln as stoic as he seems?"

Edwin had thought about it for a moment. "Yes and no," he finally said, reaching for the full glass of beer the server handed him. He took a sip. "I mean, he has to be, to an extent. He is the president, after all. He can't just say what he wants at any time. Everything is calculated in terms of politics. Much of it's a show, really."

James lowered his brow and took a gulp of beer, then picked up his napkin and wiped the foam from the lower reaches of his thick moustache. "Ed, you haven't been here long enough to sound so disillusioned. I thought you liked this job."

"I do," Stanton replied without hesitation. "I just don't always agree with the popular vote."

James looked at him expectantly but remained silent, indicating he should go on.

Edwin sighed. "James, this whole administration is a mess. Lincoln is a good man. I know he means well. But…some days I just have trouble finding any token of intelligence in him, or in the crew that governs him."

James let out a low whistle. "Coming from you, that's a scathing comment," he said, then took another drink. "And unexpected. He thinks the sun rises and sets on you. You know that, don't you? He says it every chance he gets."

Edwin thought back to that morning's meeting and Lincoln's railing at the secretary of state. "Yes, I know," he had admitted, sounding defeated. "Which makes it even harder for me to say it. But it's the truth, James." Stanton looked at his friend, worry clouding his eyes. "Lincoln is just like Buchanan. I believe it's only a matter of time before he gives up too, and the whole country will fall to ruin."

In his office now, Edwin resumed his pacing, the echoes of that conversation repeating in his head. It had been the first and only time he had admitted to anyone how he truly felt about the president and his staff, and he'd done so only because he trusted James. They'd known each other for years, and Edwin had no doubt that James respected him enough not to tell a soul. They'd been two friends complaining about work, nothing more. At least that was what he'd thought at the time.

"Watch who you talk to," he repeated absently. Now he understood what the president meant.

FOUR

The Search Continues

1904, New York and Chicago

John Stanton was not sure if he was ready, but he had no choice at this point. He'd already quit his job at the Tribune, sold or given away his few belongings, and packed up his clothing and research papers. He sat on his bed at the boarding house counting out the money he'd been stashing under the mattress since he'd arrived in the city; added to his prior savings, this amounted to almost a thousand dollars, the most cash he'd ever held in his hands at one time. He divided it up into several piles of a few hundred dollars each and put one in his suitcase, one in his shoe, one in the band inside his hat, and so on. At least if someone mugged him, they would get only the small amount found in his wallet.

After giving the room a last once-over, he closed the door behind him and headed down the stairs. He'd already told the landlady that he would not be returning and given her the key to his door, so at least he could slip out quietly. He stepped hurriedly out onto the street and hailed a horse-drawn carriage. He climbed in and put his small leather traveling bag on the wooden seat next to him.

"Grand Central Depot, please," he told the cabbie, who slapped the horse's reins against the animal's rump, and off they went. The train station was in midtown, a good ride away; at least this slow mode of transport would allow John a last look at the city—and a last smell, thank God. The carriage went east up Wall Street, then north on Broadway, then picked up Park Avenue at Union Square. It was midday, and the streets were bustling all over, automobiles and horses and people all clamoring and getting in the way of one another. Before long, John was almost glad to be taking his leave of it.

Thankfully, the train he boarded at Grand Central was much plusher than local stations. He'd bought a ticket for Pennsylvania Railroad's New York and Chicago Special, which was just as exclusive as the Limited but made fewer stops and ran extra fast; it would get him to the second city in just over sixteen hours. The train was only two years old and still fairly gleaming. John's reservation was for the parlor car, better than standard coach but not as expensive as the Pullman sleeper, which was the best he could afford on his meager budget.

The train got underway just after five o'clock, and after an early supper in the dining car, John made his way to the parlor, where he could take a window seat and watch the cities and countryside blur into one. The Pennsy, as it was called, had already passed through Philadelphia, Harrisburg, and Pittsburgh; next would be Cleveland and Toledo, Ohio, and Gary, Indiana. Finally there would be an urban stretch northward into Chicago's Union Station, where Jonathon Armour—son of Phillip—would be waiting to pick him up.

"Last stop, Union Station. Watch your step as you exit the train!"

The conductor's call roused John from a fitful nap. The dinner he'd had half a day ago was like a rock in his stomach, and his mouth was dry. He sat up straight and looked around. Everyone else was standing, gathering their suitcases and topcoats and whatnot. In a daze John followed suit, going through the motions as his mind came back to full attention. He was confused by a dream he'd had, unsure what parts were real and what came from his imagination. His father had been there on the train with him and they'd been having a conversation as the scenery whipped past outside. The only problem had been that John couldn't hear. His father's face had grown red, and he'd wildly gesticulated, trying to make John understand what he had to say. But John had gotten nothing. Just silence, like he had sunken down into the dark depths of the sea.

By the time he reached the platform, he'd managed to shake himself out of his stupor, though the vision of his father's face remained: his pleading eyes, the spittle that shot from his lips as he tried so desperately to get his point across.

He wants to tell me something, John thought, as if it hadn't been a dream at all but a message about his current situation.

He got so wrapped up in the idea, he didn't notice the young man in front of him until they'd collided.

"Sorry, sorry," John muttered, backing away and looking up. The other man was maybe forty years old, with a prim mustache and an oval face; the top of his head was bald, but sprouts of hair stuck out just over his ears.

"John Stanton?" he said, and John looked around himself, to the sides and back, as if he did not know the man was speaking to him.

"Uh, yes, yes, that's me," he said. He thought for a moment. "Are you—"

"J. Ogden Armour," he replied, stepping forward to shake John's hand. "But I go by Ogden. I thought it might be you—you're the only straggler left, and you look a little lost."

John laughed at his own expense. "Guilty on both counts," he replied, then followed Ogden down a nearby staircase and onto the street. He paused, taking in his very first view of the city of Chicago. It was crowded like New York, maybe even more so. It was just after nine in the morning, and everyone, it seemed, was out—on their way to work, hawking their wares, going in and out of shops. The buildings here were much taller than in the city John had just left, the downtown area crowded with them, a network of concrete canyons with the people pouring through them like rivers.

The din was incredible, a constant low buzz of voices. A breeze blew in from nearby Lake Michigan, cooling the already tepid air. John took a deep breath, glad to be free of the inescapable odor of manure for a moment.

"This way," Ogden said, gesturing to his right, then he took off at a brisk pace, politely pushing his way through the crowd until he'd reached the corner. John did his best to keep up but was not such an expert at maneuvering among so many people. By the time he got into the alleyway to the right, Ogden was climbing into an automobile parked there: a Buick Model B Touring, black with white wheels and a double set of soft red seats. It looked like it was brand new.

"Is that yours?" John asked then realized the absurdity of the question. He went over to the passenger side and got in. "Well, of course it is," he went on with a laugh as Ogden started up the engine. It came to life, filling the alley with an acrid smell.

"Is that—" John paused as his eyes began to water. "An internal combustion engine?"

"Yes," Ogden shouted above the noise of it. "Gasoline powered. Fresh from Detroit." He gave John a smile and raised an eyebrow then pulled out of the alley, honking the car's little horn, making the pedestrians all around scatter. Out on the main thoroughfare, he glided the Buick into the flow of auto and equine traffic.

John clutched his leather bag to his chest and let out his breath. He hadn't realized he'd been holding it.

"Have you been in an automobile before?" Ogden asked, making a hard turn onto South Lake Shore Drive. The street was much quieter there, with less people. John breathed a sigh of relief.

"Yes, yes, I have," he replied. "A couple times. Just not in a city like this. And not an automobile this powerful."

Ogden smiled again, gripping the steering wheel, leather

driving gloves on his hands. He looked from side to side for a moment, then made a left turn onto Adams Street. At the corner of LaSalle, he stopped and brought the auto to the curb. "Here we are," he said, and then jumped out and motioned for John to do the same.

In the lobby of the Home Insurance Building, Ogden stopped to speak to the guard on duty. It seemed his company had been receiving threats lately from unionized laborers, so he had a man posted at the door at all hours.

"It's all right, he's with me," John heard Ogden say, then the two men climbed the nine flights up to the Armour Packing Company's offices, went straight through the lobby, and back into private office. John noticed the name still on the door: "Phillip Armour, President."

"Ogden, I was very sorry to hear about your father," John offered as soon as the door had closed. He hadn't been sure when the right time to say it would come up, but this seemed as good as any. "I didn't know him personally, but I have read much about him. He was a great man."

Ogden paused for the first time. He was a man in perpetual motion, it seemed—understandable for someone who had just taken over the vast holdings of what really was a family business empire. His famous father's death had come unexpectedly after a short bout of pneumonia, but he'd prepared Ogden well, training him for years in every aspect of the company's operations. Phillip had left some very big shoes to fill, but Ogden appeared to have landed on his feet.

"Yes, he was," he replied softly, and John thought he saw a trace of tears in his eyes. He sympathized. He knew what it was like to face the world without a father. He felt he should say something to convey his empathy, but he couldn't think quickly enough. The door of the office opened and in walked Malvina Belle Ogden, Phillip's widow. She wore a black mourning dress with a high-neck collar and belled sleeves. Though she was at least seventy years old, her eyes were bright, and she strode into the room with purpose.

"Good morning, Ogden, dear," she said, her chin held high. Then she turned her sights on John. "And you are?"

He withered a little under her stare. "Uh, John Stanton, ma'am," he sputtered.

"You remember, Mother," Ogden chimed in. "The reporter from the *New-York Tribune*, here to do a story on Dad?"

John cringed a bit more and felt a flush in his cheeks. In all the excitement of arriving in a new city and the raucous ride in Ogden's Buick, he'd forgotten he'd told that little lie.

"Oh, yes. Blackwood's paper. Who can afford to turn down *his* requests?" She raised an eyebrow at her son then turned her attention to John, her demeanor softening a bit. "Welcome, Mr. Stanton. Please, have a seat."

She motioned toward a brown leather couch, and John made his way over. As he was taking off his coat and hat, the office door opened one more time and a young man in a tweed suit and a black bow tie came in holding a large serving tray. On it was a silver coffee urn, a plate of croissants, and an assortment of cheeses, along with two fine bone china place settings and gleaming silver utensils. He set the tray down on the low, glass-top table in front of the sofa.

"Bring one more setting for our guest, please," Mrs. Armour

directed him as she took her own seat on a chair flanking the sofa. On the other side, Ogden did the same. The boy in the tweed suit nodded and slipped back out the door.

Mrs. Armour turned to John again. "I appreciate your interest in Phillip and our company, Mr. Stanton."

"John, please," he interrupted.

"Very well, John. As you can imagine, many journalists have solicited us for interviews in the wake of Phillip's death."

The words stopped her for a moment, and she glanced out the windows at John's back, her eyes looking far away. Her husband had been dead for only a few weeks. John imagined the emotional impact was still quite fresh for her and her son.

Then she simply looked back at him. "But none from New York yet. So tell me. Where would you like to begin?"

The boy came back in the room, more china and silverware rattling in his hands. He set them down on the table before John then put out the other settings and poured coffee for everyone. Mrs. Armour thanked him. He dipped his head politely and left the room again.

"Well," John said, trying to buy some time as the other two drank their coffee. He picked his up as well and took a sip. It was dark and strong, just as he liked it. "Actually, there's one specific aspect of your late husband's story that I'm particularly interested in."

Mrs. Armour wrapped her fingers around her coffee cup, her elbows resting on the arms of her chair. She eyed John through the wisps of steam coming off her febrile drink. "And what part is that?"

John shifted in his seat and set his cup back on the table.

Ogden had helped himself to a croissant and was chewing on it slowly as he also awaited John's reply.

"The early part." John cleared his throat. "Around the time when he first started in the butchering business." He paused, waiting for a response. None came, so he continued. "When he met Tom Candy in Ohio and they struck up a business deal."

The room grew even more silent than it had been. The Armours didn't look at one another or at John; Ogden reached for his coffee cup and took a drink while his mother tugged on the sleeves of her dress and rearranged her skirt. Neither seemed to want to acknowledge what he had said, but John could wait them out. He'd dealt with much more hostile subjects in interviews past.

Finally, Mrs. Armour cleared her throat. "And where did you hear about that?" She raised her eyes slowly to John. Their brightness had been replaced by a shocking coldness.

"I didn't exactly," he said, keeping his tone of voice firm but open. He wanted them to know he was serious but also feel comfortable enough to open up to him. So far he hadn't accomplished either. "I've just managed to put some pieces together."

He stopped and brought his bag up onto the couch. He opened it and took out his stack of research papers then thumbed through them at the corners. He pulled out a sheet of yellowed newsprint and handed it over to Mrs. Armour. She held it at arm's length, squinting as she tried to read. It was an account—albeit a short one—from the *Tribune* of Tom Candy's arrival in New York City, after his successful cattle drive all the way from Texas.

Mrs. Armour handed it back to John. "And what do you think this has to do with my husband?"

He put his papers aside and held the article facing out, so the others could see it. "Well, it starts here," he said then read aloud:

> Candy, an old hand in the cattle trade of his native England, arrived in America in 1849 and shortly thereafter opened his first business, a butcher's shop on the south side of Chicago that soon became known for also developing and selling consumer products made from animals, such as glue, fertilizer, hairbrushes, buttons, oleomargarine, and even medications fabricated from slaughterhouse byproducts. It has been said that his business used "everything but the squeal."

John shuffled through his papers again. "Then, here, in this one…" He looked for a moment more and pulled out a sheet of handwritten notes. "I apologize. I couldn't get the original article, but I copied it word for word. It's a profile of Phillip Armour done just five years ago, marking the fiftieth anniversary of the start of the company. Look at this line," he said, leaning toward Mrs. Armour and pointing to a passage he had underlined.

She read: "'Mr. Armour became known for his savvy business practices. To maximize profits, he used every part of the animals he butchered to manufacture products such as fertilizer, glue, and medications.'" She paused and glanced at John, then back at the page. "'He once said he uses everything but the squeal.' Well, I don't see how that ties the two together," she said immediately and sat back in her chair. "That's a fairly common phrase. I'm sure many in the meat industry have used it at one time or another."

"True," John conceded, though mostly just to be polite. "But you have to admit, Mrs. Armour, the products mentioned are specific. And the timing—Tom Candy started his business in 1849, and Armour's fiftieth anniversary fell in 1899. The years coincide."

Mrs. Armour was silent. She picked up her coffee again, took a sip, and then put it back down. She uncrossed her ankles and recrossed them the other way. She motioned a hand in the air as if she were about to speak, but nothing came out.

Then, from the other side of the room: "Mother, he's right. Just tell him."

Both John and Mrs. Armour turned their heads toward Ogden. He was trying to dislodge croissant crumbs from his mustache with a napkin, but he stopped. He looked at John for a moment then addressed his mother.

"I know Dad didn't like to speak about Tom, but he's gone now." He paused. "What's the harm in sharing their story?"

Mrs. Armour said nothing, just continued looking at her son. He raised his eyebrows and shrugged at her. "I know how private Tom was. Dad told me the stories. But do you really think any of those old problems will matter now?"

She sat back again with a sigh. Gazing out the window, she brought a hand up to her chin as she thought.

"All right, Mr. Stanton. John. I will tell you what you want to know. But first I want something from you. Tell me *why* you need this information. Why are you looking for Tom Candy?"

"I never said—" John began.

"Well, why else would you want to know about him?" she interrupted. "Of course you're looking for Tom, and you're not the first. Over the years, there've been many inquiries as to his whereabouts. Phillip would never say a word." She glanced at her son again. "And I'm not so sure we should either."

Now it was John's turn to sit in silence for a moment. While the Armours had their secrets about Tom Candy, he harbored his own about his true purpose here. Would they understand if he told them he thought Tom might be the key to clearing his father's name from all the misunderstandings that happened before his death? Would that make them more or less apt to tell him everything they knew?

He didn't give himself time to debate it. "I need to find Tom Candy because I believe he may have information about what happened to my father."

Mrs. Armour blinked. "And who is your father, dear?"

John's mouth suddenly felt very dry. "Edwin Stanton, ma'am," he said, his voice low. "Former secretary of war under President Lincoln."

"Yes, I know of him," she replied quickly. "But I don't see the connection."

John sat back, his stack of papers on his lap, hands gripping its edges. "Honestly, I'm not sure about it either. I just know that in all the research I've done into my father's death—"

He stopped. How much did they know? Should he explain how his father had waged his own war against corrupt military generals right there on the battlefields? How that had led to most of Washington hating him, even people he'd thought were allies? Had they heard about Edwin Stanton's implication in Lincoln's death? Nothing had been proven, but the damage was done. John had never believed it, of course. And now he had the chance—possibly—to do something about it.

"In my research I've seen Tom Candy's name time and time again," he continued, feeling more bolstered with every word he spoke. "I don't know how he and my father met, or even if they did. But it's something I have to find out."

Mrs. Armour regarded him for a moment. "I heard about your father," she said at last. "And the circumstances surrounding his death."

It was a vague statement, but John took it to mean she understood the situation.

"And though it happened long ago," she went on, "I offer my condolences."

He nodded once in acknowledgment. Mrs. Armour in turn motioned to her son, who picked up the story.

Ogden cleared his throat. "John, before I tell you this, you have to promise me it will not end up in your story. It cannot be printed in a newspaper. You'll soon understand why."

John let out a nervous laugh, remembering once more the false intentions he'd passed off as his reason for being here. "All right, Ogden. No problem with that."

"Good. Thank you." Ogden took a last sip of his coffee then set the cup down on the table again. "In the summer of 1849, my father was twenty years old and loading cordwood onto boats on the Ohio River. His pay was two dollars a day. He was poor by most standards but ambitious. He'd been planning to head out to California in the fall, to look into the gold trade. But before that could happen, he met an Englishman who had just arrived in America and was looking to find his own fortune."

"Tom Candy," John said.

Ogden nodded. "Tom Candy. Now, Tom was heading out west as well, but not for gold. That had been his original aim, but he had a background in cattle tending and had found great opportunities here for a man with his skills. When he met Dad, he was full of ideas—one of which was opening a butcher shop then driving cattle there to slaughter and sell. They got along well, and Dad was ready to move on, so he agreed."

"But then he slept on it," Mrs. Armour chimed in. "And he realized he didn't know this man. Tom could have been a criminal for all Phillip knew, and he wanted Phillip to be his business partner? It just sounded fishy. So he backed out."

"Of course Tom tried to talk him back into it," Ogden continued.

John looked back and forth between them as if watching a tennis match. He smiled a bit at the ease with which they told the story together.

Ogden smiled too. He rarely got the chance to tell this story, John imagined, and doing so clearly pleased him.

"He told Dad not to go chasing gold. But of course Dad didn't listen. He headed to California."

"And did he come back a millionaire?" John asked, and both of the others laughed.

"Heavens, no," Mrs. Armour replied. "My husband was

dead broke. Phillip was always so generous. He'd spent the money his family had given him to make the trip on his traveling companions on the way there, and whatever he earned from panning gold disappeared just as quickly."

"So how did he and Tom find each other again?" John asked.

"Phillip did come to Chicago eventually, and he started a small grocery store. Several years later, Tom was passing through with a herd of cattle and looked him up."

"And they went into business then," John said, looking from Mrs. Armour to Ogden, who answered the question.

"Actually they didn't go into business together at all. Tom advised Dad to open and then expand that butcher shop they'd talked about because he had been down South and saw the unrest that was fomenting there, the grudges over the North's growing insistence on abolishing slavery. This was many years before the war broke out, but Tom predicted it would happen, and all the smart ranchers and herdsmen would sell or move their steers north."

"And this time he took Tom's advice," John said, though almost to himself. He was thinking back to that time when the North and South were at each other's throats. His father had not been in office yet, and was still just a private-practice lawyer. John wondered if Edwin had seen it coming too. Maybe this was the point where he and Tom had intersected.

"Yes, he did," Mrs. Armour said, her voice gentle, bringing John out of his thoughts. "Phillip started the Armour Packing Company with Tom as a silent partner. Tom brought in local cattle, Phillip butchered and sold the meat, and they both made a pretty penny. Thus began the Armour empire. All thanks to the advice and help of Tom Candy."

As always happens at the end of a profound story, a hush fell over the room. Its three occupants looked at one another, then away, then out the window, their eyes not settling on any one thing at which to look. The Armours, perhaps, were thinking about their beloved deceased, whose presence still somehow filled this office.

John's mind, of course, was on Tom Candy.

"So, where can I find him?" he asked, breaking the quiet.

Mrs. Armour looked puzzled for a moment, then understanding washed across her face. "You mean Tom?"

John nodded. "Yes. I really must speak with him. Especially now that I've heard your story."

"Why, we haven't seen him in years, my dear." She said it plainly, sounding almost apologetic. John felt his stomach drop to his feet. Mrs. Armour looked over at her son. "And I have *no* idea where he ended up. Do you, Ogden?"

He pursed his lips and shook his head. "I'm afraid not." He paused, his brow lowered as he thought. Then his face brightened, and he snapped his fingers. "But I can give you the names of some other men who might."

FIVE

An Ally Is found

1904, Chicago

John left the Armours' office with his head so full of thoughts, he could barely focus on putting one foot in front of the other. All the way back down the nine flights of stairs, his mind raced, and he stared at the paper he held in his fingers: a list of three names Ogden had given him. Any of these men might know the whereabouts of Tom Candy and perhaps something about what had happened to John's father. Or maybe they would know nothing. He tried not to get his hopes up too high, but it was difficult. This was the most solid lead he'd ever encountered in the ten or so years he'd been pursuing this story.

Outside, John snapped back to reality with the blaring honk of a Thresher Electric automobile, made for four but precariously loaded with seven or eight men, several of whom stood on the running boards. As he stepped back up onto the curb, the car careened by, and John feared it would tip, spilling its passengers into the manure cesspool running down the gutter. But the vehicle righted itself back onto four wheels and kept going. One of the men on the back grinned at John and tipped his hat as they sped away.

John wandered back up Lake Shore Drive and stopped by the Chicago Yacht Club to look eastward across Lake Michigan. He eyed the list again. Joseph McCoy, Abilene, Kansas. Opened up the first cow town in Kansas, at the north end of the Chisholm Trail, according to Ogden Armour. John Clay, general manager of the Swan Land and Cattle Company of Chugwater, Wyoming, and one of the foremost cattle men of the West. He'd even written a book on it.

Last was Charlie Goodnight in Colorado, who had blazed the Goodnight-Loving trail from Texas up through Palo Duro Canyon and Trinidad, up to the ranch he started in Pueblo. He would likely be the most knowledgeable about Tom Candy and cattle driving in general, Mrs. Armour had added—if he would agree to talk to John. Goodnight was known to be about as irascible as the longhorns he rousted out of the Texas brush country. He was a good man but a tough one, and mostly kept his mouth shut. If John could get him to open up, he knew he might find out what he so desperately needed to know.

John walked briskly back toward the city, noting as he went the strange anomaly between the skyscrapers, electric trains, and automobiles and the city's thousands of horse-drawn wagons and carriages. *Old world meets the new*, he thought, as usual framing his mental wanderings as catchy newspaper headlines. He couldn't stop thinking like a journalist. Though he'd always loved writing, he'd fairly stumbled into the profession en route to his larger goal of gaining justice for his father. Either way, he had come to like it and made some friends along the way. One of them was George Hollings, now an editor at the *Chicago Tribune*. He'd come to do a story a while back and simply stayed because he'd liked the city so much. Plus, he'd confided in John, the pay was better, and it was nice not to be under Blackwood's thumb for once. John already realized the truth of that statement for himself.

It was early afternoon, and the lunch crowds were heading back to work. John stopped at a nearly empty cafeteria to have a cup of coffee and write down some notes on what the Armours had told him before it slipped from his memory. "Met on Ohio River, 1849," he jotted. "Philip to California for Gold Rush. Tom predicts war's effect on cattle trade."

This had all been good information. But still the one thing—the one person—he needed eluded him. John put down his pen and looked out the wall of windows at the front of the cafeteria. He tried to imagine the streets as they had been fifty-some years earlier, when Tom Candy and Phillip Armour had plied their trades. He pictured a herd of cattle lowing and chuffing as Tom prodded them up the thoroughfare toward Armour's butchering operation. It must have been quite a sight to see, and even more so when Tom reached New York with his longhorns several years later. It had been a spectacle and had made Tom into a celebrity. So why was it so difficult to find him now?

John left the cafeteria and made his way toward the *Tribune* building. Though he had wired ahead that he'd be in town, he had no definite appointment with George Hollings but hoped to find him in. During their days at the New York *Trib*, George had lent a sympathetic ear more than once, so he knew all about John's father. Now John needed a sounding board again and was glad his old colleague was so close by.

At the *Tribune* building, a receptionist welcomed him in then went down a hallway to find George. The two returned to the lobby momentarily.

"John, old boy," George said, a big grin on his face as he approached. He grabbed John's hand and shook it vigorously, clenching John's bicep with his free hand. Then his smile faded, and he peered into John's eyes. "You look tired. Are you all right? Come on, let's go sit down."

He led John, who had not said a word yet, back down the hallway and into his office, which was much nicer than the space they had shared in New York. A cherry wood desk, high-back leather chairs, several full bookshelves, a wall full of windows.

"You've done very well for yourself, George." John smiled as he sat down in one of the chairs before the desk. George went around to the other side and settled into his own leather seat.

"Thanks," he said, turning a bit red. He'd always been so humble. "But tell me, what brings you out here? And how have you been?"

John let out a long breath, trying to decide where to start. "I quit my job at the *Tribune*." It was the first thing that came to mind.

"No!" George hissed, his hands splayed out on the blotter

of his desk. His face portrayed his genuine shock. "Was it Blackwood? Did he force you into it?"

John laughed. Their old boss was so volatile, it was no wonder George found him suspect.

"No," John said then paused. "Well, maybe yes, in a way. I proposed a story, and he shot me down. So I left to pursue it on my own."

George let out a low whistle, obviously quite impressed. "What's the story? Has to be something good."

John shifted in his seat. He coughed once. "It's about my father."

George sat up straight, his face suddenly very serious. "You've found something?"

John smiled at him. He'd known he could trust George not only to be on his side but to be interested in what John had to say. "Again, yes and no. I have a lot of leads, but unfortunately nothing solid yet. I just met with the Armours of the Armour Packing Company. Phillip, the former head of the company—"

"Now deceased," George interjected.

John nodded. "Yes. Now deceased. His widow and son told me, though, that Phillip had known a man named Tom Candy, who I believe might know something about the conspiracy against my father."

"Tom Candy." George repeated the name quietly to himself a few times. "It rings a bell. Who is he?"

John pulled up his bag and retrieved the article he'd shown Mrs. Armour earlier about Tom's cattle drive to New York City. He handed it to George, who looked it over quickly, his editor's eye catching the meaning with just a scan.

"Yes, I remember this," he said, putting the article down. He took off his glasses and rubbed the bridge of his nose. "Rather, I've heard about it. Of course, it was way before my time and yours." He replaced his glasses and blinked a few times as he looked at John. "And it is a fascinating story. But why is it of interest to you? What's it to do with your father?"

John sighed and just looked at his friend for a moment. He held a hand up in the air, indicating his exasperation. "I don't know," he finally admitted. "I just don't know. That's why I'm on this trip. I'm hoping to find Tom Candy, and maybe he can tell me something I don't already know."

"I wish I could do something to help you, John. I wish I could give you some sort of lead." He picked up the article again and eyed it, obviously trying to think something out. He handed it back to John. "But you know, if T. Burton Blackwood doesn't want the story, I'll take it."

John took the paper, placed it back in his bag, and then secured its clasp, never taking his eyes off George. "What are you getting at?" His tone sounded just as suspicious as he felt.

George smiled and leaned his forearms on his desk, folding his hands in front of him. He spoke low, conspiratorially. "I'm saying you can send me your dispatches from the road. If you want to, of course. You know how I love a good investigation. A little muckraking." He sat up straight, letting out a loud, gleeful cackle. He even rubbed his hands together, completing the picture of the dastardly villain. "Come on, John. Don't you want to burn Blackwood's hide a little?"

John moved in his seat and smirked. "Well, when you put it that way…But what sort of stories do you want, George?"

"Well, to start with, give me fifteen inches, half a page, on Tom Candy and his cattle drive. Then, say, twice a month double that on whatever news you've found out. We'll make it a treasure hunt, the prize being this mysterious figure of the Old West. I'll pay you ten dollars an article for as long as you deliver."

John paused. He liked the idea, but… "Can I write about my father in these articles?"

George nodded. "Whatever you're comfortable sharing, John. The space is yours."

He considered it a moment longer. These assignments would keep his writing chops up and, perhaps more important, give him an ongoing source of income. He'd barely dipped into his savings yet, but he wanted to make it last as long as possible. He had no idea how long this journey would last.

He put his hand out. "Thanks, George. I'm grateful for the opportunity."

George shook his hand as both men stood up. "I look forward to reading your work again," he said. "You know how much I admire your writing. Now come. Let's go see Martin, our bookkeeper, about getting you an advance on that first report."

SIX

The War Correspondent

1862 Washington City

Edwin Stanton trailed his spoon through the bowl of beef stew on the table in front of him. It was more broth and potatoes than anything else, but given what the men were eating out on the front lines of the war, he could hardly bring himself to complain. He'd been out there and seen how dire it was, how lacking they were in basic supplies, and for this he felt responsible. As the secretary of war, he was second only to President Lincoln in orchestrating and executing the pushback against the Confederate rebellion, but he couldn't be everywhere at once. Though his crusade to end corruption had reached an impressive breadth—including even generals, senators, and members of Lincoln's cabinet—sometimes undetected dishonesty cropped up. He'd only just found out about the underhanded merchants who had been keeping the food they were supposed to give the Union troops and selling it to the highest bidders.

He took a tentative bite of the steaming stew, which scalded the surface of his tongue. He chewed quickly and swallowed then picked up his mug of ale and drank deeply. Edwin had never been much for alcohol, but lately he'd found a pint or two helped to quiet his mind on evenings when he couldn't leave his work at the office. He thought of his beautiful wife at home, waiting for him while he sat alone at this pub eating mediocre food and drinking warm, flat beer, unable to get the smell of musket powder and death out of his nose. He'd just returned from an outpost in New Orleans, where a General Banks and his troops had been held in a standoff for forty days. Banks had set upon the town of Port Hudson, aiming to overtake it, but the Confederate troop coalition there was well prepared; they needed only six thousand men to hold off Banks's army of thirty thousand.

Unfortunately, this hadn't been the general's first major mishap. He'd been a congressman and the governor of Massachusetts prior to the war and had no military training—which was perhaps why he had suffered one defeat after another. In fact, he'd never walked out of a skirmish with a win. But he was a devout abolitionist and a well-known leader in the Republican Party—two traits that would likely encourage men to join the military and others to contribute money to the Union cause— and Lincoln had appointed him personally. Aware that many other generals resented Banks because he had not trained at West Point as they all had, Stanton assigned him to areas that would befit his skills but not ruffle any feathers. He needed all the military's commanders to keep their minds on the war, not infighting over who was better educated.

So perhaps Banks's record of losses and humiliations was partially Edwin's fault. He would accept that blame; his position did, after all, make him responsible for all of the military. The generals' losses were his to bear just as much as their victories. However, Banks had his own level of ineptitude that he could not seem to overcome, and Stanton knew he would soon have to oust him, as he had already done to so many. In his quest to root out corruption on all levels, he had established a network of—well, he didn't like calling them spies, but that was what they were: military men, journalists, even suppliers who would report back to him any questionable activities they witnessed. In this way, Stanton managed to reach out to all corners of the war arena and deep into the federal government itself, and remove those players who were not working to ensure the survival of America both militarily and politically. This pursuit of justice had, understandably, made him many, many enemies. These days, very few people were willing to talk; no one wanted to be seen as a snitch. It was a solitary pursuit, this rooting out evil and greed, but he felt it was his life's calling, and he remained committed to saving the cause of the Union from those who would destroy it from within.

He sighed and pushed the stew across the table. A biscuit sat on a nearby plate; he picked it up and shoved it in his mouth. It was dry and stuck to his teeth in a most unpleasant way, but at least it distracted him from the images of war that would not leave his head; this time, he thought of the gunfire volleying across Port Hudson, and the clouds of smoke and dirt in the air as soldiers scuffled for cover and their weapons. He had never been so close to the fighting as he had been on this last trip. Worse, he'd known that General Banks would not get most of his men out of it alive.

Edwin swallowed hard, pushing these thoughts and the god-awful biscuit deep down into his gut. While he thought at times it might be helpful to confide in someone about it all, he knew he was ultimately responsible for this war almost as much as the president was. Complaining would only waste time he could otherwise spend on—for example—providing his men on the front lines with proper sustenance.

After taking another gulp of ale to wash down the crumbs stuck in the back of his throat, Stanton took a small notebook out of the inside pocket of his coat and opened it on the table, pressing down on the spine to make it lie flat. Then he took out a pair of rectangular-lensed spectacles, set them on his nose, and bent over the book to read the notes he'd written while in the field, detailing Banks's pros and cons:

Gen. Nathaniel Banks

1861, named major general of volunteers (political connections? Influence with voters?). Brought in 30,000 volunteers from New England.

Sent to N.O. Dec. 1862, replacing Maj. Gen. Benjamin Butler. Raised Corps d'Afrique, first black regiment used in major battle.

"Secretary Stanton."

Edwin slammed the notebook closed then quickly put it back in his pocket. He took off his glasses and looked up to see who was there.

"Yes," he said. He didn't recognize the young man. He was slight but tall, with dark, wavy hair and a black mustache that hung down over his top lip. His brow seemed permanently knit, his cheeks slightly sunken, and his dark eyes stared at Stanton with an intensity that made the older man shift in his seat. He cleared his throat. "What can I do for you?"

The young man didn't speak but pulled out a chair and sat down across the small table from Edwin. He continued to stare—perhaps gathering his thoughts, perhaps waiting for Edwin to ask another question. Either way, Stanton was too tired for this game.

"What can I help you with?" he asked, his impatience and fatigue coming through in his voice.

The man waited a moment longer. "I have some information I think might be of interest to you," he finally said, then returned to his stoic state.

Edwin smiled. He'd heard this one before. Everyone in Washington, it seemed, knew him by sight. He couldn't count how often he'd been accosted by wild-eyed men and women looking to share their ideas about conspiratorial acts between the president and the leaders of the South or their beliefs that slavery was just the natural order of things—the way God wanted it, even—and so why should we go to war to try to stop it?

Edwin did not entertain these folks' ramblings. He remained

polite, but always told them he could not discuss such matters and removed himself from their company as quickly as possible. He was about to do the same now, but the young man stopped him.

"Mr. Stanton, just hear me out. I know about your efforts to end corruption in the military and I want to help. I'm here to offer my services."

Now it was Edwin's turn to pause. He put his elbows on the table, folded his hands in front of his mouth, and eyed the young gentleman. What was his angle? What did he want from Edwin? He didn't look destitute, so it probably wasn't money. What, then—power? Notoriety? Who could guess?

"What's your name, son?" Stanton asked.

The man just looked at him, as if a bit surprised by the question. "Birch," he spat out at last. "Thomas Birch."

"Well, Mr. Birch, may I ask why you're so interested in what I do? And what exactly you think you can do to help?"

Birch sat back in his chair. "I'm a war correspondent," he said. His speech was quick; the concerned, tense look never left his face. "And a good one. I've gained the trust of some very powerful men. Generals. Politicians. Even your president."

Edwin laughed. "*My* president? He's your president too, you know. Or do you disagree with Mr. Lincoln's policies?"

Thomas shrugged. "I don't involve myself in political matters. I'm only here to report the news."

"So again I'll ask: What do you think you can do for me?"

The younger man moved forward once more, leaning his body across the narrow table, getting as close to Stanton as he could. He lowered his voice when he spoke. "I have free access to all these people. They trust me. They tell me their secrets just to get them off their chests."

Stanton was sure he saw the smallest hint of a smile creep onto the man's face.

"Trust me," Birch went on. "I can tell you things you need to know."

Stanton lowered his hands to the table and looked at Birch out of the corners of his eyes. "And what makes you think I would trust you?"

Birch reached into his coat pocket and retrieved a leather billfold. From within it, he took out a thick square of paper and slid it across the table. Stanton picked it up. On it was a Daguerreotype portrait of the man seated in front of him. Inked next to it in small, straight script was his information: "Thomas Birch. Journalist. *New-York Tribune.*" Below that was the signature of the newspaper's editor-in-chief, Horace Greeley.

Stanton handed it back without a word. Though his gut told him not to trust this man, just like he never trusted anyone he met, he had to admit the *New-York Tribune* was a highly reputable paper. Yes, Birch could have fabricated the identification card on his own. But he also had to know that a simple telegram to Greeley would reveal him if this were a ruse.

"What exactly are you proposing, then?" Edwin asked, trying to sound as noncommittal as possible.

"Just that you remain open to communications from me," said Birch. "I live out in the field. Always traveling. Going where the fighting is. I talk to everyone, from the lowliest enlisted man to the top brass. That's the only way to get an objective story. And when I hear something I think might be useful to you, I'll let you know."

"What do you expect in return?" Stanton asked quickly. There always had to be some trade.

Again Birch shrugged. "The satisfaction of helping to save my country from the clutches of evil?"

He smiled, but Stanton saw no happiness in it, only a dry amusement. It gave him a bit of a chill. No, he didn't trust Thomas Birch, and he wouldn't, no matter what affiliations he claimed. There was something unsettling about him. Something calculating.

Still, what other choice did Edwin have? His resources were drying up; so few people wanted to help him anymore. He couldn't afford to look this gift horse in the mouth. Not if he wanted to achieve his goals.

"All right," he said and then repeated more firmly, "all right. You have a deal, Birch. Just remember: not a word of this to anyone. No one can know of our alliance."

Thomas Birch stood up and pushed his chair back under the table. "No," he said, taking a step backward. "No one shall. Mr. Stanton, I'll be in touch."

And with a tip of his hat, he melted back into the crowd at the bar and disappeared.

SEVEN

The Hunter Is Hunted

1904, Colorado

Pueblo, Colorado, was a big place. Or so John Stanton had heard. He'd never been there and had no idea where he would start to look for Charles Goodnight once he arrived. Unfortunately, the Armours couldn't be more specific than to say he was within the confines of the city—probably, or at least last they'd heard. Sitting on the train again, watching the world speed by outside the window, John thought, not for the first time, that this was some wild goose chase he'd gotten himself involved in.

The rails would bring him westward to Denver first, then John would change trains for the last one hundred miles south to his destination. At just over a thousand miles, the trip would take around twenty-five hours, give or take—plenty of time for John to get some sleep, review his notes, and prepare for his upcoming meeting with the rancher. What would he ask? Where would he even start?

"Remember you have to find him first," he told himself quietly. Outside the train, the cityscape turned to the rural farmlands of western Illinois, the gray streets exchanged for waving fields of green and grain. "If he even exists."

John let out a laugh. This wasn't the first time he'd had this thought—that maybe this was all a ruse. Just some old cattlemen and meat packers having fun with an Easterner, a New Yorker who had the audacity to think he could know anything about the West. Maybe this was a fable, with Tom Candy instead of Paul Bunyan and a herd of longhorns in place of his big, blue ox. Everyone knew of the Englishman, but at the same time no one knew a thing about him. It just didn't seem possible.

But if John chose not to believe, he might as well get on an eastbound train and go right back home. Abandon his search for Tom Candy and forever put to rest the unresolved case of his father's innocence. And that was something he most definitely could not do. No, he had to have faith that it was true, that Ogden Armour and his mother had set him on a viable path. Tom Candy had to exist, he told himself. Because if he didn't...

John shook his head to dismiss the thought then leaned his forehead on the cool window glass. The sun touched the horizon in the west, growing smaller and smaller even though the train raced it westward. He closed his eyes. When he opened them again, the sky outside was as dark as ink. Pinpoints of light, hundreds of tiny stars, glittered across an open expanse of plains covered in low grass as far as the eye could see.

John sat up straight, rubbing his fingers into his tender neck. He'd passed out in an awkward pose and slept so deeply, it seemed, that he hadn't moved. He stood up slowly, arched his back, and then reached his hands up toward the ceiling of the car. When he felt properly stretched out, he looked around. Some of the other passengers were asleep; some chattered quietly among themselves. A baby cried, then another joined in, and their mothers shushed and rocked them back to silence.

Bending over, he peered out the window again, trying to discern which state he was in. But he couldn't tell from the scenery—or, more accurately, the lack thereof. Just mile after empty mile of untouched and uncultivated land. A man coughed at the end of the car, catching John's attention, and he stood up straight again. The man—middle aged, with a large, bulbous nose, beady eyes, and a bowler hat a size too small for his head—was focused on John as if on purpose, as if he had been watching him for quite some time.

John managed a weak smile, then slunk back down into his seat, slumping down low so the other man could not see him. In the distance, he could see the Rocky Mountains just coming into view, a mass of dark rock against the dark sky. The train wouldn't reach Denver, at the mountains' base, for a few more hours. Would that man stare at him the whole way? John didn't like the idea, but he couldn't hide the whole time either.

"Oh, for Pete's sake," he muttered, sitting up suddenly and leaning down to retrieve his suitcase from beneath his seat.

With his coat over his arm and the leather satchel with his notes clutched tightly to his chest, he stepped out into the aisle and turned, heading in the opposite direction, away from prying eyes. When he reached the door of the car, he pulled it open and stepped onto the platform outside. The door slid closed again behind him.

The noise out there was immense, filling his whole head, making his chest vibrate. The chugga chugga of the engine, the whine of steel against steel. John held his free hand up to cover one ear, as if that would help, and hopped onto the platform of the next car. The door stuck, but he pulled and it finally gave, admitting him to another parlor car full of sleepy passengers and soft conversation. He found an empty seat about halfway in and set his things down, then settled in to try to get a little more rest. His sore neck complained just a little as he leaned his shoulders back against the seat and tucked his chin to his chest. He crossed his arms and closed his eyes.

The car door opened and slammed. John bolted upright.

Craning his neck to get a look over the top of the seat, he saw the man from the previous car—the tiny bowler, his eyes like a rat's—looking around as if he had lost something. John turned around and looked straight ahead.

You're just being paranoid, he told himself. *You're tired from traveling, and you're in an unfamiliar place.* It was natural to be nervous and wary in his situation.

But then he looked back, and the man was approaching him, an unmistakable look of intent in his eyes. John grabbed his things again and hurried down the aisle. Through the next door was the dining car, which was much livelier than the parlors. People sat at tables eating and smoking, laughing and drinking. There was a bar to one side. John went toward it. He'd never been much for alcohol, but he needed something to calm his nerves.

"Whiskey, please," he told the barkeep as he slid up onto a stool, suitcase and traveling bag still in his hands. He looked around furtively then deposited his belongings underneath his feet. When he sat back up again, his drink was waiting for him on the bar, and he downed it in a gulp then motioned for another. The whiskey burned a fiery trail through his chest and stung his belly like a swarm of bees. He resolved to take the second one slower.

In the dining car, the cacophony of voices rose and fell, rose and fell, falling into a rhythm with the rocking of the train on the tracks. The sounds, the movement, and the liquor all conspired to dull John's racing thoughts, and before long he was feeling better. By the third drink, he felt *good*. He smiled at the passengers around him and raised his glass to toast them, as if they were at some big, moving party. The thought brought a laugh to his throat, and he let it out freely, so thankful for the reprieve from the stress of the past week. Quitting his job, leaving New York, setting out on this crazy trip with only the clothes on his back and all his money in his pocket…

"Ay, barkeep! Gimme a whiskey, and fast."

The voice behind John was loud and gruff. He whipped around; the action made his head spin, and he closed his eyes, grabbing at the man to keep from falling to the floor.

"Ya'd better slow down," the voice said, sounding almost amused. "Looks like ya can't hold yer drink."

John squinted one eye open. "You," he said, pointing a wavering finger in the man's face then reaching up to flick the rim of his little bowler hat. "What do you want? Why are you following me?"

The man picked up his drink and tossed it back, then wiped his mouth on the sleeve of his coat. He was tall, looming over John in a threatening way, and bent over to whisper in his ear.

"I know what you're doing," he said, "and I strongly advise you against it."

When the man stood back up, John looked at him with his brow lowered. "What are you talking about? What am I doing? I can drink as much as I want, you know. That's my business, not yours. I don't even know you."

The man leaned over again, this time putting his weight against John's smaller frame, nudging him off the stool and pressing him up against the bar. "You know exactly what I'm talking about." His voice came out now as a low growl, as menacing as a grizzly's. John cowered—he couldn't help it—and felt suddenly, painfully sober.

"I—I still don't know what your meaning is," he stuttered, trying to inch away from the man, but it was no use. His broad torso had John pinned. "I think you've got the wrong—"

"I know exactly who ya are!" the man boomed, and all heads around them turned. The man scowled back at them, and they returned to what they'd been doing right quick. He turned his attention back to John. "Reporter from the *New-York Tribune*. Diggin' up old dirt that shouldn't be touched. Ya need to go back from where ya come. Go beg that old boss a' yours to give you your job back. Forget about all of this. Understood?"

The two men eyed each other in silence. A river of questions flooded John's mind: Who was this man? Had someone sent him here? How did he know so much about John's life?

However, only one word came out when he opened his mouth: "Understood."

And with that, the man eased up. He stepped away, grabbed John's drink from the bar, and tossed it down his throat. He took a couple steps backward, holding John's gaze, then turned and headed for the door.

"Understood," John said again to himself as the man exited the car. But really he had no intention of doing a thing the man had said.

EIGHT

Good Advice

1852, Illinois

"I'm curious," said the man at the next table. "Is it true what they say about the English?"

Tom Candy tipped back his drink, allowing the last drops at the bottom to slide down onto his tongue. He set the empty glass down on his own rough-hewn wooden table and looked at the man, with whom he'd exchanged cursory greetings when he'd sat down. "Pardon?"

The stranger smiled, leaning back in his chair and tossing a packet of papers he'd been holding onto the tabletop. "Is it true what they say?" he repeated. "That the English really like their drink?"

Tom shrugged. "Well, I don't know who *they* are," he said, "but they're right." He picked up his glass and tapped the bottom against the table. "In fact I'll have another right now." Looking over his shoulder toward the bar, he raised his hand and motioned to the bartender.

The man at the next table laughed quietly as he looked out over the crowded room, a makeshift bar at the back of a general store, designed for immediate consumption of its primary goods: brandy, whiskey, wine, and rum. Tom had been partaking of the latter, but the syrup-sweet liquor had not yet gotten to his head.

"Then my next question," the man said, peering back at Tom, "is what on Earth are you doing here in the middle of America?"

Tom took a drink, then wiped off his top lip with the cuff of his shirt. It was already dirty, so he figured it didn't matter much. He'd just come from delivering a herd to Armour's shop, where Phillip and his men would slaughter the cattle, butcher them, sell the meat, and then return half the profits to Tom.

"Business," he replied. "What else does—say, what's your name? If we're going to have a proper conversation, we should know what to call one another, don't you think?"

"Lincoln," the other man replied, holding out a hand to Tom. "My friends call me Abe."

Tom reached over and shook his hand. "Abe it is. Glad to be counted among them. I'm Tom Candy. A pleasure to make your acquaintance. Or as you say here, *nice ta meet ya*," he added in an exaggerated accent. "As I was saying, why does anyone come to this country if not to make money?"

Lincoln nodded. "Money or land. It's always one or the other. Or sometimes both."

The two men were silent for a while. Tom continued enjoying his rum and noticed, not for the first time, the conspicuous absence of drink on Abe's table. Lincoln watched the patrons of the bar—all male, mostly drunk. His gaze settled for a while on a table at the far wall, where a couple of men were involved in a heated conversation. It had been growing louder and louder over the short time that Tom had been there.

"So what kind of business are you in?" Lincoln asked Tom, his gaze lingering on the men.

"Cattle driving," Tom said. "Small herds, a few dozen head. I go down into southeastern Illinois mostly—Springfield, Decatur, that area—and bring them back for my partner to butcher and sell. Just got in with a herd today, as a matter of fact."

Lincoln looked at him now and nodded. "That's a good business to be in. There's always big demands for meat and leather around here. Have you been outside Illinois much? Seen the cattle trade in any other territories?"

Tom shook his head. "No. We've talked about branching out, maybe going as far as the Minnesota Territory or to see what we can find in Wisconsin, but we just haven't had the time to plan anything yet."

"You should," Lincoln said quickly, sitting forward in his seat. "But where you should head is down south. Missouri, Arkansas, that's where you need to be…or Texas. Now, that's the place to go if you want to find cattle. There's millions of wild longhorns down there, all yours for the taking."

Tom lowered his brow. "No offense, but isn't Texas a long way from Chicago, and vice versa?"

Lincoln laughed lightly and sat back again. "Yes, yes, it is. You're right about that. But I'm telling you, there are enough cattle there that you could do a drive of—how many head did you say you bring in with each herd now?"

Tom held his hand out flat and teetered it side to side. "Two to three dozen, give or take."

"Well, I'm sure you could bring a few hundred or even a few thousand from Texas and sell them for enough to make the trip worthwhile." Abe looked at Tom in silence for a moment, his head cocked to the side as if a thought were turning over in his brain. "Here's another one for you. Completely unrelated, but it just came to me. In your cattle drives here in Illinois, have you ever thought of taking them farther? Maybe…out to New York City?"

Tom lowered his brow again. "New York City?" He pondered the thousand-mile drive from Texas, then almost doubling that by adding another eight hundred miles to New York—quite a distance by anyone's reckoning. Now he was curious. "Why do you ask?"

"Well, I've just returned from a visit to New York," Lincoln said. "I'm a lawyer, had to go out there for a bit of business. Have you ever been?"

Tom remembered the short while he'd spent in the city with Orville and Sarah Pritchard, and a pang of guilt hit his chest. He'd said he would see them again, sometime when he passed through Cleveland, but it had been three years and he hadn't managed to call on them once.

"Yes, I have," he told Lincoln. "But only in passing when I first arrived in the country. Not long enough to get a good impression of the place other than that it's very fast paced. Everyone seems to be in a hurry in New York. But what makes you think they have a need for cattle there?"

Lincoln stood up slightly and turned his chair around to face Tom. Though he was bent over at the waist as he did so, Tom could see he was a man of enormous height. When he sat down again, he crossed his arms over his chest—normally a hostile pose on any man, but on his gaunt frame it merely made him look relaxed.

"Well, to be honest, the meat they have…" Abe screwed up his face into a look of immense disgust. "It's certainly nothing like what we have here. I'm sure if you could bring something of quality to the area; you'd have buyers falling all over themselves to price each other out. What do you make per head here?"

Tom, in the middle of a drink, waved his hand, a dismissive gesture. When he finished, he put down his glass. "To be honest, I don't give much thought to the price of dressed-out beef. That's all my partner's affair. I prefer to be out on the trail, doing the buying and driving. I tried butchering once, but the blood and the guts…" He shivered involuntarily. "It just wasn't for me." He thought for a moment and took another swig. "Mostly, though, I didn't like being cooped up in the shop all day."

Lincoln nodded again. "Can't say I love being in an office all day either, so I suppose I know how you feel. But it's a means to an end, right? A man has to make money if he wants to get anywhere in life."

Tom swallowed the mouthful of rum. "Too true, friend. Now, tell me, how do you know so much about business yourself? Pricing per head, all that?"

Lincoln smiled, and his hand wandered unconsciously back to the sheaf of papers on the table. "Well, I'm the owner of this establishment. Or was until about an hour ago. Just before you arrived, actually, I signed over the deeds to this store and two others to my business partners. I'm just waiting for them to come back from the bank to complete our transaction."

Tom regarded him for a moment, nodding his head slowly. "But I've noticed you're not drinking. Isn't this an odd business to be in for someone who's a teetotaler? That's what they're called here, yes?"

"You're right, I don't drink," Abe replied, "except for an occasional drop of champagne, just to be civil. But liquor's a family business for me. My parents were farmers, but in the off seasons my father was a barrel maker at a small distillery in Knob Creek, Kentucky. I used to bring him down his lunch and hang around when he'd let me. Sometimes I helped out with odd jobs around the plant."

"And why, may I ask, are you getting out of such a lucrative business? One that brings joy to so many people?" Tom smirked and took another sip of his drink.

Lincoln sat up straight and cleared his throat. "Well, as I mentioned, I'm a lawyer, and…well, I've been elected to Congress. And with the temperance movement gaining so many followers, it's just not prudent for me to have a hand in this particular barrel. I have to represent my constituents' interests."

"Well, congratulations!" Tom reached out to shake Lincoln's hand again. "I didn't know I've been in the presence of such an important man."

Abe waved at him, dismissing the compliment.

"No, it's true," Tom continued. "A congressman. It is a shame, though, that you have to give up your businesses. All joking aside, it looks like this place at least is running a pretty good profit. I assume your other shops do as well."

"They do. All three, they do." Lincoln again looked at those two men across the room, whose voices had just grown another level louder. One of them was out of his seat, leaning across the table, jabbing a finger into the other man's chest.

Tom, seeing his new friend's distraction, turned around to look too. "Do you have an off-duty constable or someone who can take care of them?" he asked. "I can tell you, every pub I've been to in England has at least one. And they certainly earn their pay some days."

Lincoln rubbed his long, clean-shaven chin, his bushy eyebrows lowering as he kept an eye on the men. "No one official. We try to give men a chance to calm down on their own. Liquor makes them rowdy, but most of the time they mean nothing by it. They'll be fighting one minute and swearing their undying allegiance to one another in the next."

Tom smiled at him. "I like you. You seem like a very level-headed man."

Lincoln again motioned to him to stop, another gesture of humility. "I try to be," he said quickly, but before he could say more, the men across the room began to shout. One stood up so quickly, his chair fell over behind him, hitting the floor with a clatter. By the time Tom turned far enough around to look, Abe was halfway across the room to them.

"Listen, gentlemen," Lincoln said in a tranquil voice, so kind and gentle it actually made the irate men stop to listen. He put a hand on each one's back, guided them both to their chairs, and then pulled one up for himself. He sat with them and talked quietly for a minute. Their eyes remained on him, nodding as he spoke, looks of deep concentration on their faces.

Back at his table, Tom watched the scene with a growing fascination of his own. Within a few minutes, Abe had the two former enemies shaking hands and even embracing one another. Then they headed out the door together, and Abe returned to his seat.

"That was amazing!" said Tom. "What did you say to get them to calm down? They looked like they were about to murder one another before you got there."

Lincoln bowed his head, a small smile on his lips. "I listened to their problem and tried to mediate it for them. Thankfully, they were able to come to an agreement." He looked up toward the front of the tavern to make sure the two men had actually left. "Then I told them to stop drinking and go home to their wives. Hopefully that's what they're doing."

"Well," said Tom, "I have to say, just seeing that, I can tell you'll be an excellent politician."

"I hope so," Lincoln replied with a laugh. "My wife tells me I'm far too honest for politics."

Tom raised his eyebrows and his near-empty glass. "I'll drink to that." Then he downed the rest of his rum and pulled out his pocket watch to check the time. Almost eight o'clock, and he hadn't eaten dinner yet. He'd be staying with Phillip and his wife, Malvina, who was an excellent cook and undoubtedly had a plate of something delicious waiting for Tom. Plus, he had to be up at five the following morning to help Phillip sell the meat his men cut up overnight. Tom wasn't fit to be a butcher, but a salesman—that he could do, and do well.

He let out a contented sigh. "Well, Mr. Lincoln," he said, pushing his empty glass away from him on the table, "it's time for me to take my leave. I thank you for your hospitality."

Lincoln closed his eyes solemnly and bowed his head for a moment, a gesture of sincerity. He looked back at Tom. "The pleasure was mine. I hope our paths will cross again someday."

"Here, here," Tom replied as he took some money from his pocket to give the bartender—enough to cover his drinks and a generous tip. Then, with one last acknowledging nod toward Abe, he headed out the back door of the shop, toward the stable to retrieve his horse.

NINE

The Burly Rancher

1904, Pueblo, Colorado

Charles Goodnight spent half his time at his ranch, about five miles west of Pueblo proper, and the other half living out of a hotel in town, near to where he maintained an office from which he ran his business affairs. As a former Texas Panhandle rancher, he dutifully applied vigilante justice to any of the area's outlaws and cattle thieves who dared cross his property lines; he was a cowboy through and through, a legend of his own making.

However, he was also a shrewd and immensely successful entrepreneur, and though he was on in years, he'd never given up the reins of his ranch or any of his other many investments, which included a partnership in an interstate land company that sold shares in property along the Texas-New Mexico border. Goodnight managed his considerable wealth down to the penny, but he was not a miser. To the contrary, he was generous to a fault, contributing regularly to his local community's charitable and philanthropic organizations.

John hoped to find him at the hotel in Pueblo, and so he headed there as soon as he disembarked from the train. It wasn't a long walk from the depot, and he took it briskly, glad for the opportunity to stretch his legs. He was still haunted by the threatening encounter with the beady-eyed man on the train. Who would be following him next? If he moved swiftly, he thought, at least he'd be a moving target.

It was near eight o'clock in the evening by the time John found the place. He rented a room first, where he deposited his bags, and freshened up with some cool water from a pitcher and basin a housekeeper came by to deliver. Then he went down to the dining room, both because he was starving and because he knew it would be the gathering place for the hotel's regulars. If Goodnight were in town, this was surely where he had to be. John seated himself at a table in a corner, ordered a plate of steak and potatoes, and surveyed the other guests as discretely as he could.

But it didn't take long to identify the man he had come to see. Charles Goodnight was a giant of a man, tall and thickset, though he seemed to be fairly light on his feet, ready to spring at an instant if need be. He had thick, gray hair and a heavy mustache, with chin whiskers that protruded for several inches below his stern mouth and square jaw. He wore what seemed to be an eternal scowl, and his furrowed brow appeared to be chiseled out of stone above his penetrating stare. Standing in front of the fireplace on the far side of the room, a fat, ashy cigar clenched in the corner of his mouth, he nodded solemnly at some story a smaller, weasely-looking man was telling him.

John's food arrived quickly, and as he ate he watched the older man, trying to learn something about him that might give him an in—a way to introduce himself and simultaneously get into Goodnight's good graces. Charles had an infamous hatred of the press and anyone representing it, or so Ogden Armour had told John, this due to a scandal surrounding Goodnight's land company many years ago. The state of Texas, it seemed, had thought enough of him to invest public funds into his venture, but then he and his partners were accused of some questionable divesting of this money. When it came to light, true or not, newspapers across the country censured him for it, claiming he had robbed money from Texas schoolchildren to further his own standing as a leader among the big cattlemen. He was a proponent of their interests, they said, and nothing more than a criminal.

As a result, and understandably, Goodnight felt pressured to reduce his holdings and eventually sold out his entire interest in the company. The negative publicity affected his own ranching activities as well, which was the last straw for him. He never granted another interview to any reporter lest they twisted his words and used them to strike him down again.

Looking at him now, though, John wouldn't have known he'd ever gone through such a rough period in his life. Goodnight was the picture of abundance, surrounded by men and women both, a glass of port in his hand and the tables around him strewn with a smorgasbord of foods. All this on a Tuesday, too; John wondered what the weekends were like for a man like Charles Goodnight.

As the server took his empty plate away, John wiped grease from his mouth and took a deep breath, steeling himself for what was about to come. Knowing how much Goodnight detested journalists, he fully expected to be rebuked when he approached, if he weren't flat out thrown from the establishment. Still, he had to try. Newspaper men were aggressive by nature and stubborn to the core; they would press on until there were no more possibilities to be tried.

And Goodnight was an extremely important possibility to John. The old rancher might be the link he had searched for between his father and Tom Candy, part of the key to figuring out the mystery of the unjust accusations against Edwin Stanton and his untimely death. So John needed an approach that would work, something that would soften the old cattleman and get him to talk without it seeming like John was trying to interview him.

"Here goes nothing," he muttered as he stood up, then he smoothed his jacket and strode across the room to introduce himself.

"Mr. Goodnight," he said, his voice barely registering above the loud conversations all around. He cleared his throat and raised his voice. "Mr. Goodnight! I'm John Stanton, and I wish to speak with you about some personal matters." He did not attempt to sound familiar or to imply that Goodnight somehow owed him any time, and he certainly made no mention of his former ties to the *New-York Tribune*. John didn't even hold out his hand for the older man to shake.

But this indifference made no impression on the big man. He scowled at John and tapped a large chunk of ash from his cigar onto the carpeted floor, his eyes on this intrepid intruder the entire time. Without a word he turned away, like a long-horn bull deciding his adversary was not a worthy opponent.

"Mr. Goodnight, Ogden Armour told me I might speak to you about—about the history of the cattle movement." John congratulated himself silently for coming up with this falsehood on the spot. It wasn't a lie exactly, just a bending of the truth. Tom Candy was, after all, quite a large part of that history. "I've just come from the offices of the Armour Packing Company in Chicago, where I met with Ogden and the Widow Armour."

Goodnight turned to look at John but only over his shoulder. His eyes showed a blink of recognition this time, his stare boring down on John for a long moment. Again, however, there was no response, and the cattleman turned his back once more.

All of a sudden, John felt desperate, as if this were his last and only chance to get the man to listen to him. "They told me to speak to you about Tom Candy," he blurted before he even knew what he was saying, and had to hold back from slapping his hand across his mouth, covering it up so no other bad ideas came rolling forth in this one's wake.

The big man paused his conversation again and this time turned completely around to take stock of the young man who was brash enough to interrupt his dinner, and on top of that to mention the name Tom Candy. John did his best to stare back with unblinking eyes and keep his body's nervous shaking at bay, but both were difficult. Charles Goodnight was an intimidating man.

Then his scowl softened. Just a little, almost imperceptibly. But the shift was there; John saw it with his reporter's eye for detail. He also thought he saw a bit of a twinkle of remembrance in Goodnight's eyes. Maybe the mention of Candy's name had brought back a flash of his own heyday in the cattle trade, when he'd once earned as much as six hundred thousand dollars in ten years. Those had to be some good memories. John hoped they would work on his mind.

And it seemed, after a moment, they had. The furrows around the older man's brow relaxed, and he extended his hand slowly, with what Stanton took for a smile, though it was halfway to a grimace.

"I'm Charlie Goodnight," he announced, taking his chawed-on cigar out of his mouth with the other hand. "And if the Armours sent you, then I guess you're all right. But don't ever mention that name in public again, you hear?" He pointed at John with the two fingers between which he held the cigar. Its smoke trailed up in a tendril that wrapped itself around John's face.

"Yes, sir," John replied, stifling a cough.

"Good. I'll be leaving for my ranch in the morning. Be ready to go at eight."

"What—I—" John stuttered, not knowing at all how to respond.

"Be gone now, boy," Goodnight interjected, flicking his

hand in a shooing gesture. "I don't want to see your face until tomorrow morning."

John felt compelled to obey. If this was how he would get the information he needed from Goodnight, then so be it. The old man wanted to order him around? Great. Wanted to call all the shots and bring John onto his own land, setting him at a clear disadvantage? No problem. The journalist in him knew to play along. This was how deals were struck, how bonds were forged, and how the most reticent witnesses were slowly enticed to state their claims. If Goodnight wanted to call all the shots, John would let him—as long as in the end the cattleman delivered what John wanted to know.

With a polite nod, John left the dining room and retired to his sleeping quarters, where he lay in bed and stared at the ceiling until the following morning.

Promptly at eight o'clock, John found Charles Goodnight already waiting in a carriage outside the hotel. It was a two-seater, and the older man, a newly lit cigar between his thick fingers, waved John over and motioned to the empty seat. John put up his small valise and leather bag, then boosted himself up.

"Good morning," he said, tipping his hat to Charles. "I want to thank you for—"

"Luke, let's get on the road," Goodnight shouted over John's head to the lanky driver at the reins. He in turn called to the next driver up ahead, and John turned around to see there was a line of horses and carriages stretching to the end of the block.

"This is quite an entourage you have," he said with a laugh, turning back to Goodnight. But the cattleman did not smile. He just looked at John, blinking slowly as his tongue worked the end of the freshly cut cigar between his teeth.

In moments the caravan was underway, slowly at first, then picking up speed as they cleared the town limits. They left Pueblo heading to the west, following a rough road that paralleled the Arkansas River. After five miles of rolling hills and cuts descending into the river plain, the road opened up into a sheltered valley, a natural barrier that kept the winds and snow of the Rocky Mountains from pummeling the immense Rock Canyon Ranch, Goodnight's headquarters, visible off in the distance.

"This is good land to winter cattle," Goodnight offered, the first thing he'd said to John for the entire ride. "The wooded foothills offer them decent shelter, more so than they'd find out on the unprotected plains. We've got about twenty-five miles here bordering on the river, over to Hardscrabble Creek in the west and to the Greenhorns in the east, right at the junction of the St. Charles and the Arkansas Rivers." He paused, puffing on his cigar, which wasn't even halfway diminished yet. "We lay up hay in late summer and have running water year round. It's comfortable for all of us."

John nodded and looked around. He didn't know a whole lot about ranching but could see some telltale signs that this place was a good environment for it. The land was well-watered and covered with uncropped grama, which was said to put tallow on a steer rivaling that of corn-fed stock. Thanks to a little research George Hollings had helped him with before he'd left Chicago, John knew Goodnight had invested his earnings here after his droving partner, Oliver Long, had died and Charles had given up on that life. He'd needed a home base, somewhere he could settle down and raise a family. Which he had done—he'd married and had several children, all grown now with families of their own. Along the way, he'd single-handedly built this range into a cattle empire totaling more than fifty thousand head.

As the carriage descended the last rise of the great Arkansas River valley, John saw that the rains had been good that spring. The grass was a bold emerald green and already about a foot and a half high, a blue grama strain that was hearty and drought resistant even in the worst years, then lay dormant all winter to emerge the following April when daytime temperatures rose again.

The main ranch house came into view as the carriages trundled along, slowing their pace now that the bulk of the journey was done. They rode through stands of trees to the west and north, a shield of extra protection against severe winter winds. Closer to the main house, an array of deciduous trees gave welcoming shade in the hot summers and lost their leaves to let the spare sunlight of winter pass through to the grounds and house. Ponderosa pines and blue spruces formed the outermost windbreak lines, with shorter trees and heavy bushes closer to the compound's buildings.

"Everything must be so calculated," John mused aloud, looking over at Goodnight. "The plants, the stables, everything must be in perfect order for the entire operation to run as it should. It's an amazing feat of engineering."

For only the second time since they had met, John saw what he guessed might be a grin tease the corners of the old cattleman's mouth. But they just as quickly turned down again, leaving him to imagine that it hadn't been there at all.

"We've got an apple orchard out east, between the big house and the sandstone barn," Goodnight noted, jabbing his cigar in that direction. "Twenty acres. More than enough for the animals and ourselves. Don't think I've gone a day without a bite of apple pie in the last twenty years."

To John's surprise, Goodnight let out a wheezing, sputtering laugh, his ruddy face turning even redder and a splash of tears springing from his eyes. John couldn't help but laugh too, not so much at the joke but at the older man's unexpected gaiety after so many hours of stoic silence.

As the carriage pulled up in front of the big house, the ranch hands and their horses continued on to the barns and the stables beyond. Molly Goodnight, Charles's wife, was waiting to greet him at the door. She was in her mid-sixties, John figured, but showed no signs of her age other than a few thin silver streaks in her dark hair, which she wore twisted up in a bun.

"Welcome, welcome, Mr. Stanton," she said as John stepped out of the carriage, her face bright with a beaming smile. "Luke," she told the driver, "please see to Mr. Stanton's things. Third room on the right in the upstairs hall."

The sleepy-looking cowboy nodded and jumped down from his perch, releasing a stream of rank tobacco juice from his mouth onto the grass as his boots hit the ground. "Yes'm," he mumbled, but with a smile at Mrs. Goodnight that made it very clear he would do anything she asked him to.

"Thank you so much," she told him sweetly, and John could see why any of the hands here might fall over themselves to heed her call.

Molly had an enormous early dinner spread waiting for them and all her husband's ranch foremen: roasted chicken, warm biscuits, greens cooked in bacon grease, and a variety of preserved fruits and vegetables Molly had canned herself throughout the year. She sat right down and ate with the men, talking and laughing loudly at the stories they told of their time on the trails.

"I don't get into Pueblo all that often myself," she said to John as she poured him another glass of tart lemonade. "And that's just fine with me. I prefer it out here in the hills. But I do enjoy hearing about city life from these fellas once in a while."

When they'd had their fill, the hands scattered to go about their afternoon business. Some headed out to check up on the herds; others went to work on shoeing the horses after their long ride. A few, John noted with some amusement, laid themselves down under those enormous elms out front, cocked their hats over their eyes, and took naps.

Charles invited John into his office at the rear of the first floor of the big house, which also served as his library; although Goodnight could neither read nor write, he liked to collect books he thought he might be able to read someday, when he had less work and more time to learn the skill. So far, he hadn't gotten to it. He showed John his collection with pride nonetheless, then showed him to a soft leather chair in front of the room's large, log fireplace with massive, moss-covered stones set into it, culled from the shaded canyons where the river mist created patterns of the living green and gray lichens.

The fire was lit; even though summer steadily approached, the evenings were always cool in Colorado, sometimes even downright cold.

"So, where do you want to start?" Goodnight asked, then took a drag off his favorite meerschaum pipe.

John didn't know what to say. He'd grown comfortable in Charles's presence, had even grown to like the somewhat curmudgeonly man. Underneath that rough exterior lay an old cowboy with a wicked sense of humor and a shrewd businessman's mind, a combination John had to admit he found fascinating. He'd listened with great interest to Goodnight and his men telling uproarious stories about things they'd experienced while droving and ranching, but now that the focus was turned on to him, he found himself at a loss for words.

Goodnight clearly picked up on this. "Don't be shy, son. I told you if the Armours sent you, I'm sure you're okay, and you haven't proven to me otherwise. Now, I don't know what your dealings are with Tom Candy or even how you know his name, but when you said it, you got my attention." He motioned with his pipe in his hand. "So go on. Tell me what you know and what you want from me."

John let out a long breath, gathering his thoughts as well and as quickly as he could. "Mr. Goodnight," he began. "You seem to be a man who doesn't mince words, who appreciates a direct approach. So I will be as forthright as you have been. What I want to know is how you know Tom Candy and where I might find him today, as I have some questions of a personal nature I hope he can help me answer."

Goodnight regarded him for a moment, his eyes narrowed.

Then he turned his attention to the fireplace. "That's a broad enough request," he said, his voice sounding a bit far away. "So I guess I'll have to start at the start. After the Confederacy lost the war, the market for cattle in the South just dropped out—particularly in Texas, where I was doing all my business in those days. We all had to find other avenues, other ways to sell our herds. I drove into New Mexico, taking a chance that if I could cross the dry plains, the army at Fort Sumner would buy my steers to feed the thousands of starving natives they were trying to help out there."

"The Navajos," John interjected quietly. "That was a terrible time for them."

"Indeed," agreed Goodnight, then he continued on with his story. "Fortunately my plan worked, but other cattlemen weren't as fortunate. It was so hard to find a market even in nearby states. So everyone starting looking toward the North."

"No one had driven that far before?"

Goodnight smirked at John and released a stream of smoke from between his lips, blowing it in an upward plume. "Jesse Chisholm. Back before the war, he'd planned a trail through Kansas and into Chicago. He found some good markets there and thought, well, why not set up a steady trade route to the north and then head east?"

"Wait, I thought Tom was the first one to do that," John interrupted again, shaking his head.

"He was, he was," Goodnight said, his tone of voice veering toward irritated. "Chisholm only had the idea. He never did it himself. Tom was the only one to have the guts. He went right up the Shawnee trail—the only route open at the time—to St.

Louis, then to Chicago, then out to New York City. And this was back in 1854, a good fifteen years before we all started driving to the markets in Chicago."

"Tom was really ahead of his time," John noted, to which Goodnight nodded.

"And he was rewarded for it. He did a few more drives north before the war started and got himself wealthy in the process. And he had bigger ideas than Chisholm, let me tell you. Tom used to talk about making a national cattle highway, running all the way from Texas to the Canada border. Said he had something like it back in England, from where he'd come. Somersetshire to London, if I'm not mistaken, but it's been more than a few years, so don't quote me on that."

John laughed nervously at Goodnight's inadvertent reference to his journalist roots and looked to change the subject quickly. "But the highway never happened."

"No. What's that saying? Too many cooks spoil the soup. Other drovers wanted a piece of the pie, but they all wanted things done their own way. There was never enough consensus to actually go forward with the plan. But Tom didn't let that stop him. He went on with what he wanted to do, and he pioneered two of our most-used trails. I'd say at least two million head passed through them, all from south to north, over about twenty years." He stopped, took a drag on his pipe, and then added sadly, "Tom was a visionary. It's a shame things had to end up the way they did."

John sat forward in his chair, recognizing this comment as his chance to pounce. "How *did* Tom end up, Mr. Goodnight? See, that's the one thing I've had some trouble getting a handle on. No one seems to know where he is or even if he's alive or dead. And if they do know, they won't say. There's a great cloud of secrecy around the man."

Goodnight shook his head sharply. "Not secrecy," he said. "Protection. We all just want to keep Tom safe."

The two men were silent. Only the crackling of the roaring fire filled the room. John put his elbows on his knees and folded his hands out in front of him, a pensive pose. Staring deeply into the flames, he tried to craft what he would say next very carefully. However, he didn't get a chance to speak.

"And what about you, John?" Goodnight asked, his voice very measured and even. "What is your real interest in Tom Candy?"

John laughed nervously and sat up. He leaned back in the chair, which released a puff of air as he sank into it. "I told you before." He tried to keep the nerves and agitation he felt out of his voice. "There are some personal matters I'm hoping he can help me with."

The cattleman looked at John through the smoke of his pipe, opening and closing his mouth as he puffed and puffed away. "And those are?" he finally asked. Then, when John did not respond, "You have to understand my curiosity. A stranger—an easterner—who knows so much about the Old West approaches me out of the blue and asks me all these questions about things that happened a lifetime ago...You can understand my trepidation."

"Of course, of course," John said, feeling his throat constrict and beads of sweat form on his brow. He knew that all Goodnight had told him so far was a matter of public record—nothing he couldn't find in old newspapers or from other less scrupulous participants in the old cattle trade. Now that John wanted to delve into more personal information, though, the older man put up his guard, and John couldn't help but feel intimidated. "Well, my interest is—"

"What did you say your last name is?" Goodnight asked, cutting him off.

John cleared his throat. "Stanton, sir. John Stanton."

Goodnight looked at him for a moment, nodding his head as the wheels inside it turned. "That name is familiar to me." He puffed on his pipe, never taking his eyes off his young guest. "I remember a military man. No, a war leader. From the Union? With the same last name. Was he any relation to you?"

John shifted in his seat, crossed his legs, and then uncrossed them. He looked around, wishing Molly would come in with more lemonade to help with his suddenly parched tongue. "You probably mean my father," he said. "Edwin Stanton. The secretary of war under President Lincoln. He was in office during the War Between the States."

Charles Goodnight sat back in his chair and grinned. He held his pipe in his hand, pointing its stem at John. "Yes, yes! That is exactly who I meant." Then his face grew serious all at once. "Now, I also remember some rumors, if I'm not mistaken. Regarding the president's assassination? Conspiracies and speculation…but your father wasn't involved in it, was he?"

"No, uh…no, he wasn't. I don't think." John didn't know what to say. He looked down at his lap and picked at some dirt underneath his fingernails.

"Listen, I'm sorry," Goodnight went on, his voice gentler

than John had heard it yet. "That's impolite of me to ask. It must've been rough on you as a young fella. You don't have to talk about it with me if you don't want." He lowered his head a bit, trying to see John's downturned face. "I can see the hurt is still fresh. It never really goes away, does it?"

An instant pressure came up behind John's eyes as tears threatened to come out in a rush. He raised his head and looked at Charles, surprised by the old man's tenderness when so far he'd shown only grudging tolerance. "Actually," he said, swallowing back his emotions, "that's part of why I've come to see you."

Goodnight lowered his brow, his normal gruffness returning to his voice. "Because of your father and Lincoln's assassination?"

John smiled politely. He understood how odd the idea must have sounded. "In a way, yes. You see, I do believe there was a conspiracy, one built wholly to implicate my father and protect the powerful men who actually were responsible for the president's death. He had nothing to do with it or with letting the real assassin escape, of which he has also been accused. Edwin Stanton was a man of honor and morals. And he believed in Lincoln. They had their disagreements, as all colleagues do, but in the end they really did support one another. Or so my mother has told me. Unfortunately, my father passed away just before she gave birth to me."

"Oh, I'm sorry," said Goodnight, true sympathy in his voice. He eyed John for a moment before speaking. "And you think this all has something to do with Tom Candy?"

"Yes," John said, sounding defeated. He closed his eyes

and rubbed them with the tips of his thumb and forefinger. "It sounds absurd. I know it does."

"Well, maybe it's not as far fetched as it seems."

Goodnight's statement was plaintive and low; John wasn't even sure for a moment if he had heard it right. He opened his eyes. "Excuse me?"

Charles sucked on his pipe for a moment as he gathered his thoughts. Then he nestled back into his chair, getting comfortable for what might be a long story to tell.

"I didn't mention that I served in the army during the war," he began, looking to John for verification. When he shook his head, Goodnight continued. "And I met your father on a few occasions, when he was out to the battlefields, checking up on the generals."

He paused to let that sink in. John's eyes widened, but he didn't say a word, only nodded to Goodnight to indicate he should go on.

"And in the course of conversation, I told him I'd worked in the cattle trade before I'd joined the fight. He thought about that, I guess, and in the next month or so I received an order to report to the capital. The secretary of war, it seemed, wanted my advice on how to keep the army fed and get meat to the civilian populations in the North that had been cut off from trade routes because of the war."

"He wanted you to drive cattle?" John asked.

Goodnight shook his head, smoke trailing from between his lips. "No, he just wanted to know if it could be done. And I told him, not without regret, that it would be damn difficult." He counted off on his fingers as he spoke. "You had the battlefields to navigate. Then there were the Indians. They didn't want anyone crossing their plains for any reason, and if you did, they'd kill ya. If you were Union, you couldn't go through Confederate states and vice versa. And then there were areas like bloody Kansas, which was split right down the middle, Northern sympathizers on one side, Southern rebels on the other. God help any man or steer who tried setting foot in that forsaken territory."

"So it couldn't be done," John affirmed, leaning forward in his seat once more, enthralled by the turn in this story.

Goodnight laughed, that raspy, airy sound coming from his lungs again. "Son, there's no *can't* in cattle driving! If there's a will, there's a way, as we used to say. And I woulda' done it, but I was in a cavalry regiment and not fixin' to leave until the war was through. However, I told your father I knew another man who not only *could* do it but would most likely welcome the challenge."

"Tom Candy," said John.

"Tom Candy," Goodnight affirmed with a grin.

"So my father met him, then." John sat back again and brought his hands up to his head, as if that could keep his mind from reeling. This was a breakthrough, a bomb that shook the ground beneath his feet, an opening in the heavens. His father and Tom Candy had known one another. He brought his palms down over his face, pressing them into his eyes, holding back another flood of tears. All the years he'd been searching and guessing, all the hypotheses and predictions he'd made, all of them came down to this moment. And now he knew: His suppositions were right.

Still, he had such a long way to go to find the truth.

"Please," he said, putting his hands down and looking at Goodnight. His voice was low and rough. "Can you tell me where to find Tom Candy?"

Goodnight paused but then shook his head, the expression on his face one of sincere regret. "Sorry, son," he replied. "I just can't. Tom's been a recluse for years. I don't even remember the last time I saw him. And if he wants to be left alone, he's got his reasons, and I have to respect them."

John let out a long, slow breath. He sat up straight and brought his hands to his knees with a bit of a slap. "Okay," he said, nodding, looking straight out in front of him. "Okay." He'd hit so many walls already, and he'd been sure, only moments earlier, that this time he would find a door—the one that would lead him to the object of his pursuit. But no such luck...again.

He looked at Charles Goodnight. "Sir, I thank you for the information you've given me. It is most helpful, and I appreciate the time and the hospitality you've offered." He stood up as if to leave, though he had no idea where he would go. It was too far back to Pueblo to walk; he was at the mercy of Goodnight's willingness to provide him with transportation. Still, John did not want to ask. An anger slowly rose to a boil inside of him, and his reaction was to deny that he needed anything further from this man who would not give him what he ultimately needed: the present location of Tom Candy.

"John, wait," Goodnight said, sitting forward in his chair and reaching out to grab the sleeve of John's coat. "Wait. Listen, I feel awful about not telling you where Tom is, but I just can't.

Whether you understand or not, I can't. But I *can* tell you that you're looking for answers in the wrong place. What you need isn't here. You have to go back the way you came."

The two men looked at one another in silence for a good minute, John trying to decipher the message Goodnight was trying to impart to him.

"Thank you," John finally said, his voice calmer than it had been. "I'll take that advice into consideration." Then he shook Goodnight's hand and strode directly out of the room.

By the time John made his way back to the front vestibule of the somewhat sprawling ranch house, Molly Goodnight had caught up with him.

"John," she called as he bent to pick up his bags where they'd been deposited, just inside a large, doorless closet for storing coats and boots. He stood up straight and turned back toward the hallway.

"Yes, Mrs. Goodnight. How are you?"

"Well, I'm fine, John. And how are you? Do you need something from your bags? I just spied you walking by the kitchen doorway and thought I'd see if there's something I or one of our domestics can help you with." She smiled up at him sweetly. She was a petite woman in height and frame, and John had a hard time feeling angry in her presence. His shoulders slumped a little as the tension left them.

"No, ma'am, there's nothing I need. I'm just—" He paused, a thought occurring to him. "I'm just getting ready to leave," he continued, holding his hat against his chest, "and I could use a ride back into Pueblo, if that's not asking too much."

Mrs. Goodnight opened her eyes wide. "Oh," she said, sounding surprised. "Oh, you're leaving?" She looked back down the long hallway, toward the end of the house where her husband's office was situated. Then she looked back at John. "Did something happen between you and Charlie? He can be a brute at times, I know. He tells it like it is, though sometimes he shouldn't. I hope he didn't say or do anything that offended you."

"No, no," John was quick to reply. "Not at all. In fact our conversation was very productive. I'm grateful for his help with—with a project I'm working on. I just have to get back into the city now."

Molly narrowed her eyes. "And Charles didn't offer to get you a carriage?"

John laughed nervously. "I, uh, didn't ask him."

She continued to glare at him for a moment longer, as if trying to figure out what was really going on here. Then her face softened, and she reached out a hand to John's cheek—a motherly gesture the likes of which he hadn't felt in a very long time. He closed his eyes for a moment and let the warmth of it wash over him.

"No bother, dear," she said to him, her voice gentle. "I'll just call up Luke from the stables. He'll take you right away. And I'll pack up some food for you to take in case you find yourself hungry later."

With another pat on his cheek, she smiled and retreated to the kitchen. John watched her go, peering past her as well to see if Goodnight had come out of his study at all to see where he had gone. But nothing down that end of the hallway stirred. John shook his head a bit, then put on his hat and went outside to wait for Luke.

"I can take a hint," John wrote, then shook his Waterman pen a bit, trying to discern how much ink was left. He'd filled it that morning but had then written so many notes about his time here in Pueblo, he was afraid it would run dry in the middle of his missive. However, it seemed to be all right for the time being.

"And it was obvious there was nothing left for me to learn there. So I left," he wrote. Then he paused and reread the letter he'd been composing to his friend George back in Chicago. He'd laid out all he'd learned so far—and what Goodnight had withheld from him. Just seeing the words, the anger bubbled up in him again. He put pen to paper and kept going. After all, he had a train to catch.

"Goodnight's last message—that I should go back the way I came—is, of course, more frustrating than I can describe. Why was he so cryptic? Why take me all the way out to his ranch just to tell me, essentially, that he couldn't help me?"

John stopped again, holding the blunt end of the pen against his lip as he thought. He gazed outside the nearby window; the sun had just crested the horizon out over the eastern Colorado plains, and a few people now roamed the streets. He remembered T. Burton Blackwood's penchant for scheduling break-of-dawn reporters meetings back in New

York and laughed a little, glad that he didn't have to see that sour face so early in the day anymore.

John turned back to his letter. "And I've decided that perhaps he's correct," he continued, writing of Goodnight and his admonition to get out of Pueblo. "I have some information but not enough, and no direction in which to go next. It feels like I'm running in circles, getting nowhere. So I've decided to go back to New York to regroup—to collect what evidence I have and see how I can try to piece this enormous puzzle together. Of course, I'll have a stop in Chicago along the way. I'll look you up; perhaps we can have dinner together, or a few good, stiff drinks would suffice."

John finished the letter with his signature and got it ready to post, then he went around the small hotel room to make sure he'd packed up all of his belongings. Satisfied that he'd left nothing behind, he put on his coat and hat, collected his bags, and went down to turn in his key. After a brief stop at the post office next door, he headed toward the train station. The day was warm already; although it wasn't even May yet, spring had swept in on cat feet when John wasn't paying attention. If it weren't for the ever-present gutters full of animal waste, it would almost be a pleasant day.

On the platform of the station, John found he'd arrived just in time: His train was to leave in just under fifteen minutes. With the departure so close, the crowd waiting to board was thick. There was no line per se, just a mob moving slowly toward the doors of the train cars. John joined up at the back, ticket in hand, and shuffled forward every chance he got. At least, he thought, no one was pushing or complaining.

When he stood a few feet from the conductor taking tickets outside the parlor car's entrance, John took out his pocket watch. Ten minutes had passed, and he wondered if the train was going to leave on time. Not that he had anywhere to be right away, but he was anxious to get moving in both body and mind. As he snapped his watch closed and put it back in his vest pocket, he looked around, trying to gauge how many passengers were left on the platform and how long it might take for them all to board. Twenty on the left, maybe half that on the right, and—

John froze, his feet so heavy he couldn't move. People began to pool around him, moving toward the doors and not giving him a second glance. Over the tops of their heads, he could see one person standing out: a man with a rounded nose and eyes like a snake, the bowler hat on his head about to pop off because clearly it was a size too small. And he was looking right back at John, meeting his gaze through the hectic scattering of the crowd, his thin lips curled into a grinning snarl.

John turned to look straight ahead, swallowing hard. *It can't be*, he thought. *You haven't slept and your mind is playing tricks on you.* But the guy certainly looked like the one who had stalked him on the train to Colorado, who had threatened John to give up on whatever it was the stranger thought he was doing. What was his purpose now? To make sure John indeed was going back to New York? To beg Blackwood to reinstate him at the paper?

John shuddered at the memory of the man's words, at his eerie knowledge of John's life. Suddenly he felt claustrophobic, as if the crowd were closing in on him, and he took a few steps toward the train, pushing himself in between a couple, separating them by force to let him pass.

"Hey," the man said, pulling the woman close to him in John's wake.

"Sorry, sorry," John muttered, looking over his shoulder to check if the man was still there.

He wasn't.

John whipped his head back and forth, searching one end of the platform and the other, but saw nothing. He turned his body around in a full circle, afraid maybe the black-eyed monster was planning a sneak attack. Again, there was no sign of him.

"Ticket, please," a voice behind John said, causing him to start. Turning again, he found he was standing directly before the conductor.

"Ticket, please, sir," the man repeated. John took his from an inside coat pocket and flashed it; when the conductor waved him through, he bounded up the steps to the train's vestibule and on into the car. He didn't stop until he'd reached the last row of seats, where he could position himself with his back to the wall.

No surprises that way, he thought, then he stowed his bags underneath a seat and dropped down into it. He looked out the window next to him, checking for the intruder, and saw only the rail yard where out-of-service cars were stored. With a sigh he sat back, crossed his arms, and let his body relax a bit, though for the first hour of the ride he remained vigilant, his eyes moving in a constant arc between the car's two doors. No one came or left—not the conductor, not even a porter to help someone with luggage.

Finally, as the train passed over the border of Colorado and into Nebraska, John let himself believe that the mysterious man had not boarded the train. Which left him wondering: Had it all been a hallucination? Or another threat of some kind? Maybe he didn't intend to hurt John, just to scare him.

He really had no way to know. But he felt safe for the moment, and so he let down his guard. Leaning his head back against the seat, he closed his eyes and allowed himself to drop off into a fitful sleep.

TEN

The Way to Texas

1853, Missouri

Tom Candy had never much liked trains. He hadn't ever seen one in his youth; they hadn't existed where he'd lived back then, and when they did come around they certainly didn't reach all the way out to his family's lands. It wasn't until he'd immigrated to America that the great, noisy steam engines began to be a regular sight. But still he didn't ride them. Mostly he just stopped to look as they passed him on the trail. He traveled exclusively by horse or by foot.

That was how he'd seen most of this country so far, or at least the parts around Ohio, Wisconsin, and Illinois through which he herded the cattle for his business. But he hadn't crossed to west of the Mississippi, and he was itching to see that part of the country. He'd traveled on foot between Chicago and Wisconsin a half dozen times already, maybe, with two drives per year if possible. He was so used to the route, he barely even saw the scenery anymore—the dense forests along the Wisconsin River, where settlers set up blast furnaces and sawmills; the steamships transporting stores of grain out of the Ohio Valley on the Erie Canal, en route to the East Coast; the fertile open prairies of southeastern Illinois, cut through with wood-plank roads for the stagecoaches. These were all great and wonderful things, truly fantastic sights to behold…but he no longer even cared to raise his eyes as he made his way past them. All he thought about was getting them to Chicago, selling the meat, and getting his money. And that was not at all how he wanted his life to be.

Perhaps, he sometimes thought, it was time for a change. Some different scenery, at least.

"Well, where do you want to go?" Phillip asked Tom when he brought it up. He could tell his business partner and friend had been different lately—bored, maybe, of the routine of his life, the constant back and forth of it. But Tom, as he had learned, would not speak his thoughts until he was ready, and so Phillip hadn't pushed him about it.

Tom shrugged as he slapped the rump of a steer moving into the pen at Armour's plant. He'd just arrived with a new herd, and the two men were watching as Tom's hands—two Irishmen he'd found just wandering the countryside, looking for employment of any kind; they now accompanied him on every expedition—corralled them into the enclosure.

"South, maybe?" he shouted at Phillip over the bawling of

the cattle. "See some new land, find out what the cattle trade is like elsewhere. Who knows? Maybe I could find some new suppliers for us." He paused, adjusting his worn, dirty leather gloves as he figured out how to approach the idea he'd had in his head for some time. "I've heard these stories about Texas, actually, how there are just millions of wild cattle down there. I could head down that way and see if what they say is true."

Phillip smirked at him over the cattle moving by. "And who are *they*? Who put this notion of going to Texas in your head, Tom?"

"As a matter of fact, I heard it from a *congressman*."

Now Armour had to laugh. "A congressman? Where on Earth did you meet someone like that around here?"

Tom shrugged as if it were no big deal. "I met him in a tavern he owned—rather, he had just sold it due to his new career in Washington City. He was a lawyer as well, from somewhere around Springfield, and quite an intelligent man. He said Texas is full to bursting with longhorns. You'll never find that many cattle anywhere east of the Mississippi."

They watched the steers in silence for a few minutes, each man lost in his own thoughts. Finally, Phillip shared what was on his mind.

"And what about the business?" he asked, crossing through the line of moving cattle so he wouldn't have to yell to Tom. "What will I do for meat while you're out exploring?"

The question could have seemed blunt, even accusatory, but Armour paired it with an amused smile, making his delivery soft. Tom picked up on his partner's dry humor but still felt a pang of guilt. He'd thought of this, too: What would happen to their business if he left? He was responsible for fully half of the operation, without which the other half could not survive. Tom's leaving would essentially force Armour out too.

But he had given this conundrum some consideration.

"I wouldn't want to put you on the spot, Phillip," he said as they left the pen and went inside the building where Armour's men butchered the meat. Though they hadn't yet begun on this herd, the scent of blood lingered in the air. Tom resisted putting a hand up to cover his nose and mouth; Phillip didn't seem to notice the stench.

"And I have thought about some alternatives for you," Tom continued. "I'm not the only cattle driver in America, you know."

"But you are the best," Phillip replied. "And you're the reason I got into this business in the first place. It wouldn't be the same without you."

They walked the length of the room in silence, then through the door into Phillip's office. He took a seat behind his desk while Tom pulled up a chair in front.

"I know that, and I'm sorry," Tom began, but Phillip waved his words away.

"No apologies, friend. I'm only ribbing you a little bit. Of course I'd love you to stay, and I wish we could be partners forever. What we've got here is good, and I think it could keep going for a while. But if you're ready to move on..." He shrugged exaggeratedly. "Then I suppose I'll have to make myself ready as well."

Tom sat up straight in his chair. "No, Phillip, you can stay in business. My two hands out there"—he looked out the door, back in the direction from which they'd come—"are ready and willing to take over. They know the routes backward and forward, and I've taught them everything I know. I'm confident they can keep you supplied, so you can keep the business running smoothly...until I come back from Texas with the biggest and best herd of cattle you've ever seen." He smiled slyly.

Phillip considered his friend for a moment. He had known this day would come, when Tom would want to branch out. He was new to this country and still had so much left to see and do—not like Phillip himself, who had been around and seen just about all he wanted to, he thought. This cattle operation of theirs had been the first endeavor of his that had truly been a success, and he enjoyed doing it to boot. It wouldn't be the same with Tom gone. But Phillip had to keep going.

He nodded once. "All right. Once the steers are in, let the boys clean up, then we'll talk about it. Have you broached the idea with them?"

Tom grinned. "Oh yes, and they are excited about it. They'll be very pleased that you've agreed."

Phillip rolled his eyes, once again putting on his comical face. "Oh boy. Well, I haven't agreed to do anything but talk yet, so let's not put the cart before the horse."

There was no direct road to Texas. Tom couldn't just hop on a trail in Chicago and follow it all the way down. Though he hadn't seen any of the lands between the former and the latter, he'd read what he could about it and asked advice from anyone who would listen to his traveling plans and might know a thing about it. Some gave him good directions on which ways to go and what areas to avoid; some told him he was crazy and should abandon the idea altogether. Either way, the consensus was this: he truly would have a difficult row to hoe.

The distance was a little more than a thousand miles, which Tom estimated he could do in six to eight weeks, giving him plenty of time to stop and rest and look around along the way. He camped when he was tired, setting up in a meadow or woods with the bedroll he kept slung across his back. He cooked his dinner on an open fire, ate with the company of whatever local wildlife joined him, and fell asleep under the stars—or a protective bough if it started to rain. And everywhere he went, he wrote down notes in a small book he kept tucked in his coat pocket, a pencil stub tied to it with a string. Though he wouldn't put much thought into it yet—the cart and the horse, as Phillip had noted—he hoped he would be traveling back this way someday, and it would be helpful to have some notes on the terrain and such.

Though he didn't keep strict track of his time, when he finally stopped in a proper town—figuring he could do with a bath, some clean clothes, and a more hearty meal than whatever he could forage or trap—he found that he was right on schedule. It had taken him roughly two weeks to cover the nearly three hundred miles between Chicago and Union, Missouri, just west of St. Louis. He had picked up a southeast trail out of Springfield, crossed the Mississippi, and then traveled west to Union. After all that time alone on the road, he was surprisingly glad to see some civilization again. First he visited the town's tailor to be fitted for new pants and a shirt, then he paid for a bed for the night at the town's only tavern, which thankfully had a vacancy—and hot water. He took a good, long soak, waiting until the water had grown cold to get out. Then he slipped on his crisp, clean new clothes and went to the tavern downstairs in search of food. He dropped off his soiled clothes with the laundress on the way.

Union was a fairly new city, established in 1826, just a little less than thirty years prior. It was small, only about nine square miles, and set right on the twisting, crooked Bourbeuse River. No railroad lines had made it there yet, and there didn't seem to be a defining industry at work. Still, a year after its inception, a caucus of commissioners appointed by the state had named Union the seat of Franklin County, and thus many businesses, it seemed, had sprung up around that distinction—especially taverns.

The one attached to Tom's hotel was crowded that evening, with most of the benches and dining tables taken. There were leather chairs before a large, roaring fireplace to the left and a bar to the right, both with available space, and Tom chose the latter. He made his way through the room toward the bar, where he sidled up between a tall, young man and an old cowpoke who, Tom figured, was probably passing through like himself. He nodded at the older gentleman and tipped his hat, and the man returned his gesture, then went back to studying the glass of whiskey before him. He had a worn-out look in his eyes that Tom hoped he would never see in his own.

"What can I get you?" the bartender said, coming over and leaning on the bar.

Tom smiled at him. "What meal are you serving tonight?" He wasn't sure why he asked—to be polite, he supposed—because he would have eaten anything the man put before him at this point.

"Bison stew, cornbread, comes with a pint."

"I'll take it," Tom said, and the man went off to get his order. There were no seats at the bar, so Tom just leaned on it while he waited, trying not to look around all that much. This place seemed respectable—it was clean and fairly quiet, even had a separate ladies' parlor in the back—but only travelers stayed at taverns, and one could never know exactly who was standing nearby. There were pickpockets, con men, thieves—

"I wouldn't eat the cornbread if I was you," said the tall, young man beside Tom, drawing him out of his thoughts.

He shook his head. "Sorry, what?"

The young man turned fully toward him, holding a pint of ale in his hand. His words were slurred a little as he spoke, his movements languid. "The cornbread. Dryer than a dirt road. Feed it to your horse, he'll like it."

Tom still kept his guard up, but the young man's demeanor made him laugh a little. "Well, thank you for the advice," he said. "But I don't have a horse."

The man raised his eyebrows slowly and brought the glass to his mouth. When he was through drinking, he set the glass down again and let out a satisfied sigh. "No horse, huh?"

Tom looked at him for a moment. He didn't seem like a crook, but his mannerisms *were* odd. He was slow, but he didn't seem drunk. Perhaps it was the way people spoke in this part of the country.

"Say, where are you from? You've got an accent," the man said, as if he could read Tom's mind.

"I'm from England," he replied. "And yourself?"

The young man laughed and shrugged his shoulders slightly. He looked around the room as if trying to think of a good answer. "I'm from all over," he finally replied, looking back at Tom. "I'm kinda what you'd call—what is it?—a drifter." He snapped his fingers. "Yeah, that's the word." He paused, his face growing more serious. "Been spendin' some time here recently, though."

The bartender came back with Tom's pint and let him know the food would be out soon. Tom tipped the glass back and took a long swallow, feeling the warm ale sliding down his throat. He put the glass back on the bar. "For work?" he asked the young man. "What do you do?"

The man shook his head. "No, not work." He went to take a drink again, leaving Tom staring at him, waiting for a further reply. The silence sat between them for a moment, the sound of other men's conversations drifting by them on the air. "I was in jail," he finally said. "That's what I'm doin' here. I stole something, I was caught, and I was incarcerated for three months."

Tom nodded his head and turned back toward the bar. He had been right about the thieves. This man was just another average tavern patron. Best to go on about his own business.

"But I was only stealin' food," the man went on, his words drawn out in the same slow accent. When Tom did not reply, the young man reached out and put a hand on his sleeve. It startled Tom, and he turned abruptly.

The young man drew his hand back quickly, his entire

body freezing. "Look, I don't want no trouble," he said. "I—I just didn't want you to think I'm gonna rob you or somethin'. I was stealin' food 'cause I was hungry, that's all, and the sheriff here didn't care none. He locked me up with a man who shot his own wife and another who had tried to rob a bank." He laughed again. "Here. In Union. The county seat, where every other person is in politics or law."

The joke, as it were, softened Tom up a little. The irony *was* amusing. He let the muscles of his body unclench, and he took another drink to try to steady himself. "Sorry," he said, keeping his voice even. "But I'm somewhat of a drifter myself. You know how it is. Can never be too careful about strangers in a strange town."

"Ain't that the truth," said the man, then he stuck out his hand for Tom to shake. "I'm Shawn O'Reilly, by the way. Now that you know all my business, you might as well know my name, too."

Tom took his hand. "Tom Candy," he said.

Shawn grinned. "That's a funny name. So, where are you headed, Tom Candy?"

The bartender was back again, this time with a metal dish piled high with steaming stew, a hunk of crumbly cornbread shoved in it at the side. Tom took the plate, eyeing the bread. It looked like Shawn had been right.

"Look, a table's opened up," Shawn said, turning around to grab Tom's glass and his own from the bar. "Come on. Bring your plate."

Tom watched him walk across the room, making a beeline for a table and a couple of empty chairs. He had really been looking forward to a nice, quiet dinner and turning in early for the night. Shawn seemed all right, his criminal activity notwithstanding, but Tom just wanted to dine in peace.

However, he also wanted his drink back. With a sigh, he held his plate tightly with two hands and followed in the young man's steps.

The table was in a good location, in a corner away from the door. The people occupying the seats around them spoke quietly, their conversations little more than murmurs.

Shawn was seated already but had pulled out the other chair for Tom, who set his dinner on the table and then lowered himself. He'd barely touched the wooden seat before he had the first forkful of stew in his mouth.

"That looks good," said Shawn, breaking the trance Tom had fallen into as he chewed. The bison was a little tough, but the gravy was hot and delicious, the potatoes nice and soft. He looked up at his companion, another forkful already halfway to his face.

"Sorry," Tom said, lowering it back to the plate. "Would you like some?"

"No, no," Shawn said right away. "I already ate. Still ain't got no money, but the owner here's nice. Took a little pity on me, just gettin' outta jail and everything." He looked at Tom intently. "I'm not gonna steal again, if that's what you're thinkin'. I only did that outta necessity, and—"

Tom held up a hand to make him stop. He finished his bite of stew before speaking. "It's all right. You don't have to explain yourself. What you do is your business."

Shawn smiled at him, a very big and toothy grin that really

showed, Tom thought, just how young he was. Shawn had the face of a child, with chubby, rosy cheeks despite his overall thinness. The hair on his head was dark and curly, his eyes a piercing green. Looked like every other Irishman Tom had seen in America, probably the son of the son of an immigrant.

"Speaking of business," Shawn said, "what brings you into town, if you don't mind my askin'?"

Tom finished chewing once more and set down his fork. "I'm a cattle driver," he replied.

"Ain't no cattle around here, mister," Shawn interrupted, the look on his face so earnest, Tom had to stifle a laugh.

"Yes, I know," he said, trying to keep his tone kind. "I'm not *here* for cattle. Just passing through on my way to Texas. I've heard the cattle are abundant there."

Shawn slapped the table, the sound and sudden movement making Tom jump a little. He'd been holding his drink in his hand, and some ale had spilled on his new trousers. He picked up his napkin to dry it.

"I'm from Texas!" Shawn exclaimed, all smiles on the other side of the table, continuing on with no inkling of Tom's annoyance. "Born and raised in San Antone. Best state in the nation, if you ask me." He went to hit the table again but, seeing Tom's glare, pulled his hand back to his lap. "That, uh, that's very excitin'," he said, visibly trying to compose himself. "Where in Texas are you expectin' to go?"

"Not sure," Tom said distractedly, then finally gave up on the pants. He didn't care so much about the stain—he'd be back on the road tomorrow, and the pants would be covered in dirt and dust in a matter of hours—but the warm wetness of the cloth was making his leg itch. He looked up and went back to eating his meal. "I suppose I'll know when I get there and look around. If the longhorns are as plentiful as I've been led to believe, it shouldn't be difficult to find them."

Shawn shook his head sharply. "Oh no, no, Mr. Candy. They won't be hard to find at all. Mostly they're south of San Antone. And I'll tell ya, that's where all the trails start."

Tom watched him, waiting for the rest of the story. But Shawn was looking around the room again, one elbow on the table, chin propped in his hand. For all the world looking like he wasn't a criminal, just a young man who's finding himself a little out of his ken. The way he eyed the other patrons in the tavern was like a boy watching men, a look of fascination on his face.

"Excuse me," Tom said to get his attention. "What trails?"

Shawn looked at him again and smiled. "Oh, the cattle trails. You haven't heard of 'em?" He stopped again, and Tom shook his head, hoping it would urge him on. Thankfully it worked, and Tom continued eating. "Well, the ranchers in Texas send their steers out *all* over—even out to California. Go right through the Indian Territory. It's pretty dangerous, from what I've heard."

Tom was chewing. He nodded his head in silent thought, then he put down his fork. "How about north?" he asked. "What sort of drives do they do up this way?"

Shawn thought for a moment, sticking out his bottom lip and squinting his eyes. Tom tried to hide his smile. The kid was comical, with his exaggerated faces and dramatic declarations.

"I'm not sure, you know?" he finally said, shaking his head

and smiling at Tom like he just couldn't believe his own words. "I know there's trails from Illinois and Arkansas, but they're all going out west too. And there's drives *into* Missouri to supply the trains taking people out that way. I'm tryin' to think... are there any going north out of Texas?" He looked up at the ceiling, sticking out his lip again, then returned his gaze to Tom. "I don't think there are. None that I've heard of anyway."

Now it was Tom's turn to be silent for a while. He ate and thought, drank his ale, and pondered the information from this strange young man. "How do you know so much about driving?" he finally asked, pushing his empty plate away.

"I got family in the business," Shawn said. "Uncles who worked on ranches where the drovers get the cattle. They were my ma's brothers. Liked to tell stories when they came to visit."

"Have you ever worked on a ranch yourself?" Tom asked tentatively, a hint of a thought forming in his brain. "Or with cattle in some other way?"

But Shawn shook his head. "Nah, not me. I liked to hear my uncles talk about 'em, but I never had a chance to myself." He looked down at his lap. "When my ma died," he said, his voice cracking a little, "we all kinda lost touch."

These words shook Tom. He'd lost his own mother when he was young. One day it seemed she'd come down with a cold; within a week she had departed from this world. "How old were you?" he asked, his voice low and gentle.

Shawn sniffled and looked up at him. "Ten, sir."

Tom nodded. "I was twelve."

The two men exchanged a long, knowing look, as if to tell each other that they understood.

"Shawn," Tom said at last, sitting forward in his chair as that thought he'd been fighting finally came in clear. He put his forearms on the table and leaned in. "Let me propose something to you. How would you like a job?"

ELEVEN

A Crooked Trail South

1853, Missouri

The trail—though there was really no definable path to speak of in most places—from Missouri to Texas was a dirty, wandering way full of traps and sinkholes, long stretches of dirt plains that offered no relief from the blazing afternoon sun for miles and miles. Even if they'd been on horses, Tom thought, this would have been a difficult trek. That he and Shawn O'Reilly traveled exclusively by foot did not make it any better. At least he found that O'Reilly had a good knowledge of the trails and an unerring sense of direction, and so was more than adequate as a guide.

"Mr. Candy, sir, could we stop and rest for a spell?" Shawn paused and whipped his old, frayed brown slouch hat against his leg, then ran the back of his wrist across his sweaty brow as he gazed out across the plains.

Tom did the same, though he blotted at his forehead with a rag he kept in his pocket for just that purpose. They'd left Union ten days ago; they had to be nearing the border of the state by now. He just didn't know where exactly they were. This was truly no man's land—no towns, no signposts, not even a clutch of local animals to show them where the nearest watering hole lay. Just hot, dirty land as far as the eye could see.

"Yes, Shawn, let's rest," he said, and heaved his pack from his shoulders. He dropped it down onto the ground with a thud, then lowered himself right next to it and reclined back a little, elbows resting on his bedroll. Shawn sat right on top of his own, as if he didn't want to get his pants dirty. Tom laughed a little; both their pants could probably stand up on their own by now. There'd been no way to wash them since leaving Union, and even their spares were filthy.

"We should stop in the next town we see," he told Shawn. "Get a good meal and wash our clothes, replenish our supplies."

The younger man smiled. "Sounds good to me," he replied then took a small sip from his canteen, wary to avoid using up his daily water ration. He swallowed with a satisfied sigh then set his sights on Tom. "So have you given any thought to what you'll do once we get to Texas?"

Tom just looked at him for a moment, trying to figure out the question. "Well, I'm going to look into the cattle trade there," he began slowly. "And see if it will be worth buying a herd and driving it north. Isn't that what we've discussed?"

Shawn put his hat back onto his head, mashing down its

top against his skull with the palm of his hand. "Yes, sir, that is what we talked about when we met. I was just wondering if you're planning to do this alone, or..." He left the rest unstated but gazed at Tom with a look that was at once expectant and a bit hangdog. Was he trying to ingratiate himself?

"Well, no, Shawn, I assumed you would be coming along with me."

At that, the young man perked right up. A big smile grew across his face; he quickly capped the canteen and strung it back onto his pack. Then he stood up again, and with a bit of a spring in his step he pranced around as he got his pack back onto his back.

"Well all right, Mr. Candy. Thank you for that. That puts my mind at ease. Because I sure do like workin' for ya so far." He held out a hand, and Tom grabbed it and pulled himself upright. Once he had his pack on as well, they set off in a southerly direction again, Shawn chattering like a magpie as the sun blazed overhead and a hot, dry wind blew in from the west.

The next day, they found a town. An unexpected one; Tom had not seen it on the small map he carried with him. Indeed, it seemed like an unknown place without even a main road around which to situate itself, just a dusty expanse with shops and homes gathered loosely at its sides.

"Mr. Candy," Shawn began, his voice almost at a whisper. "Does this place look...*strange* to you at all?"

As they walked down the center of the small town's main street, Tom tipped his hat back a little, just enough to still keep the sun out of his eyes. It was late afternoon, and the hard orange beams of the impending dusk shot out from the horizon. He scanned the buildings: A post office. A saloon. A barber. A general dry goods store. A physician. Some boarded up, others with windows knocked out or doors that hung sideways from broken hinges. Tom turned in a circle, taking in the entire place. Was this a ghost town? He'd read about them but never thought that they were real.

"Hello?" Shawn called out, cupping a hand around his lips. His voice rang back off the shoddy, leaning walls around him and Tom. "Hello!" he tried once more when the first shout received no response. Then he just looked at Tom and shrugged.

"Come on," Tom said, waving his hand at his companion as he continued through the middle of the town. "I don't think there's anyone here."

Shawn didn't follow right away. He stood where he was and just looked around, as if he didn't believe what Tom said. As if at any moment, the entire population would come spilling out of the saloon, or maybe through the hallowed doors of the abandoned church at the end of the lane.

When it didn't happen, he shuffled along to catch up with Tom.

"Should we look inside any a' these places?" he asked. "Seems a shame to come all the way here and at least not see if there's anything we can use. Maybe there's no people, but they could've left behind some cans of food, or a knife, or…

hey, maybe some clean clothes!" He seemed delighted by this thought, rubbing his chin as he eyed what appeared to be the residences a little farther down.

Tom looked that way for a moment, too, then shrugged his shoulders. "All right, let's go look," he said, and took off in that direction.

The stairs up to the first house they approached were caving in toward the middle; Tom and Shawn stepped lightly, avoiding the cracks in the wood and the gaping hole where the third step should have been. The whole house seemed to creak at their touch, as if complaining of having to support their weight. The sound of it filled the silent air of the empty town.

"Hey, what are you doing there?"

Tom heard the call and stopped in his tracks, a hot feeling spreading through his belly, heart thumping in his chest. Seeing as this was, he'd believed, a ghost town, he hadn't expected to hear any voices other than Shawn's and his own. Already on the porch of the house, he turned as quickly as he could without disturbing the already crumbling structure any further. Beside him, Shawn did the same.

"Who are you?" the man demanded. He walked toward them warily, one hand on the six shooter in a low slung holster on his hip, leather thong already released; his other hand was held out in front of him as if he approached a wild animal. He wore a black waistcoat with a shiny, star-shaped badge pinned to the lapel. "What's your business here?"

Shawn shot his hands up in the air automatically, as if he were under arrest. "Nothin'," he said, shaking his head. "Nothin', sir. We're just...looking around is all." He glanced over at Tom, who still stood with his arms at his sides, eyes on the lawman.

"Are you the sheriff here?" Tom asked him, and the man stopped his approach but did not remove his hand from the gun.

"That's right. Sheriff Merle Davis. Who are you? What's your business here?" he asked again, his tone a little more forceful.

"I'm Tom Candy, sir, and this is Shawn O'Reilly. We're cattle drovers. Traveling to Texas to purchase livestock. And, well, we just stopped here looking for a respite for a day or two. But…" He gestured out toward the town. "Can I ask, Sheriff… what happened here?"

Davis kept his stance for another moment, eyeing the two strange men, but then relaxed a bit when he saw that neither wore a gun. At least he moved his hand a little farther away from his holster, hooking his thumb instead over his belt. He let out a sigh, its utter weariness apparent to Tom.

"Smallpox," the sheriff said, then paused, looking past the men as if a memory had hit him. He shook his head to clear it away. "We were hard hit. A lot of our people didn't make it, and most of those who were lucky enough not to get infected left town." He stopped again, eyeing the two men. "I advise you to do the same."

The two men on the porch glanced at one another. Tom could see the hope draining out of Shawn's eyes—he'd so been looking forward to sleeping in a bed or at least being able to clean up a bit. Any small comfort after being on their feet for so long would have been a blessing.

"Look, son, it's for your own good," Sheriff Davis went on, directing his speech toward Tom, who clearly appeared to be the leader here.

Tom turned back to him and smiled. "Yes, I understand, Sheriff. Thank you for your concern. Much appreciated. We'll be on our way."

"Aw—" Shawn began to protest, but Tom held up a hand to quiet him. Putting a hand on his younger friend's shoulder, he guided Shawn back down the rickety stairs, until they stood directly in front of Davis.

"Sorry, gents," the sheriff said. "I wish there were some other way. There's only but a few of us left here now, and most of 'em are wary of looters and strangers. After all they've been through, you can understand, I'm sure."

"Of course," Tom said with a nod and another kind smile. He too was disappointed that they couldn't get what they needed here. His feet ached, his head throbbed, and his whole body was one big itch. The fleeting thought of a deep, hot bath ran through his mind, leaving behind a feeling of longing. "We wish you the best, Sheriff."

He reached out to shake Davis's hand, but the lawman simply looked at Tom's fingers—no doubt wondering where they had been and what sort of unseen diseases they might bear. Smallpox, Tom remembered belatedly, was spread through touch; some even believed that breathing in the same air as a victim of the illness could fell a man. He brought his hand back and wiped his sweaty palm on his shirt. Better not to take any chances.

"Yes, well, best of luck to you," he said, nodding politely

at Sheriff Davis, and behind him Shawn did the same in mute silence.

"The same to you, Mr.—what'd you say your name is?"

"Candy."

"Yes, Mr. Candy. And you're going to Texas to…to drive cattle? Is that correct?"

"Yes, sir!" Shawn broke in. "This here is the smartest man in the cattle business. He's gonna take those steers all the way back to Chicago, where he's from."

Tom looked at his friend and laughed a little. "Actually, I'm from England," he told the sheriff, turning back to him. "Though Shawn is right—if all goes as planned, we'll be driving a herd back this way, en route to Chicago. Probably in a few months' time."

The sheriff grinned for the first time during their entire exchange. "Well," he said, "wouldn't that be some sight to see." He glanced around his town, its empty shops, and shutters flapping in the breeze. "I'd tell you to stop by on your way back, but…"

Tom nodded once. "Understood, Sheriff. Then let's just say it's been a pleasure to make your acquaintance, and best of luck to all of us."

"Best of luck to all of us," the sheriff replied, his voice low and sounding sad now, with the reminder of how little he had left of his home. Then he turned to watch as the two men walked back down the center of the town, nothing but the whistle of the wind accompanying them on their way.

Fifteen days out from Union, Missouri, Tom and Shawn finally crossed over into Arkansas. Entering through Benton County on the eastern border, they bedded down on that first night at the edge of where Benton and Washington Counties met. Lying under the thousands of stars up in the clear night sky, Tom was thankful to have a cushion of grass beneath the blanket on which he slept. This land, in complete contrast to the state they'd just left, was green and fertile, cool and welcoming, thanks in large part to the fledgling cotton industry that had taken root here. In just the last few years, a dozen or more massive plantations had cropped up across the state, one of which lay just a stone's throw from Tom and Shawn's campsite. As the sun went down, he had seen the slaves in the distance, hauling their day's work out of the fields in bundles and on wagons. He still had an ill feeling in his stomach just thinking about it.

"Mr. Candy," Shawn said, rolling over onto his side and propping his head up on an elbow—clearly unable to sleep. "Do you know what I've heard?"

Tom smiled to himself in the darkness. The young man loved to tell stories, and the majority of them started out with that very question. Apparently Shawn O'Reilly had heard a lot of things—many of which, Tom was sure, were not at all true. But they were entertaining, and his traveling companion's rambling did help to fill the silence over the many, many miles they had walked together.

"No, I don't," he said now. "What have you heard?"

Shawn smiled too, glad that Tom had played along. "I've heard that Arkansas has quite a cattle trade, too. Not quite on the same scale as Texas, but not bad if you take it all on its own."

Tom didn't reply right away, wondering why Shawn hadn't mentioned this information earlier. If the cattle here were so good, why were they going all the way to Texas? He asked the younger man as much.

"Oh, well, in Texas you've got quantity *and* quality," Shawn said, taking on an authoritative tone. Which was fine—Tom had known since the day they'd met that for all his eccentricities, he knew a lot about the cattle in this country. He surely liked to play the clown's role at times, but Shawn was a smart man underneath it all. Shrewd, even, Tom would say.

"And here they have...?" Tom asked, prompting him to go on.

"Here they have smaller herds with lower breeding. Tough, but not as meaty as you'll find down south. And think about this: You take some five-dollar steers from Arkansas and bring 'em out west, say to the California gold fields—which a lot of people do; there's some sort of established connection between here and there now—you'll sell 'em for fifty bucks a head. Now..." He pushed himself up on his elbow a little more, peering over the embers of the fire that smoldered between him and Tom. "Think about that, and think what you might get for a *Texas* steer way up in Chicago."

Tom gazed up at the sky again, letting that thought roll over in his mind. If the longhorns they were traveling to see were really as good as Shawn said, then certainly they'd demand high prices in a big city like Chicago that had no cattle trade of its own. Also, because this would be something new—something novel. And this was the land of innovation, was it not? With railroad tracks quickly making their way steadily westward and telegraphs sending messages between people hundreds of miles apart—it was an amazing time to be in the United States of America. Tom was thankful every day that he had made this trip.

"So how much—" he began, turning his face toward Shawn, but he didn't finish. The young man's soft snoring drowned him out.

A hurricane? A tornado. An earthquake! Did they have those in this part of the country? Tom couldn't recall ever hearing of one. Maybe it was just his imagination. Yes, a dream. He was, after all, only half awake.

No, wait. Tom sat up abruptly, clutching the blanket that lay over him. The one underneath was bunched up on the ground, moved around from his fitful rest. He looked around. The fire was long dead; the sun was just rising, and a cold dew had settled on everything in the night.

"Shawn?" he called, then cleared his throat and shouted the young man's name again. On the other side of the campfire, his blankets lay in a heap as if he had thrown them off in a hurry. There was no sign of O'Reilly.

Tom got to his feet, that low, persistent rumbling moving right along with him. The sound changed from a dull thudding to an expansive, thunderous wave higher up, growing louder and louder by the second. He turned in a circle. The boy had probably just gone off to relieve himself behind a tree somewhere.

"O'Reil—" he began, but as his body rounded toward the west, he stopped. Because he saw O'Reilly. The young man was running back toward camp at a sprint, his long johns dirty and saggy around his lanky frame, his boots unlaced. When he spotted Tom, he began waving his arms wildly, gesturing and pointing toward a copse of trees about three hundred feet to his right.

Tom glanced over at it. Was that the source of the noise? Were trees falling, crashing to the ground, shaking the earth that way? No, he saw no movement at all in that direction. And besides, no tree could make that ominous thundering sound.

It grew louder again, and he turned back to Shawn, who was now just a dozen or so yards away. And he was shouting now—at least it appeared that way. His large mouth was opening wide and closing, but Tom couldn't hear a sound above that noise. Oh, God, it was so *insistent*. He looked up to the sky. Could it be the thunderstorm to beat all thunderstorms rolling in?

Tom reached up to cover his ears, to try to block out the reverberation that battered his skull. He looked at the young man, who had diverted his path toward the small arbor he had pointed out. He still waved his arms that way, now trying to beckon Tom over to join him.

"Run!" O'Reilly screamed, his voice cracking and hoarse from the effort. "Tom, run! Go, go to the trees. Come on! Run!"

"What?" Tom called back, removing his hands from his head, still not understanding the message. "Why—"

But he didn't finish his question. He didn't have to. Now he saw why all hell was breaking loose.

Stopping only for a moment to pick up his boots, Tom set off toward the trees while behind him a herd of buffalo crested a hill to the west, a massive, dark cloud moving as one, spilling out into the valley below and headed, Tom now saw, directly for their campsite. He pushed his legs as hard as they would go, his muscles burning by the time he reached the stand of tall oaks.

"Mr. Candy, you made it," Shawn said, pulling Tom behind the tree where he hid. "You made it," he repeated, as if saying it made it more real.

Tom bent over, hands on his knees, taking in big gulps of air. Behind him Shawn hugged the tree's trunk, his eyes wide and fixed on what was happening out in the field.

"How…" Tom began, but he hadn't quite yet caught his breath. A few more breaths, then he was able to speak. "How did you know, Shawn? How did you know they were coming?"

The young man shouted without looking at him, the herd commanding his full attention. "I was up, about to start a fire for some coffee, and I heard the hooves." He made a low, guttural noise that in no way approximated the deafening pounding of the animals as they ran. "Or at least I heard somethin'. And I know the northern herd migrates north of the Arkansas River round this time of year. So I went to look, and sure enough—"

He stopped; the herd was almost on them. The two men watched from behind the trees as the enormous animals—all matted hair, muscle, and chipped horns, their breath coming out in snorts and chuffs—barreled by, trampling anything in their way. The campsite where the men had slept would be nothing but a pile of rubble and torn cloth by the time the buffalo passed. Tom put his hands to his ears again while Shawn stood up tall and raised his face to the sky, letting out a series of whoops and hollers, clearly enthralled by the stampede.

"How can you be so excited?" Tom asked him when finally the thundering of the hooves had receded to a low murmur in the distance. "All our supplies are gone. Our blankets, our water, our food."

O'Reilly turned to him, a glimmer in his eyes. "Yeah, but we're *alive*," he replied. "We're alive, Mr. Candy. Everything else can be replaced."

TWELVE

Danger to the President Escalates

1863, Washington City

Edwin Stanton had always opposed slavery. The indentured servitude of any human being was wrong, in his opinion; add in the violence inherent in the system and it became a simply evil practice that he could not abide. Hell, its immorality was one of the biggest reasons leading up to the War Between the States, as far as he was concerned. Lincoln said his only mission going in was to keep the Union together, to keep the South from breaking away, and he still purported that to be true. But the facts, the political acts thus far enacted, did not lie.

Just two years ago, with the war in its infancy, the president, in his annual letter to the Congress, had praised the country's free-labor system as valuing human rights over property rights and endorsed legislation to address slavery—though only in those states that remained loyal to the Union, of course.

The following year, the leader of the House, Thaddeus Stevens, had called for an escalation of the war to include emancipation of all slaves within the rebelling states. His purpose, sadly, was less about humanity than it was about crippling the rebellion's economy, but Edwin took it as a positive step nonetheless. In times like these, he knew, one had to remain hopeful and take whatever scraps of goodness one could find.

In the subsequent months, Congress had risen to Stevens' challenge. In March, they approved an additional article to the proclamation of war that forbade Union soldiers from returning fugitive slaves to their owners. Only a few weeks later, they ordered the federal government essentially to pay slave owners to free their slaves—Congress referred to it as *compensation*, a word showing that indeed slaves were still considered property, no matter what the law said.

June saw slavery abolished in all United States territories—again, another step forward, but Edwin's vision of releasing all slaves in all states was still a long way off.

"We have to bide our time," Lincoln had told him when he'd brought it up again, during a private, informal meeting in the Oval Room.

Stanton had looked around, not knowing how to reply. He remembered the last time they'd met behind closed doors like this, when the president had told him to tone down his quest to end corruption. He grimaced. Maybe this was where Lincoln called Edwin to whenever he felt he had to reel him in.

He returned his gaze to the president. "If not now, when?" he asked, remembering a phrase a former law colleague, an older Jewish man, used to say from time to time—a quote from the Torah, his sacred book. Edwin was not well versed in any religion, but he knew wisdom when he heard it. "We've been working up to this for more than a year. The time is long past due."

Lincoln sat back in his yellow damask chair and stretched out his long, thin legs. He held up a hand to Edwin, palm out—a signal he often gave the secretary of war. *Stop*, it said. *Hold on. Let's not get ahead of ourselves.*

Edwin found the gesture infuriating.

"Slavery will end when it needs to," Lincoln said, his voice low and calm. Tired, actually. Edwin knew the president slept just as little as he did these days. "And that day is not today. You know I support the cause. And *I* know I hold the power to make it happen. And I promise you, Edwin, I will do so. But I must wait until the time is right."

"Not the time, sir," Edwin said quickly. "It's more like the *timing*, right?" He knew, after all, that Lincoln, Stevens, and the entire Congress and House for that matter, saw slavery as a political issue—as leverage they could use against the Confederacy when they needed to. It was their ace in the hole, the card they kept tucked into their shirtsleeve for when they needed to turn the tide of the game. As far as Edwin was concerned, that time had come. He just had to convince his boss of the same.

And so he had kept on Lincoln, bringing the topic up as often as he could—at cabinet meetings, when they shared meals, or whenever he could steal a moment of the president's time. Edwin Stanton was nothing if not persistent, especially when something so important was at stake. Lincoln, to his credit, always listened in what Edwin assumed was quiet consideration.

It had taken Edwin only five months to convince him.

Now here he stood, behind the president's chair, as Lincoln, ink pen in hand, readied himself to sign the Emancipation Proclamation, an edict stating that as of this day—January 1, 1863—the Union's explicit goal in the war effort would be to outlaw slavery and grant full citizenship to all ex-slaves. Toward that end, the president, as the commander-in-chief of all armed forces, used his authority to free all slaves within the ten states that had not yet surrendered or fallen to the Northern army and been subsumed back into the Union. This amounted to the release of three million slaves from bondage.

The problem? The proclamation was not a law, and there was no way to enforce it within the Confederate states it intended to target. It would come into effect as the Union army came to control these areas, but it would be a long and slow process. These souls would indeed be freed, but it would not happen overnight. Once more Edwin reminded himself: *At least it's one more step.*

As the president's small, unevenly spaced signature dried

at the bottom of the document, he sat back in the creaky wooden chair and massaged his sore right hand. He had dedicated much of the previous day drafting the document himself; today he had spent the morning and a portion of the afternoon at the customary New Year's reception in the Blue Room, then hurried back to his study to complete the writing. Due to the late hour when he finally finished, there was no special convocation for the signing. Any cabinet members still in the White House were invited to the executive office to be witnesses, as were Lincoln's two personal secretaries, John Hay and John Nicolay. Unsurprisingly, a few journalists had found their way in as well.

While Lincoln took a few moments to field questions from the reporters regarding the proclamation, Edwin slipped out into the hall, where another correspondent waited. Stanton found him in a shadowy corner, out of view from the office.

"Birch," he said, quickly shaking the man's hand as he scanned the corridor up and down. He kept his voice to a whisper, aware how well conversations could carry down these hallowed halls.

"Secretary Stanton," the man replied, withdrawing his hand and reaching to an inside pocket of his coat. "I have something for you."

He produced a slim, off-white envelope and handed it over to Stanton, who turned it over to view both sides. There was no writing on the outside, no indication of what it was. He looked back up at his informant, eyebrows raised.

"It's a letter," Birch said, voice low but sounding exasperated. Edwin recoiled a bit. This spy of his was certainly surly.

They'd met only a handful of times since Birch had introduced himself that night at the tavern, but each time he'd seemed fouler than the last. If he didn't provide such good and useful information, Stanton might have dropped him long ago.

"From whom?" he asked when no explanation was forthcoming. He looked down at the envelope again and slid a finger under the flap, preparing to break the wax seal.

Birch grabbed his hand. "Not here. Not now." He too glanced down the hall, only releasing Edwin when he was sure they were alone. "It's from a man who as yet is unknown to me," he continued, looking back at Stanton. "He wants to meet with you. I can't tell you much about him other than that he is a stage actor, and he claims to have some information about a plot that could be forming as we speak."

Edwin tried not to roll his eyes. On top of the negative demeanor, Birch was a bit on the dramatic side. Always trying to sound very cloak-and-dagger. Again, if what he delivered to Edwin were not so valuable—

"A plot against the president," Birch went on, drawing Edwin's immediate attention. He looked at the young man for a minute, blinking and trying to process what he had just said. Edwin was tired and thought perhaps he hadn't heard it right. There had been dozens if not hundreds of such reports about threats against the president—too many even to check out. Still, he had to take each threat seriously and do his best to verify the level of danger, if any.

"What sort of plot?" he asked tentatively, brows lowering, looking at Birch out of the corners of his eyes.

Birch leaned his back against the wall, grimacing a bit as

he did so. Edwin assumed he'd suffered some injury out in the field. Birch had come to him before with broken fingers, or with his head wrapped in bandages with blood seeping through. A hurt back would be no surprise.

"That part I don't know. Not yet anyway," the young man said and let out a sigh. "This actor is an elusive man. I've never met him face to face. I know him only through a go-be-tween—one I trust explicitly, mind you." He nodded toward the letter, still in Edwin's grip. "I don't vouch for it personally, but if there's anything of use in there, I'd believe it if I were you."

Edwin looked down at the envelope as well. Suddenly it felt hot in his hand. He slipped it into his pocket.

"I'll read it later, when I get to a private place," he said, and cleared his throat. "What else is there? What have you heard out there?"

Birch shook his head. "Not a lot, I'm sorry to say." He tilted his head and looked at the secretary for a moment. "This war is wearing everybody down," he said at last, his voice still low but now almost soft sounding, not on a note of weariness but with a rare trace of compassion in his tone. "The men are exhausted and hungry. They have holes in their boots, feeble horses, and not enough ammunition."

Edwin put a hand over his eyes and bowed his head. This was not news to him; he had been doing his best for months to get the troops what they needed to survive. But with such an expansive arena, so many states and miles over which they were spread, it was his greatest challenge.

He looked back up at Birch. "Well, when you go out next,

at least you can spread news from the independent press that food is on the way. I just hired a man—a drover—to bring in a herd of cattle from Texas. And he will continue to bring in more herds until there's enough for every outpost and every man on the Northern battlefield. I know provisions have been sparse, but—"

"A cattle driver?" Birch asked calmly—almost too much so. His demeanor had shifted, but what was it that Edwin read in the young man's eyes? Concern? *Anger?*

"What's his name?" Birch asked, interrupting Stanton's thoughts.

"Tom Candy," he replied. "One of the soldiers recommended him to me, a man by the name of Goodnight. Charlie Goodnight. He was a rancher prior to joining the war effort. He said—"

Edwin stopped talking. The look on Birch's face alarmed him. His mouth had turned down into a severe frown, his brow set low, and that strange look was still in his eyes.

"What's—" he began to ask, but once again Birch interrupted him.

"I have to go," he said. "I'll be in touch." He'd barely finished the words before he turned, stepped out of the darkened corner, and then strode right down the middle of the hall. Hanging back, Edwin looked around again, hoping they were still alone. He watched Birch until he'd turned onto the stairway that would lead him down to the front foyer, where he could blend in with the reception guests who had lingered a little too long.

Realizing he'd been holding his breath, Edwin let it out in a long, slow push. He patted his coat pocket once, checking that the letter Birch had given him was still there, then headed back into the president's office, where Lincoln and the cabinet awaited him.

THIRTEEN

A Clue Is Found

1904, Chicago

John debarked from the train with a sigh. He'd been doing that a lot lately, unable to contain the disappointment that welled in his gut. All the time he'd spent traveling, all the money he'd spent, not to mention that he'd quit his job—and he was hitting walls at every turn. The walls being, of course, the impenetrable fortress of friends Tom Candy had somehow erected about himself. Everyone who knew him wanted to protect him, it seemed. From what? John could only guess.

But then, he was through with guessing. That was the decision he had made during the train ride from Pueblo, and he reaffirmed it now as he trod slowly, aimlessly, through the city streets. It was still early in the day, not quite nine in the morning; the train had been a red eye, traveling through the night to arrive in time for the start of business in Chicago. John planned to see his friend George at the *Chicago Tribune* offices but knew from his own time as a reporter that he would probably be busy with meetings all morning. To kill some time, he ducked into a cafeteria and ordered some coffee and breakfast—fried ham and eggs on toast, a sandwich that had been popular since the war and had become one of John's favorites. It went mostly untouched. Gazing out the window next to his table, he drank his black coffee and watched all the people outside walking along, looking as if they had purpose in life. John was sure now that he had none. It didn't do much for his appetite.

Back on the street, he lugged his leather satchel full of papers—notes, news clippings, even a photograph or two—that he'd been accumulating since he was back in New York. They all had been about his father; it was John's evidence to clear Edwin Stanton's name. Now there were folios for Tom Candy as well, holding telegrams from his friends, more newspapers, maps, and John's handwritten musings, often scribbled down while on a fast-moving train. This bag used to be his rock, the one object that he felt kept him anchored in this world. Now it felt like dead weight, a thousand-pound problem that he couldn't detach from his hand.

"George Hollings, please," John said as he dropped the satchel down by his feet. It didn't make as loud a sound as he thought it ought to. Standing in front of the receptionist's desk in the lobby of the *Tribune* building, he crossed his arms and waited while the woman—young, blond-haired, and smiling at him, though in his distracted state he didn't notice—called his old friend to inquire if he was free.

"Just had the telephone installed," she said as she picked up the receiver and brought it to her ear, glancing at John, a blush coming to her cheeks. "I'm still learning how to use it."

John nodded, still feeling as if he were a hundred miles away. He absently watched her dial a few numbers, speak a few words, and then replace the receiver gently on its cradle.

"Mr. Hollings will be out to greet you shortly," the woman said. Her voice was so soft and pleasant. Finally, John recognized her cordiality and returned her smile.

"Oh, uh, thank you, miss. Much appreciated," he said, then retrieved his bag and paced the floor until George came bounding out from a back hallway and into the reception area.

"John, John," he said, striding over with his hand held out, then grabbing John's, his other hand gripping John's shoulder firmly. "Got your telegraph—so glad you decided to stop by on the way home. Come on, let's go talk in my office."

John followed him without a word, the receptionist still smiling at him as he walked past.

"So tell me what happened out in Pueblo," George said, sitting down behind his desk, which was piled high with papers, just as messy as John remembered he'd been back in New York.

He shrugged, hands held out in front of him. "There's not much to tell, I'm afraid."

George waited for a moment, to see if John would continue. When he didn't, George jumped in. "Well, did you get enough for a story? I was hoping you'd come to hand one in. I've been saving a space for you on page two."

John smiled. "That's flattering, George, thanks. But I'll have to apologize. I just didn't find what I was hoping to out in Colorado."

For the next half hour or so, he recounted to Hollings all he'd learned from Charlie Goodnight. By the end of the tale, George seemed appropriately dumbfounded.

"He just told you to go *home*?" he asked, sounding incredulous. He sat back in his chair and rubbed his chin, trying to figure this out.

"Not in so many words, but yes," John replied. Just remembering Goodnight's admonishment to him to give up his search left a sour feeling in his stomach.

"Well..." George began, rocking to and fro in his swivel chair. He stared at John absently, his hand still on his face. John raised his eyebrows, waiting for the thought George was working on to come to light.

"Well," George said again, more definitively. Then he bent over and opened a drawer at the bottom of his desk. He pulled out several newspaper pages that had been folded a few times in order to fit in the drawer. He put the stack on the desk, pulled in his chair, and laid his palms on top of the papers.

"While you were gone," he continued, putting on his professional voice—the one he used when he wanted to seem like a respectable journalist. John knew it well from the old days, and hearing it again made him laugh. George grinned as well, but kept talking.

"While you were gone," he repeated, "I thought quite a bit about your situation. And I thought about this Tom Candy. I told you last time you were here that his name and his story sounded familiar to me. So I asked around the office here, to see if anyone else knew who he was. Just out of curiosity, you see."

John nodded, then sat back and crossed his legs, feeling a little more relaxed. It was good to be back in the company of someone he knew, and who knew him well. Someone who wasn't trying to keep secrets from him.

"And it seems Tom Candy is rather a local legend. No one here actually met him, but many had stories their parents or grandparents told them about Candy's cattle drives—how all the children would line the streets to watch him bringing the steers down to Armour's butchery, how friendly he was on sale days, when the shop would sell all the beef he'd brought in. Seemed like an upright fellow. Everyone liked him."

John nodded. He raised his arm and folded his hands atop his head, a pose of thought. He gazed out the many windows lining the west wall of his friend's office and considered what he'd said. He'd rather gotten the same view of Tom from all the people he'd talked to—that Candy was a good friend, a wise businessman, an innovator, and a man of good humor. There had to be something special about him, John thought, because these people didn't just like him; they were *loyal* to him. Even fifty years later, they held the bonds of their friendship tight.

"However," George went on, "though everyone seemed to know *of* Tom Candy, no one I spoke with knows whatever became of him. There were rumors—he went back to England, he finally made it to California and panned out his weight in gold. But nothing very definite. So."

He looked down at the newspapers he'd taken from the

drawer, patting them with his hands. Then he looked back up at John. "I took it upon myself to do a little sleuthing."

George picked up the first newspaper page, unfolded it, and turned it around for John to see. John sat forward in his chair, forearms leaning on the edge of the desk, and took the paper gently. It was old, yellowed. He didn't want it to end up crumbling in his hands.

"Second column, right-hand page. Toward the bottom." George peered at John, waiting for him to scan the article.

"'Cattle Driver's Son Meets Tragic Fate,'" John murmured, then scanned the words underneath. This was definitely about Tom Candy—he was named in the first paragraph and referred to as "the man behind the historic Texas-to-New York City cattle drive of 1854." A good twenty-five years later, the paper said, Tom's nineteen-year-old son, William, was killed. The young man was bringing a trainload of cattle from Abilene when the train derailed and crushed him under a carload of steers. It was said that Tom was supposed to have been on the train but instead gave in to his son's request to deliver the cattle. Tom never forgave himself, especially since foul play was suspected—it was found that someone had tampered with a switch, and that had caused the accident. If it even *was* an accident.

"Gruesome," John commented, looking up at George, who nodded in agreement.

"A sad story to be sure. But interesting because it happened in Illinois—in Springfield, actually."

John quickly read the article again, looking for this detail that he'd missed. Sure enough, the train had been approaching the Iles Junction station when the accident had occurred. "So do you think…"

"That maybe Tom Candy could be somewhere in that area?"

The two men looked at one another in silence. Then George reached back to his papers.

"This one puts him in Auburn a year earlier. This one"— another paper—"close to Toledo in 1893. Mason County. Champaign. Back in Chicago."

With each new location, George slapped another sheet of newsprint down on the desk before John.

"It seems he liked to travel," said George, then he added with a laugh, "but I guess we already knew that. Now, if I—"

He ceased speaking abruptly, prompting John to glance up from the papers. George's gaze was aimed over John's shoulder, and he turned in his seat to see. Beyond the doorway, the windowless hall was dim; John could just make out just the tip of a shoe and the edge of a hat brim peeking out from behind the right doorjamb.

"Excuse me, can I help you?" George called, his voice firm. The shoe and the hat pulled back, and the sound of fast footsteps receded down the hall.

John turned back around to the desk. "What was that all about?" he asked.

George shrugged, then he got up and crossed the room. He glanced out in the hallway, left and then right, then ducked back in and closed the door with a quiet click.

"Not sure," he said, returning to his seat. "Maybe just a reporter who's too scared to talk to me."

John paused, remembering the man from the train, the one who'd told him to go back from where he'd come. "Or maybe he was here for me…"

George laughed. "You? Does anyone even know you came to see me today?"

"No, but…" John shook his head and laughed. "You're probably right. But George, a reporter's scared of *you*? Well, you *have* changed since we worked together."

George smiled. "As I was saying, if I were you, I might try to visit these places. Ask around, see what people know. Maybe strangers would be more forthcoming about Candy. If they're not his friends, they won't have anything to hide for him."

FOURTEEN

The Trail Drive Begins

1853, Texas

"Ahhhh." Shawn O'Reilly took a deep breath in through his nostrils, let it out strong and hard, and then released this satisfied moan. He'd stopped in his tracks and turned his face to the sky, eyes closed and brim of his dirty, dusty slouch hat bent up to expose himself to the sun.

Directly behind him, Tom stopped as well. He took his hat off completely and wiped his brow with his sleeve.

"What is it, Shawn?" he asked, sounding just as weary as he felt. They had agreed to keep walking into the afternoon, but by the sun's position he guessed it was only about one o'clock. They still had a long way to go, and these little rests his partner took were starting to add up.

O'Reilly looked back at Tom and pushed his hat down to its normal position. "You don't smell that?" he said, smiling so wide he almost appeared giddy. "Go on, Mr. Candy. Take a whiff. Go on."

Tom just looked at him through half-closed eyes for a moment. He was in no mood for tomfoolery. But then Shawn looked so happy, he couldn't help but oblige. He took in a breath just as the younger man had but let it out slowly, calmly.

"Okay," he said. "Now what?"

Shawn guffawed. "You don't get it, do ya?" Still laughing to himself, he turned around and kept walking.

Tom stood still, incredulous, watching him go. "Shawn!" he called, starting out to catch up.

Hearing his name, O'Reilly turned around. He paused again, holding his arms out from his sides, palms upturned. "Mr. Candy," he said, shouting a bit to cover the distance between them. "We're about to cross over from Indian Territory into Texas. Can't you smell it? The Red River is just over this here hill, and that's Lone Star air!"

He let out a whoop, turned on his heel, and practically skipped down the dirt path they'd been following since sunup. Tom followed him, smiling now, marveling at the rugged and expansive river valley just coming into view. The air smelled moist and clear. This Texas must indeed be a marvelous place.

"That's Texas across on the far bank!" exclaimed Shawn.

True to their plan, they crossed the river while hanging on to a floating log and walked on until almost sundown. With no civilization in sight—Shawn, the Texas expert, estimated they were fewer than one hundred miles from Dallas—they camped out in the wooded edge of a prairie. Both fell fast asleep almost as soon as their heads hit the ground and managed to sleep past dawn.

The next few days and nights went more or less the same. Shawn was a surprisingly good scout and guide; he knew a little bit of something about every area through which they passed, could always point out a little flower, a type of bird, or the color of the dirt and expound on it, sometimes for hours. It did grow tiresome, but mostly Tom was thankful for the break from the monotony. O'Reilly also knew shortcuts that would take them around hills, marshy land, treed areas with more wildlife than they wished to encounter. In a handful of days they were in Waco, then another few brought them to Austin, the state's capital, and home, so Shawn said, to a distant branch of the O'Reilly clan.

"Oh, they'll be right happy to see us," he assured Tom as they approached the sprawling homestead, which looked to cover about five hundred acres. The back of the property butted up against the Colorado River; Tom could hear the rush of the water the closer they got to the ranch. A small band of horses, brown and tall and strong, stood in the pasture, watching the two men pass. Closer in, the smells of hogs and hay filled the air.

Much to Tom's surprise, the husband and wife living here did actually know who Shawn was. The man was an uncle's cousin's cousin twice removed or something like that. Tom couldn't quite follow the string of names and associations they went through upon meeting. Nor could the couple recall how long it had been since they had seen O'Reilly—not since he had been a boy for sure. They'd been to San Antonio for his mother's funeral, bless her soul, so that was probably when.

Regardless, they welcomed in the pair of grimy travelers and immediately fed them. Tom ate slowly, nibbling on a crust of bread for what seemed like hours, savoring the taste of the freshly cooked and baked foods after so many weeks of eating beans from tin cans and dried strips of meat. When his plate was finally clean—every drop of gravy sopped, not even a bit of potato skin left—the farmer's wife ushered him into a room at the back of the house, where a galvanized wash tub, just big enough for a full-grown man to sit upright, was already filled with steaming water. It was the most beautiful thing that Tom had ever seen.

"You get your fill, now," she told him, her voice kind and gentle. She was older, not elderly, getting on in years but still had the hale, hearty look of country folk. "Shawn can wait. He's family. You're our guest."

She cracked a grin, backed out of the room, and closed the door behind her to give Tom his privacy. As he sunk down into the nearly scalding water—someone must have filled the basin from the wood cookstove only moments before he'd come in— he had a fleeting feeling of pity for O'Reilly, who would have to suffer through the bathwater after he was through with it. Given all the dirt on his body, it was likely to be nothing but a big bucket of mud by the time he was done.

And as the woman had instructed, he did take his time. There was a window nearby through which he could hear the rushing of the river again, and he closed his eyes, imagining the still water in which he sat was an eddy out there, the Colorado's torrents flowing over him, washing him clean. When he stepped out of the tub, he found a fresh, clean nightshirt had been left on a chair for him. He held it up for examination. It looked to be just the width and height of the man of the house. It was a little big on Tom when he slipped it on over his head, but the old, worn flannel was a comfort to his sun-dried skin.

They stayed for two days with the distant O'Reilly family— one more than Tom had planned on, but in the end he agreed the respite had been good. The farmer's wife washed and mended their clothing, and filled their packs with jars of fruits and meats she had preserved herself over the last year. This made their loads heavier, but Tom was sure that would be worth it too.

As Shawn had promised back at their first meeting in Union, Missouri, the travelers found the most steers south of San Antonio. They arrived in the city proper four days after leaving Austin and asked around before deciding on which ranch outside of town to visit. The overwhelming majority of men they queried told them the Double Diamond down toward Castroville had the best longhorns and the best prices. A couple of days later, Tom and O'Reilly stood in a pasture with the proprietor, listening to him enumerate the Spanish cattle breeding lines, weights, and demeanors of his abundant herd. The man certainly was proud of his Texas stock, although they were mostly wild range cattle he and his ranch hands had rousted out of the mesquite breaks in the hills. One young cowboy in particular, name of Charlie Goodnight, was said to be fearless in crashing his cow pony directly into the dense mesquite thickets in hot pursuit of an errant longhorn bull. The two men shook hands and agreed on a price of two dollars a head—more than a fair price for both.

"And if you're lookin' for help," he added as they walked back to the ranch house, where they would discuss numbers, "I know a good droving assistant you can talk to, and a vaquero if you're interested. And I'll have Charlie Goodnight cut out four spare horses for each drover, so's you can keep fresh mounts under 'em. I'd loan you Chuck for the drive, but I need him here."

At that, Tom noticed, Shawn's normally bright expression soured. He hung his head and kicked his feet into the dark green grass of the pasture.

"Don't worry," Tom assured him with a smile. "I'm not looking to replace you, Shawn. But we will need some hands to move a herd this large."

The younger man glanced at him and gave a laugh, but he was still obviously upset. He remained silent through the rest of the negotiations.

The rancher sent for the men he'd mentioned, and they arrived the next day. Tom was surprised to see one was an Indian and the other a Mexican, and they seemed just as taken aback by him, most particularly his accent. Always a straight talker, he took it upon himself to clear the air right away.

"I understand your apprehension," he told them both as they stood outside the rancher's corrals, where several mounted riders were partitioning off his herd. "I suspect you've probably had some bad dealings with strangers like me."

Neither of the men said a thing; they just looked at Tom,

waiting, he supposed, to see what he had to say. How far he could put his foot into his mouth. But he had no intention of that.

"I assure you," he went on, keeping his expression grave, "you will receive no ill treatment from me or from my assistant, Shawn."

Tom turned and motioned toward the young man, who straddled the fence on the other side of the corral. He was watching the hands tally up the steers too, but even from that distance Tom could tell that O'Reilly had one eye on him and the new men. And he didn't look pleased.

"I'm a businessman, fair to a fault," Tom continued, turning back. "You put in the work, you get your pay. End of story, as far as I'm concerned."

The Mexican vaquero, called Charro, seemed to soften a little at that. Where his shoulders had been tense and hunched before, they now slumped a little, and he relaxed his stance. He held his wide-brimmed sombrero in both hands at his front. Tom smiled at him, and he nodded back. But when Candy did the same to Ahote, the Indian, he got nothing but stoic silence in return.

Regardless, he cleared his throat and went on. "Now, I will provide what you need on the road as far as food and any incidentals along the way. You'll have to bring your bedroll, though, and your own horse and saddle. And you won't get paid until I do at the end of the drive, when we reach New York. How does that sound to you?"

The Mexican raised an eyebrow. "New York?" he asked.

Tom grinned. He'd been anticipating the question—and

the incredulity with which it was asked. "Yes, New York. I know, it's never been done before, taking cattle from Texas all the way out to the East Coast. But I believe it's possible, and I know there will be ample profit in it for all of us. I have it on reliable authority that New Yorkers are in dire need of quality meat, and it is my aim to bring it to them."

Charro nodded his head. "Si, señor," he said. "I will go with you. I can get my supplies ready and be back here within a day."

Tom smiled and nodded at him. "Well," he said, reaching out to shake the man's hand. It was dry and rough, callused from years of handling an oxhide riata. "Glad to have you along on our journey."

Next he stepped over and stood in front of the Indian, who still regarded Tom silently but calmly. "And for you?" Tom asked.

Ahote looked at him for a moment longer then nodded his head slowly. "Is good," he said, his voice deeper than Tom had expected. He smiled at the unexpected utterance.

"Excellent," he said, backing away from the man. "Excellent. Ahote, can you return with your supplies tomorrow as well?"

Again the Indian nodded, and with that Tom thanked and dismissed them both. Then he looked across the corral for Shawn. He wanted to share this good news. His young companion, though, was nowhere to be found.

FIFTEEN

The Homestead Is Found

1904, Illinois

Traveling was a dirty business. John was a city boy at heart—born and raised in Boston, transplanted most recently to New York City—and so was used to a certain level of cleanliness and order in his life. Lately he'd found himself disheveled and unwashed, spending days at a time wandering with no clear destination in sight. In the last week, he'd traveled from one side of Illinois to the other and from bottom to top—first Auburn, then Toledo, then Mason County and Champaign—following the list George had produced of Tom Candy's possible whereabouts.

So far he'd gotten nothing but blank stares and a whole lot

of silence. Once again, if anyone had information, they weren't willing to share it.

Now, standing just outside the Springfield Junction train depot—it hadn't been Iles Junction since 1898, he'd learned—John stopped and looked around. He'd sworn that at the last stop, he'd seen a man getting on the train—the one who'd seemed to be following him in Colorado. Same funny hat and large nose...but then again, he hadn't slept in days. Not really, just catnaps here and there when he could catch one. Perhaps he'd imagined the man.

Still, he thought as he surveyed his surroundings, *can't be too careful.*

Once he was sure there was nothing out of the ordinary happening here, he continued on his way, though really he had no way at all. He would just do as he'd done in all the other cities and towns—roam, stop to talk to people who looked friendly, sidle up to other patrons at a tavern or restaurant, and ask what they knew about Tom Candy. And, mostly, hope and pray for answers.

Surprisingly, he got some here. Perhaps it was because this was the town where Candy's son had been killed, but at least the name was familiar to people.

"Oh, sure, Tom Candy," said an old man sitting on a milk crate in front of a barroom, holding out his hat for donations. He face was dirty; his two front teeth were gone. His hair was a frightening near-white nest upon his head. He looked almost as bad, John thought, as John himself felt.

"So you know him?" John asked, his ears perking up with interest.

"Oh sure, sure," the man repeated, nodding and gazing out past John to the street, where a string of noisy automobiles trundled past.

John waited for the man to go on. When he didn't, John prompted him. "And how do you know him?"

The man looked at him at last. His eyes were watery and red, the tip of his bulbous nose a spider web of bright red arteries. His breath, now streaming fully into John's face, reeked of bathtub gin. "How do I know who?"

John sighed. He reached into his pants pocket for some coins, then dropped them into the man's hat.

"Ah, thanks, mister!" the old man said, his voice suddenly loud and bright. John tipped his hat slightly, smiled gently, and walked away.

None of the interactions he had for the rest of the day went much better, not even when those he approached were sober. Some genuinely did know of Tom Candy, like the nice woman working at the small cafe where John stopped for lunch, but that knowledge was about as far as it went.

"I didn't know him firsthand, of course," she said, her voice so lilting and feminine, it sounded as if it could blush. "But my granddaddy's told me some stories 'bout Tom Candy's cattle drives. He was known all over these parts, I guess. Always comin' and goin', bringin' herds back to Chicago to butcher and sell." She smiled sweetly at John and shrugged. "Granddaddy used to talk about him like he was Wild Bill or somethin', except without all the guns. You know? Like a celebrity. Everybody knew someone who knew Tom Candy back then."

In that, John surmised, not much had changed. He thanked the girl for her time and left her a generous gratuity.

By evening, John was exhausted, though he hadn't thought he could be any more tired than he'd already been. As the sun burned low on the horizon, he was ensconced in a small room at a boarding house, lying in bed with the blanket wrapped around him like a mummy's shroud. He wanted to block out all sights, all sounds, and all sensations, and just drop into a deep, deep sleep, preferably for a week or two. The fatigue that gripped him had taken its toll not just on his body but his mind as well, and even though he'd put the former to rest, the latter could not stop its frenetic pace.

Just give up, it told him. *You're getting nowhere. You're tired. Just pack your things and go on home.*

This idea was strongly appealing. John had run up against so many walls headfirst, it was a wonder he hadn't cracked open his skull by now. How much longer could he carry on in the same way? Was finding Tom Candy worth sacrificing his health? His sanity?

He fell asleep before an answer came to him. But in the morning, he felt no different. He awoke feeling lethargic and groggy. Swinging his bare feet onto the floor, he put his elbows on his knees and his head in his hands and stayed that way for quite some time. John could not will himself to move. His legs ached from all the walking he'd done, miles and miles of pounding wooden boardwalk and dirt road in search of the truth. His skin felt scaly, dried out from the wind and sun, the sere heat of the Midwest.

No more, he told himself silently, his fingertips absently scratching at his scalp. He just couldn't make himself get up and continue this search for one more day. A fleeting image of his father ran through his mind—Edwin Stanton, secretary of war; his solemn, bearded face; his stony, troubled eyes gazing off into the distance. John had seen him only in a small daguerreotype his mother had kept in a locket around her neck. The jewelry had been buried along with her, the image of both his parents gone forever.

John sighed, long and deep, filling his entire body with air and releasing it again. Then he stood up. Slowly, he made his way to the basin across the room, washed his face, and wet his hair. He shaved, dressed, and gathered up his two bags— one for his clothes and belongings, the other with his notes and discoveries so far. He'd added only a few pages since he'd begun this journey. He'd thought he'd have more by now. What little he'd found didn't seem like enough to justify any further pursuit.

Before leaving the room, he took count of how much money he had left—at least enough for a train ticket back to New York. He should have just gone straight there, as Charlie Goodnight had told him to, he thought now, a pang of regret hitting his gut. Or was it just hunger? He laughed bitterly at the thought, but decided to head downstairs for breakfast. Better to make the long journey home on a full stomach. *Home. But I wonder where that is now,* he thought bitterly.

"Good morning, Mr. Stanton," said the proprietor of the boarding house once he reached the dining room. There were six or seven tables scattered about the room, mostly full. "There's a place right over here for you, if you don't mind sharing," she said, then guided him over to a long table where one other man was seated, a mug of coffee and a half-eaten plate of eggs and bread in front of him. He and John nodded at one another as John sat down, then the other man returned his attention to the newspaper he was reading.

"Be right back with your breakfast," the woman told John, laying a gentle hand on his arm. "I hope you like eggs? That's what we're having today."

"That will be fine," he replied, mustering a smile for her, then concentrated on the coffee she had left for him. He took a gulp; it burned his throat as it went down.

"If you're interested," the other man said, sliding his paper across the table to John as he stood up. The man tipped his hat, nodded once again, and then took his leave.

"Thank you," John replied to the man's back, and then reached out for the paper. Not that he cared much about the goings-on in this part of the state—not anymore, not since he'd made his decision to go back to New York. But at least the newspaper would give him something to focus on, something to keep his mind from wandering back over and over again to his dejection and disappointment.

"Two Lives Lost in Auto Accident," read the front-page headline. The second page featured community news—Miss Edith Wood would be leaving to attend Cornell University soon; Bessie Colby, age thirteen, would be spending the last month of the summer with her grandmother in Ann Arbor, Michigan; Miss Mary Richmond held a dinner in honor of a visiting educator from Connecticut, then took the entire party to the theater for a production of *Ranson's Folly*, a comedy about army life that was touring the country after a successful run on Broadway.

Perhaps these tidbits were of interest to those who lived in the area, but to John it was all blather. For the first time in months, he found himself actually missing the *New-York Tribune*. He might have been the odd man out in the newsroom, but there was no denying the talent that paper employed. Its reporters were diligent, the news they reported important and hard hitting. He felt a small swell of surprising pride at having been a part of it even for a little while.

He stopped short, however, of fondly reminiscing about his former boss. T. Burton Blackwood had done nothing but make John's life exponentially harder in their time together, not to mention the many ways in which he had blocked John's attempts to get to the bottom of his father's death. The memory of it still ate at John; a hot flame of anger flared up inside him. He dropped the newspaper to the table, sat back, and closed his eyes.

But his peace was short lived. "Here you go, dear," said the older woman as she set a plate down right on top of the paper. "There's butter and jam right there for you." She indicated both at the center of the table, where they sat alongside a dish of salt and a stack of napkins. "Raspberry preserves, actually, from the bushes out back. Cooked and canned by yours truly."

John looked up at her and smiled. "Looks delicious. I'll be sure to try it."

Happy with the compliment she'd been fishing for, the woman moved on to another table, leaving John alone. He looked at the food she had brought—slightly runny eggs, a rasher of overcooked bacon, and a roll that had probably been fresh at dinner two or three nights prior. He glanced at the pot of jam and decided against trying it despite his promise.

But he was hungry, so he tucked in, eating quickly to avoid having to look at the meal. When he was done, he set his knife and fork across the plate and pushed it away, then sat back, hands folded on his stomach. It was already rumbling. He put a fist to his lips to stifle a sour belch.

Leaning forward again, he reached for a napkin from the pile to wipe his mouth and brush the crumbs off his shirt and pants. As he did so, he glanced down at the newspaper, still spread out on the table before him. The word "cattle" stuck out from underneath his plate, and of course it caught his eye. He pushed the dish farther away, revealing the entire text:

HOMESTEAD CATTLE
Moweaqua, Illinois

High-Quality Shorthorns
Available for Breeding and Butchering

Caroline Candy, Proprietor
Telephone, B 1556 West

John's eyes froze on the paper, his hand on the plate. He felt as if time itself had stopped as the name—*Caroline Candy, Caroline Candy, Caroline Candy*—glared out at him from the page in rhythm with the blood rushing to his head. He read the advertisement over and over again, just to make sure he had it right.

Then he snapped out of his trance. Shoving his chair back from the table, he reached for his leather satchel and pulled the heavy bag up onto his lap. Inside it he leafed rapidly through the edges of papers until he found what he wanted: one of the articles George Hollings had given him. The one about William Candy's untimely death.

Pulling it out, he scanned it quickly, almost reaching the bottom before he found what he wanted.

"Yes!" he hissed and landed his fist on the table, making the jam jar and his silverware rattle. Then he read in a quiet voice: "William Candy is survived by his parents, Tom and Elizabeth, and his sister, Caroline."

Suddenly it looked like John wouldn't be returning to New York so soon after all.

SIXTEEN

The Herd Is Blocked

1853, Missouri

Tom Candy had never been one to doubt his own abilities. He'd known men like that all his life—too wary, too unsure of themselves just to get things done. Tom had long prided himself on his straightforwardness, his drive, his success at most things he tried. That didn't mean it came easily to him; he was no stranger to hard work, but the difference was that he loved doing it. The bigger the challenge, the more he desired to overcome it.

But this…he had to admit it had been the truest test of his faith in himself.

The Shawnee Trail was the route most early drovers and their small herds took out of Texas to the north. Its main stem ran through Austin, Waco, and Dallas, then across the Red River at Rock Bluff and over the state's northern border, into no man's land. This territory still belonged to the Indians, and Tom would be following a trail they often used for hunting— and for raiding parties of settlers coming down from the Midwest. He'd heard accounts of terrible violence out there, including scalpings and deaths at the end of a spear. He fully expected to meet trouble at least once along the way.

But he tried to keep that fear in check and retain a rational mind on the matter. On the one hand, Tom couldn't blame the native tribes. They just wanted to protect their families and their land, which white men were taking away thousands of acres at a time. But on the other, all *he* was doing was moving steers. He didn't see why that could warrant brutality in the least.

Plus he had Ahote. He still didn't speak much, even after they'd spent several weeks together. But Tom knew this man was a strong and fearsome presence. At all times he sat erect atop his horse, one of the forty the cattle rancher had sold to Tom for the journey north. Each drover—Tom, Shawn, Charro, Ahote, and four others Tom had hired—needed at least five horses for the trip, to switch between them as they went; sometimes one man would wear down three mounts in one day. Ahote rode out in front of the herd at point and was always on guard, scanning the trail ahead and to the sides for any signs of danger. Tom was thankful to have him for the help he provided with the animals but also for the security he granted the entire drive for both cattle and drovers.

Whether due to Ahote's presence or not, he couldn't say,

but Tom and his party passed without issue through the edge of the Indian lands. In fact, it wasn't until the route split off into several branches just north of Fort Gibson that things began to go wrong. On Shawn's advice, Tom had opted to follow the trail leading to St. Louis, as it seemed to be the most direct route, and if need be they could sell off some of the herd in that city. He thought that might be a good idea and hoped to cull some of the slower steers, the ones that Charro always seemed to be bringing up at drag, driving them hard to catch up with the herd.

Well, that might not be a problem anymore, Tom thought now as he pushed himself up to sit on a slat of the wooden fence. He looked from side to side, down the lengths of the barrier, which covered all possible routes for the trail herd.

"Mr. Candy, I'm real sorry," Shawn said, kicking the toe of his boot in the dirt of the trail off to the side of where Tom sat. Behind him, the herd of longhorns milled, picking on tufts of grass and leafy bushes wherever they could reach. Ahote, Charro, and the other men patrolled the perimeter, making sure they all stayed bunched and didn't stray too far in search of graze.

"I thought that all of this was over with," Shawn went on without looking at his boss. He seemed ashamed almost, embarrassed at least that his advice had turned out to be so bad. "From what I'd heard, I thought there'd been a truce."

Tom sighed and just looked at the young man. He could choose to be angry at Shawn, and he would have every right. O'Reilly had known there might be blockades up this route, but he'd failed to mention it until they'd come upon one:

this fence, which blocked all possible routes northeastward through these canyon hills toward St. Louis, erected by local farmers to keep the drovers out of Texas from passing through with their herds. Seemed the cattle from that area were known for bearing infected ticks and for leaving them behind wherever they bedded down. The bugs then found their way onto the local livestock, which didn't have the immunity the Texas herds did due to their previous exposure, leaving them sick and dying, or at the very least unfit to sell.

Tom could see the farmers' point. But that didn't make his situation any easier, and it didn't quell his ire. He eyed Shawn, wanting to give him the lashing of his life—verbal or physical, he wasn't sure yet. But he also knew he'd do no such thing. As angry as he was, he could never take it out on Shawn. He was just a boy. In the many weeks they'd spent together, Tom had come to know his assistant and see that although O'Reilly appeared to be a full-grown man, his mind was like that of a child: petty sometimes, oblivious, and lacking in common sense.

"It's all right," Tom told him, trying to sound as gentle as he could, though it was difficult. It was only the early afternoon, the sun just starting its downward trajectory in the sky, but already they'd had a trying day. A dozen or so of the steers seemed to be coming down with an illness; they were losing weight and had discharge from their eyes. Even with all their pooled experience, none of the men could tell exactly what it was. But it was worrisome.

Tom got back on his mount and rode to the top of a nearby hill to survey the area for any way around the barricades.

But even with the long view from up on high, all he saw was impenetrable, fenced-off canyon passes for miles and miles. He breathed out slowly and just sat there for a while, looking down on his herd and pondering what to do. Should they go east or back south and then west? Which was more likely to provide an opening at some point? There was no way to know. They might as well flip a coin in the air and call heads or tails.

He took off his hat, scrubbed his hair back, and wiped his brow. Down below, Shawn was entertaining the other men with some song-and-dance routine, as always the entertainer. It made Tom smile a little, though his chest felt empty and tight. He'd come too far to stop now. Between him and the eleven other drovers, he thought, they'd have to come up with something. Maybe Ahote or Charro had been hit with an idea while Tom was out exploring. He yanked the horse's reins to head back down the hillsides toward the herd.

As the horse wheeled about, out of the corner of his eye, Tom saw another rider on the crest of the hill, maybe a quarter mile down—the figure of a man atop a huge gray American Saddlebred that must have stood at least sixteen hands. Tom pulled up on the reins again abruptly, stopping to try to see what this gentleman's intention was. But he just sat there, staring at Tom, it seemed, and the two thousand steers stretching back down the trail behind him for more than a mile. Obviously he had an interest in some aspect of this operation.

Still, the man made no move. Tom took it upon himself to approach the stranger—carefully, slowly, hands gripping the reins in case he would need to turn and run for cover. As he grew closer, he saw the man wore a blue army uniform and had a full, bushy, dark beard. Finally, they were within speaking distance of one another, close enough that Tom could see the silver oak leaf on each shoulder of his coat.

"Colonel," Tom said, dipping his head and reaching up to touch the brim of his hat.

The man nodded his head in acknowledgment. Then he raised a hand and pointed at Tom's herd. "You'd best turn westward," he said, his voice much softer than Tom had expected from a military man. "Take the middle branch of the trail up through Sedalia. Vigilante riders are blocking this way, to the east. They're armed, and they mean business."

Tom looked down at the herd as well, a feeling of apprehension growing in his gut. He turned back to the lieutenant colonel. "You're sure of this? You've seen the vigilantes?"

The man nodded again. "With my own eyes. I'm not trying to fool you, son. Just trying to help you out. Where are you headed with all this stock?"

Tom laughed a little, as he always did when he shared his destination with anyone who asked, anticipating the incredulous response. "New York City."

The man just looked at him for a moment, his expression unchanged. "Well then, you've got a long way to go. I'm heading west myself, if you'd like me to accompany you for a while. Perhaps the uniform might deter anyone thinking about bringing harm to your party."

A personal army escort was too good an offer to pass up, and Tom didn't. He welcomed the lieutenant colonel—Robert Lee was his name, former commandant at West Point military academy, now en route to his new post as commandant of the

Second Cavalry regiment at Camp Cooper in Texas, to help protect the western frontier. At eight thousand miles long, it was going to take more than his one small group of men. But, Lee assured Tom as they rode on toward the west, the Congress was getting ready to authorize sending more regiments and infantry to the area. There were thirty thousand Indians out there, after all, many of them widely dispersed but all of them, it seemed, set on attacking settlers with their raiding parties.

"Have you been to Texas before?" Tom asked, casting a glance aside at Ahote, who rode a short distance away. If the Indian had overheard the lieutenant colonel's remarks, he showed no outward sign of it.

"I have not," replied Lee. "But I have heard about their livestock." He nodded toward the herd behind them, a slow-moving mass in rows of fifteen head across, Ahote and Charro and the other hands at intervals on the perimeter. "Supposedly the best there is. What do you think? Do you agree with that assessment?"

Tom looked at him and grinned. "Well, if I didn't, I sure wouldn't be taking two thousand of them halfway across the country."

Lee smiled as well—the first time Tom had seen him show any sort of emotion at all. "Good point," he agreed. "I think you've found yourself a profitable business here."

The lieutenant colonel went quiet for a moment, his brow lowered, gazing into the distance ahead as if he had something on his mind. They rode on, not speaking, the only sound the din of the cattle's hooves shuffling along the dusty trail. They'd been following this route, parallel to the barricade, for several hours already without one break in the fencing through which they could pass. It was well past noon; Tom could tell from the position of the sun in the sky. He had his doubts that they would find a way through before nightfall.

"There is one thing," Lee said then, coming back from his thoughts. "I assume you have your route mapped out already?"

"Sure," Tom replied. "Notwithstanding this detour, we're heading to St. Louis, then from there northeast back into Illinois. Near Chicago, we'll load the herd on a train and get out to the East Coast that way."

Before Tom even finished speaking, Lee was shaking his head rather vigorously. "No," he said. "No. That's not the way you want to go."

Tom waited for an explanation, and when none came, he snapped his reins lightly to get his horse a little ahead of Lee's. Then he looked at the lieutenant colonel's face and gave him a questioning look.

"Sorry, I was just—debating what to tell you about this." He stopped again, looking at Tom. Finally, he sighed. "All right. There is…some unrest brewing in this area of the nation."

Tom shrugged. "Unrest? What does that mean?"

"Disagreements. Mostly political in nature. There are a lot of reasons for what's happening that we don't have to get into right now. But you know there have been some tensions between the states, yes?"

Tom nodded. "The south wants to separate itself from the north, that's what I've heard."

"In short, yes, that's what's going on. Several southern states want to secede from the union. And of course there is opposition to this." He paused, then he jumped right in. "It's clear at this point that the country is headed toward engaging in a war with itself."

Tom didn't know what to say. He had heard about the problems between the north and south, mostly over slavery—the former wanted it abolished, the latter didn't. This made sense; without slave labor, the south could not be the agricultural center of the nation it had become. They even exported goods, mostly cotton to be woven into cloth, overseas to Britain and France.

Still, Tom couldn't agree that slavery was right. To keep another person as if he or she were property...it was inhumane. It left an ugly taste in his mouth.

"Are you sure about this?" he asked.

"Not positive, of course, because no one knows what will happen in the future. But all signs are pointing in that direction." Lee sat up straight in his saddle as he said this, his back tall and stiff. A military posture. But there was, Tom thought, just a tinge of sadness in his voice.

"All you need to know right now," Lee went on, "is that war is coming, and right where you're going—St. Louis, Missouri—is going to be a hotly contested battleground. So I would avoid it if I were you. Keep following the trails to the west with your herd. Go through Kansas instead and then turn northeastward."

"Kansas," Tom repeated, trying to picture the change in routing in his head, his hand unconsciously reaching for the saddlebag where he kept his map. "All right, colonel, if you think it's for the best."

He asked Lee to excuse him for a moment, then rode around the southern flank to Charro. After a short conversation—shouted so they could hear one another over the bawling steers—Tom returned to the front and Charro went around to the other hands. Within minutes, the directive had been shared, and the herd was coming to a halt.

In total, the detour added four days to the drive. By the time they'd reached the end of the barricades and brought the whole herd around, night had begun to fall, as Tom had predicted. It was time to camp. While the men set up, Tom saw Lieutenant Colonel Lee off.

"Are you sure you won't stay the night?" Tom asked again— he'd suggested it several times already. It didn't seem safe, what with all the hostility in the area, to be out riding after dark by himself.

Lee waved a hand at him and gave him a small smile. "I appreciate the offer, but I am expected at Fort Gibson in three days. I'll keep on."

Tom nodded and looked around. They'd stopped right on the other side of the end of the fences, on some unwitting farmer's land. The irony of it gave him a wicked feeling of satisfaction. The sun was more than halfway below the horizon; Charro, Ahote, and the other four drovers rode the perimeter of the herd, using low, soothing voices and getting them bedded down for a night's rest. Shawn was gathering rocks for a fire ring, then small branches for tinder. Beyond them was nothing but green grass, nothing but pasture for miles and miles.

"Any other advice you'd like to pass on before you go?" he asked, turning back to the lieutenant colonel. He regarded him fondly; he had come to like talking to Lee as they'd rode along, and would miss the companionship. His usual conversations with Shawn were not very stimulating, to say the least; Ahote was not much of a talker, and there was a bit of a language barrier with Charro. Mostly as they drove, he was stuck with his own thoughts.

Lee was gazing out over the herd and men as well. He thought for a moment, then looked at Tom. "Keep on with your business of driving cattle to New York. Or to any of the northern states. Because after this conflict begins to erupt, there won't be any buyers in the south for you. All you'll find here will be danger and turmoil. Steer clear if you can, my friend."

"Will do," Tom said, and the two men shook hands. Then without much fanfare, Lee mounted his big grey horse and rode off.

Tom went over to where Shawn was working on the fire, throwing matches in the middle of a bundle of branches, twigs, and leaves. The dryer material caught the flame, blazed up momentarily, and then went out again.

The younger man had taken out Tom's bedroll and spread it out on the ground for him. Tom laid down on it feeling grateful, and folded his hands over his growling stomach. They hadn't eaten a bite since breakfast, and the hunger in his belly only magnified his suddenly sullen mood, brought on by Lee's departure and his dire predictions upon leaving.

"Mr. Candy," Shawn said, dropping his backside down on his own bedroll, as usual positioned right at the foot of Tom's as if Shawn didn't want any of the other men to get close to him. "Do you think we'll get in trouble for camping here? I mean…" He looked around, eyes squinted, looking suspicious. "This is farmer's land," he whispered.

"No one will see us this far out," Tom replied quickly. "And if they do, oh well. I guess we'll just have to turn back toward Texas."

"Bite your tongue," Shawn said without even thinking—as usual. Tom cast a sideways glance at him, the annoyance he felt apparent in his eyes. What he'd said had been a joke. As usual, Shawn didn't get it.

"Sorry, Mr. Candy," O'Reilly said, then he poked at the growing fire with a long stick he'd been holding in his hand. "I just mean we've come so far. And all things considered, it's going pretty well."

Tom eyed him again.

"Oh, I know we've had some setbacks," Shawn went on quickly, earnestly. "Don't get me wrong, Mr. Candy. I'm well aware of what we've all been through. It's been a tough road. But why would you go back now? I can't see wanting to give it up because of a few hard times."

Tom didn't speak for a while; he let his mind go blank and focused on his hands at work: pulling grass, tamping the dirt, and arranging the rocks that Shawn had collected to form another fire ring. When that was set, he sat back on his heels and let O'Reilly arrange the bundles of tinder and wood.

"It has been harder than I expected," he said at last, a

thought he'd been having trouble admitting even to himself. Now that he'd said it out loud, it sounded even worse.

"Aw, nothing good in life comes without a little struggle," Shawn said as he rearranged the kindling, then he pulled a small box of safety matches from his shirt's pocket to start the fire again. He opened it carefully, withdrew a stick, and struck it on the side. Tom smelled the pungent odor of sulfur as the small flame jumped to life. "That's what my daddy told me, and I've never seen anything that don't prove it's true."

Tom fell into his thoughts again. He knew what Shawn said was true. And he'd never been afraid of work no matter how hard it was, no matter how long the odds seemed of getting it done. Those were the jobs that he enjoyed the most, in fact. He thought back to his first cattle drive for his neighbor back in England. For six weeks, he and his brother had moved those surly Welsh cows, slogging through rain and mud to the Smithfield Market in London. It had been hell, but they had done it—and earned a good reward for it when they sold the herd at market. So what was so different now? The weather had been blessedly fine, and he had twelve experienced men to help him out. That was about it. Rain or shine, trail drives were always hard. End of story.

"I just don't know what I'm doing wrong," he muttered as he kicked out his feet and sat down fully on the grass. The unexpectedly hard-packed dirt beneath it jostled him as he landed.

The fire was taking off, the flame licking up from the small twigs and catching on to the bigger branches that Shawn had scavenged from a nearby stand of trees. The younger man sat back then, keeping an eye on his handiwork should it need a little nudge to keep going.

He leaned back on his hands and stretched out his legs, crossing them at the ankles. "Mr. Candy, can I tell you something straight? I mean, can I be honest with you?"

Tom looked at him, surprised by the serious tone of O'Reilly's voice. His earlier assessment still stood in his mind: Shawn was very much an overgrown child. But there were very curious moments, like this one, in which he sounded smart.

Tom cringed at the thought. *Who's being petty now?* He had to stop being so hard on the kid.

"Of course you can," he replied as he reached down to unlace his boots. Suddenly, he couldn't wait to take them off and give his sore feet a little air.

"Well, Mr. Candy, you know, I just want to say..." Shawn paused to collect his thoughts. He looked at Tom and started over. "I want to say that it's really disappointing to hear you want to give up."

Tom stopped untying his boots and looked at O'Reilly, a dirty lace dangling between his fingers. The younger man met his gaze and straightened up, preparing himself for retaliation.

But Tom had none. He was tired; there was no fight left in him. "Go on," he said, then returned back to his task.

Shawn slouched again but was smiling a little, as if he felt he'd won some sort of battle. "I don't mean no disrespect. You know how much I appreciate this chance you've given me to help you on the drive. No one's ever trusted me that much before."

He stopped again. This time Tom just waited in silence.

The fire was now almost at full burn, and Shawn gazed into it as he wrestled with his thoughts.

"Now, I know I'm not the smartest man there is," he went on at last, and Tom detected a quaver in his voice. "Or the strongest or the bravest or the richest. Maybe the handsomest, though." He looked at Tom and snorted out a laugh.

Tom grinned. "Definitely the handsomest. Hands down."

"Well there, then we agree on that. But Mr. Candy, let me tell ya." Shawn brought his legs in and crossed them in front of himself, turning his body toward Tom. He leaned in and spoke earnestly. "You are a smart man. You are strong and brave and all the things I'm not. All the things that most men aren't. There's somethin' special about you, I knowed that from the first time we talked at that tavern in Union. The ideas you've got about cattle drivin'…"

He moved his hands in front of him in circles, as if trying to grab the word he wanted. "I don't know," he said, then dropped his hands to his lap. "They're just not like anything I've ever heard. You have *vision*, Mr. Candy. You have *dreams*. And, most important, can make them happen. You're not just following everyone else. You're making your *own* trail. And if you give that up, well…then I'd have to say you're really no smarter than me after all."

By the end of this speech, Tom's gaze was riveted on O'Reilly. He didn't know whether to be hurt, angry, or impressed by the diatribe the young man had released on him. He had never liked praise, just never cared much for it, and the level to which Shawn's had risen…It was too much. It sounded like idolatry. Was this really how his assistant felt about him?

Tom had had no idea, and now that he did, it really didn't sit well with him.

"All right, Shawn," he said slowly, still looking him in the eyes. "All right. I get the message. Thank you for speaking your thoughts plainly to me."

A moment of uncomfortable silence passed; the only sounds were the crackling of the fire, the scuffling sound of the steers' hooves, and their grunts as they circled and bedded down.

"Oh, one other thing," Shawn said then, cutting into Tom's thoughts.

Tom cleared his throat. "Yes. What is it?"

Shawn sat back, leaning on his hands again. "Do you know why it's called the Shawnee Trail?"

Tom shook his head slowly. "Can't say I do. Why is it?"

Shawn paused, a serious look on his face. "No one knows. It's just called that." Then he laughed. He literally guffawed at his own wit.

Tom laughed along with forced mirth. It would be best, he thought, to stay on the man's good side.

SEVENTEEN

A Familiar Face

1904, Moweaqua, Illinois

John climbed down from his rented one-horse carriage and stood on the edge of a meadow. The green grass swayed in the breeze, mimicking the motions of the leaves on the trees. Patches of wildflowers dotted the landscape here and there, a truly lovely scattering of purples and blues and yellows. Beyond this was a fence at the far end, and behind that a corral, a set of breeding pens, and several wood-sided outbuildings.

To his left was the start of a long dirt-and-gravel road that led into the compound, splitting off halfway. One route led to the working area, one to the main house—Tudor revival in style, if John wasn't mistaken. And right beside him, at the top of the drive, stood a large, white clapboard sign. "Homestead Cattle," it read in big, black letters painted on with a steady hand. Beneath it was the silhouette of a shorthorn. John gazed at it for a long while as he tried to calm the tumult in his mind. He'd wanted this for so long and now he was so close.

But don't get your hopes up, he told himself and pushed his thoughts in that direction. Though he'd spent the entire trip here almost literally on the edge of his seat with anticipation, he had to prepare himself, he knew, in case it didn't pan out. It could be just another dead end. He didn't want to let his hopes soar. That would only set him up for a dangerous fall.

Out of the corner of his eye, he saw movement and turned to look at the house. A man had come from around the back. He wore high, black boots; white trousers; and a green coat with tails—a stable groom. John wondered if they were expecting company. He looked up and down the road behind him but saw no sign of another carriage or automobile. When he turned back, the man was gone, as if he hadn't been there at all.

"All right," John said aloud to himself, trying not to be bothered by the man's odd disappearance. "All right," he said once again to bolster his courage, and set his foot onto the drive. The gravel crunched beneath his boots. It seemed to be the loudest noise John had ever heard; it announced his arrival at the homestead all the way down to the home's stone steps.

Finally, he stood before the door. The house was larger than it had appeared from the road, with an entire wing well hidden from view by the meadow's trees and sloping hills. John cleared his throat. He took off his hat and shook the dust from it. Then, before he could change his mind, he reached for the big, black door's massive iron knocker and made his presence known.

It seemed an eternity before anyone heeded the sound. John gripped the handle on his bag of notes and made sure his vest was buttoned, his boots tied. He wanted to look presentable, as if he hadn't been living on trains and at hotels for the last few months. He needed to seem trustworthy.

Finally, the doorknob turned slightly. Then it stopped. Then it started again, and the door opened a crack. A watery, old blue eye peeked out from the crevice, a flop of white hair falling over it. John's mind immediately went back to a photograph he had seen somewhere in the midst of his research: a young man wearing wool pants with buckskin stitched down the insides of the thighs to protect against rubbing from a saddle. Leg up on the slat of a corral fence, thick leather gloves on his hands. The picture had stood out to John in particular because it was in color—a rarity for the time it was taken, sometime in the 1850s. Thanks to that, he could see the colors of the man's eyes, though they were partially obscured by a lock of hair the wind had blown across his face.

"Yes?" asked the figure behind the door. The voice John heard was tinny and cracked, dry and old but clearly male in timbre and tone. The blue eye looked him up and down.

"Are you—" John began but then stopped. His heart thumped; his stomach felt as if it had dropped right out of his body. He took a step forward on numb feet. "Are you Tom Candy?" he asked in a whisper, leaning into the doorway as much as he could.

The door, though open only an inch, squeezed halfway closed again, leaving the slightest sliver through which the man continued to peer at John. Where at first his blue eye had looked cloudy, now John saw a glint in it, a spark of recognition, or perhaps of fear. There was an awful span of silence during which John's mind raced and grasped at wild ideas. Maybe he was in the wrong place. The ad in the newspaper could have had a misprint. Maybe the proprietor's name was actually Caroline Tandy. Or maybe he'd come to the wrong ranch. Perhaps it was the one John had passed on the way in, ten or so miles back down the road. What if—

But then the door creaked, and the sound stifled the whirlwind in his head. He blinked. The door was opening, this time far enough that John could see the old man's face. It was wrinkled, weather aged, and set in a menacing scowl.

"Who wants to know?" he asked, and John could clearly hear his English accent.

EIGHTEEN

Wintering the Herd

1853, Illinois

By the time Tom reached the border of Illinois, winter was about to start and he'd lost several dozen head already. Whatever illness the cattle had brought with them, it had spread—slowly at first, but then it seemed as though every morning the men found another whose ribs were showing through its skin, whose eyes were leaking constant tears. Charro had the most experience with livestock maladies and particularly with this breed of Spanish cattle, which was now native to the southwest. Tom put them in his care.

The vaquero separated the sick ones and drove them in a small herd at a safe distance. Though he tried every remedy in his arsenal, within a month his charges were gone and he rejoined the bigger group.

"There was nothing you could do," Tom told Charro as he pulled the saddle from his horse. In the next stall, the vaquero laid a blanket over his own mount.

"I know, I know," Charro replied in a murmur. "You've told me before. But I always feel there is something more I could have done."

With their horses put up for the night, the two men left the stable. Outside, Tom put his hand on Charro's shoulder and offered a smile. "I wish it had turned out differently. You know that. But perhaps it was for the best. Imagine if the sick ones had made it all the way here."

He gestured out before them, at the corrals and pastures where their herd was gathered. Most stood in the open and turned away from the lightly falling snow, while others had bunched on the lee side of a short ridge to keep out of the increasing wind.

"In these close quarters," Tom went on, "who knows how quickly it would have spread. We might be looking at a fifty percent loss instead of only a few dozen head."

The two men stopped at the corral fence. Ahote walked among some of the corralled steers, checking their eyes, skin, and hooves. Though Tom had declared the mysterious disease eradicated, the Indian remained vigilant. He'd performed these inspections sometimes twice a day since they'd arrived at the ranch, whose owner had agreed to winter the herd for a nice fee.

"So, how long are we going to stay?" Charro asked, hitching

the heel of his high-top riding boot on the fence, its large Mexican spur clinking with a star rowel and jingle-bob.

Tom continued to gaze out over the herd, admiring Ahote's gentle way with the steers and how they responded in kind, a sort of unseen bond. In a way, he envied that a man could seem so in tune with a beast. There was something almost poetic about it—a sort of rough beauty that Tom, despite Shawn's oft-repeated compliments on his eloquence, could not express.

"Well, we're in for the winter, that's for certain," Tom replied to Charro, copying his stance and leaning against the corral's fence. "The temperature's dropping further and further every day, and the ground's freezing up, which means no grass for grazing…"

He looked out at the steers again. This was a young herd, most of them six or seven years old, with the long legs and fine, tapered horns that were characteristic of their breed. Some looked wilder than others—sparser hair, chips and scratches on their horns; their meat would be fine grained and coarse, comparable to venison and tough if not cooked right. The trick, Tom concluded, was to buy them young and feed them well for two years at least, though unfortunately he didn't have that sort of time. He had managed to stretch this drive out for close to a year already, and in that length the steers had matured. They were bulkier now than they'd been when Tom had taken possession of them in Texas.

"And they need to be fatter." Charro finished Tom's thought.

"Yes, exactly," Tom replied. "More food and less movement—that's the plan. Pack on the weight and keep it on.

Tomorrow we get started on buying surplus corn from local farmers to feed the cattle."

"Then in the spring we go to New York, and you get higher prices."

"*We* get higher prices," Tom said quickly. "We're in this together, Charro. You know that, yes?"

The Mexican drover smiled at him, a tired but content look. "Yes," he said. "We work together. We finish together."

"We get paid together," Tom added with a laugh, once again putting a hand on Charro's shoulder and giving it a squeeze. "Speaking of food, let's go see what we can rustle up. I'm starving."

Shawn O'Reilly, by his own admittance, was not a hale and hardy fellow. He'd suffered from breathing problems all his life, no doubt exacerbated by the dusty, dry clime in which he'd come of age. In the spring, when all the flowers came into bloom, he sneezed until he thought his nose might fall right off his face, and every winter he was laid up for weeks with influenza. This one was no different; of the month they'd been at the ranch, he'd already spent twelve days in bed, his body so achy that even the slightest movement left him with hours of dull pain. And despite all the rest, plus Charro's chicken soup and Ahote's native remedies, he didn't seem to be getting better.

When the third week of O'Reilly's sequestration came and went, Tom felt it was time for him to be concerned.

"Has the flu ever plagued you this long before?" he asked,

taking a seat on a rickety wooden chair next to the young man's bed. While the other men kept their distance for fear of contagion, Tom held no such trepidation. As O'Reilly himself was always quick to point out, nothing ever seemed to harm Tom—no illnesses, no injuries ever befell him even in the harshest conditions on the trail. Flus and fevers passed him by; he never even got blisters on his feet after months of walking in the same old boots.

"You're indestructible," Shawn had told him one night as they'd camped out under the stars; he kept Tom up all night then with all of his sniffling and sneezing.

Now, his head and shoulders propped up on a mountain of pillows, a quilt pulled up tightly across his chest, Shawn sneezed again into a handkerchief and let out a moaning, gurgling sigh. "No. Usually if I'm sick on a Monday, by Friday I'll be up and about again." His voice was dull and sticky, dripping with sickness. "But this…" He shrugged. "I don't know what this is."

Tom reached out and patted his shoulder. Even that was hot with the fever that had been burning through his body. Tom could feel it right through his bedclothes.

"I'm sure it will pass," Tom assured him. He wasn't sure, really, but he wanted to say something that might sound comforting. Apparently, this worked.

Shawn smiled at him with chapped, swollen lips and blinked his tired, wet eyes. "Thanks, Mr. Candy. I'll do my best to get better so I can get back to work."

Those were the last words Tom ever heard Shawn speak. The next day, he could barely sit upright; by the end of the week, he had ceased to eat. On Sunday, Ahote went to check on him and found him unresponsive in his bed. The Indian sat vigil until the last choking breath escaped the young man's ruined body.

"Blessed Mother Mary," Charro uttered in his thick accent, his eyes closed, his head bowed over the crude grave he and Tom had dug, the hole in the earth where Shawn now lay. It had been hard work, their shovels picking away inch by inch at the frozen ground. When it was long and deep enough, Ahote brought out the body, which he had prepared in the traditions of his tribe: wrapped in soft, white cloth, a tail feather laid across his chest to aid his flight into the afterlife.

"Amen," Tom murmured when Charro finished the prayer and traced a cross over his chest. The three men stood in silence around the grave, a light snow falling on their hats and the shoulders of their coats. He could barely look at the others; he didn't want to let them see his tears or the confusion on his face. Could he have done more for Shawn? Something that might have spared his life? Ever since that night when O'Reilly had berated him for doubting himself, for even thinking about turning back and giving up on the cattle drive, the tenor of their relationship had changed. Before they'd had an easy friendship, a comfort in one another born out of all those long hours together on the road. But since then, Tom had felt uneasy around him. There'd been something about the fire in the young man's eyes as he'd built Tom up, told him how great he was, and at the same time knocked himself down.

I'm not the smartest man. Shawn's words rang out in Tom's mind. *Or the strongest or the bravest or the richest.*

"But you are the handsomest," he said aloud with something halfway between a laugh and a sob. Charro and Ahote both glanced at him, smiling kindly even though they didn't understand the joke.

Tom shook his head, clearing out these morbid thoughts. This was only his grief whispering to him, trying to convince him he'd done something wrong to distract him from the unfairness of it. Shawn had been what, twenty-two years old at the most? Tom realized now that he'd never asked and a fresh spring of tears welled up in his eyes. He could have been a better friend, a better boss, and a better man—all the things one realizes when faced with his own mortality.

He took up his shovel again. No sense in lingering when there was work to do.

"Let's get to it," he said, "before the damned snow buries us all."

NINETEEN

On to New York City

1854, New York City

Spring came in like a lion that year, all warm winds and blustery, sunny days. After what had felt like an interminable winter, Tom welcomed the change, and he could tell his men felt the same. Even the cattle seemed a little happier—at least from what Ahote reported.

They waited until the end of March, just to ensure that the good weather was there to stay. When the temperature held at forty degrees for a week, it was time, and the three men, along with four other drovers, got the steers back on the road. Whereas they had set out from San Antonio with almost two thousand head, they now counted just more than six hundred, and they reduced that down by half before they left Illinois. Tom had promised his old friend from Chicago, Phillip Armour, a big herd from Texas, and he certainly delivered just that—hundreds of fat, meaty steers for which the butcher king insisted on paying top dollar. Tom graciously accepted and, true to his word, split the profits from the sale three ways between Charro, Ahote, and himself.

With that bit of business tended to, they loaded the remaining herd onto railroad cars for the last leg of the journey out to the East Coast. No one had ever attempted such a thing before—moving cattle across states by train. But to Tom it made perfect sense. The more walking the longhorns did, the more weight they would lose, and he was banking on their size as a main attraction to market them once they were in New York City. Another long drive by foot, he knew, would decrease the steers' worth and the amount of money that would wind up in his and the other men's pockets.

Unfortunately, no rail line could take them directly into New York—something about freight regulations and weight restrictions. So Tom had booked passage for the herd from Indiana into Fort Lee, New Jersey, a major stopping-off point for cotton, livestock, and other goods bound for the city. From there, they would load the cattle onto ferry boats to shuttle them across the Hudson River to their final destination.

"How many boats do you think it will take?" Charro asked, then laid down a straight flush. He and Tom were in the parlor car attached to the freight boxes carrying the steers. They'd been passing the time with endless games of poker, betting on each hand with peanut shells.

"Ah," Tom said and tossed his own cards on the table between them. He hadn't even been close. And this made what—the ninth or tenth hand in a row he'd lost? He sat back in his chair as Charro shuffled the deck. "I'm thinking maybe four or five, depending on how much weight they can take. One of us will travel onboard with the steers. The others will stay on shore, one on each side to send and receive."

Charro nodded, then smiled as he began to deal out the cards again. "Señor Tom, I have to tell you," he said with a bit of a laugh, "I honestly didn't think, back when you hired me for this job, that it would ever get this far."

Across the car, Ahote was seated by a window gazing out at the scenery as it passed. Hearing the comment, he glanced at Charro and smiled.

"Neither of us did, I think," the Mexican went on. He paused in the middle of handing another card out in front of Tom. "Not that we doubted you. It just hadn't been done before, you know? So it didn't seem possible."

Tom took the card out of his outstretched hand, one eyebrow raised in Charro's direction. "And now?" he asked.

Charro laughed again and laid the remaining deck down in the middle of the table. He turned over the top card. "Now I see the error of my ways. I have become a disciple in the church of Señor Tom Candy. I have seen the light!"

Tom tried to hide his growing smirk. "Hallelujah, and I raise you," he said and threw a handful of peanut shells into the pot.

It had been five years since Tom had been in New York City, and his stay had been brief. But in all that time since, he'd carried with him a mental picture of the place. When he closed his eyes, he always saw the South Street port with its tall ships, steamers, and fishing boats all lined up one after the other. He remembered the aromas of all the different foods the street vendors sold, a new wagon full of offerings at every corner. Sometimes, if he thought hard enough, he could remember the crunch of that soft-shell crab he'd had for dinner on his last night in the city and the sweet, buttery saltiness of the roasted corn.

Looking at it now atop Fort Lee's steep bluffs, right across the Hudson River from 155th Street in Manhattan, it didn't seem so different from back then. Tom had departed the city in the summer and now had returned in the same season—on Independence Day, of all days. Even from his distant vantage point, he could see the merriment going on across the island: parades, parties, all sorts of festivities. He could almost hear the champagne popping at the estates directly across and the firecrackers children were setting off in the streets. This was not Tom's holiday; it was not his country, not really, but he'd come to like America in the few years he'd been here, and so far it had been good to him. Deep down, he couldn't help but feel a little enlivened by the holiday.

Or maybe it's the cattle drive, he thought with an amused smile on his face. He hadn't slept in two nights, his mind racing too much with the logistics of this final push into New York. He wasn't the first man ever to bring cattle to the city; Fifth Avenue, he knew, was often blocked by smaller herds brought in by drovers for the butchers downtown. But he was the first to bring them so far, over so much land and time. In recent years, others had tried driving cattle from Texas across the United States, particularly to the California gold rush area. Missouri was also popular but not that far from San Antonio, where most drives originated, and the same went for New Orleans. A few other brave souls had attempted drives northward towards Chicago, but none had made it.

"I have," Tom said in a low voice, speaking only to himself. "I've made it." A knot of nerves mixed with pride tied up his gut. But there was no time for reflecting or self-congratulations. Below him, he saw the two ferries he had hired to transport his herd across the river just arriving at the dock, where Ahote, Charro, and the other drovers waited, keeping the steers in a long, wide line behind them, and stretching back up the narrow dirt road to the cliffs of Fort Lee above.

Besides, he thought as he headed back from the cliff's edge and over to the path leading to the shore below, he hadn't made it, not quite yet. There was still work to do. He picked up his pace down the path, eager to get it done.

In the end, Tom was glad they had arrived early. While the train had made better time than he had planned, the ferries were much slower than he had anticipated—due, he understood, to the steers' added weight. The more cattle they brought on board, the more the boats' steam engines chugged and churned through the waters of the Hudson. In all, it took six trips in just about as many hours with about fifty head per load to shuttle the entire herd to the opposite shore.

Charro and two of the drovers stayed in Fort Lee to get the animals on the ferries safely; Tom, Ahote, and another pair of men loaded their horses, and went across with the first boat and stayed there to bunch the cattle as they came in. Ahote went back each trip to bring another load and keep the steers calm during the noisy and choppy crossings.

Tom had discovered that the longer the cattle were trailed, the easier they were to handle. Longhorns held together on the trail formed attachments not only between themselves but with the drovers as well. The steers, though wild at heart, were natural herd animals, and like horses they came to understand that the drovers kept them safe and secure. It got so they depended on the drovers' prodding and soft voices and so followed them like lap dogs. This created an odd spectacle given the massive and intimidating size of these longhorns.

As the hours passed and the herd covered a quarter mile of the dirt-and-rock coastline on the New York side, a crowd of local residents began to gather—small at first, just a few curious onlookers lining up on the rough road that ran parallel to the shore, but soon they grew to number almost as much as the cattle. This was actually July third, the day before the nation's Independence Day celebration; Tom, still being fairly new to the country, hadn't realized the significance of the date but picked up as much from the snippets of chatter he heard while passing by the mob. Apparently, some of them thought this gathering of huge and strange-looking longhorn cattle had something to do with it—that they somehow fit in with the fireworks and parades and politicians' speeches. What they thought a bunch of cattle could have to do with it, though, Tom had no idea.

The longhorns, snuffling around for tufts of grass to chew and lowing at the drovers as they came around, took no notice of the oglers; the drovers tolerated them only grudgingly, and as long as they did not rile the steers. When all cattle were accounted for, Tom let all his men sit and rest for a spell while he took out his map and reviewed the route they would take to the market—the Bull's Head down on Third Avenue and Twenty-Fourth Street, a sort of sales place and social club for local cattlemen. It would be a bit of a hike, but Tom had known that before even purchasing these cattle back in Texas; he'd done all his research while still in Chicago, in fact, even placing a telegraph message to Daniel Drew, the owner of the Bull's Head, to discuss the particulars of their arrival and available accommodations for the herd.

"Señor Tom," said Charro as he came up behind him, his voice low. He held his hat in his hands, curling up its brim with his fingers as he spoke. "From what the people are saying, word is already spreading. Everyone's coming out to see the cows—that's what they call them, the cows." He laughed a little. "I hope this will not give us trouble in driving the herd to the market."

Tom sighed and sat back against the boulder where he had spread out the map. He crossed his arms and looked out at the Hudson, at the little waves that lapped against the shore nearby.

"It might, Charro," he said, looking at the vaquero. "I

won't lie. It could cause us some problems." He imagined all the tall buildings in the city emptying out, their inhabitants flowing out onto the streets like an unstoppable river, waves and waves of them trapping his herd at a crossroads with no way out.

He shrugged. "We'll just have to deal with that if and when it happens." He stood up straight and smiled at Charro. "Come on. Let's get moving. A little work will take our minds off our worries."

Charro smiled and agreed, then headed back to where Ahote was tending to the horses. After a brief, quiet discussion, they tightened up cinches, mounted up, and rode out to the other drovers around the herd. Tom repacked his map and got on his horse as well, then he rode right through the middle of the herd, surveying the steers as he went. They looked hearty, healthy, and, most important, fat. They'd packed on a good amount of weight in Illinois, and Tom felt a tinge of pride at having thought of the idea to winter them there on surplus corn. But there had been losses, too, he remembered, and his pride turned to a churning in his stomach.

"Mr. Candy! Mr. Candy!" a voice called behind him, and Tom twisted quickly in his saddle. *It couldn't be.* Only one person had ever insisted on calling him that despite his repeated efforts to get on a first-name basis with the kid.

"Shawn?" he muttered, but even as he did he realized the foolishness of it. He shook his head a bit and saw that it was only Charro riding toward him at a gallop.

When the vaquero reached his side, he pulled up on his horse's reins and came to a stop. He was a little out of breath from the effort and, Tom imagined, from the excitement of the impending drive.

"We're all ready," Charro said, a big grin on his face. "All the men are in place. Ahote will be at point. Where do you want me?"

Tom smiled too, his dizzying memories of that dark, dark time in Illinois dissipating from his mind. The Mexican drover's enthusiasm was too contagious. Tom reached out and grabbed his shoulder.

"We're all at point today," he said. "All three of us. We ride up front. If it's a parade the people want, then it's a parade they'll get. And you, me, and Ahote will be the grand marshals."

In the summer of 1854, the United States was in the sere grip of a long, hard dry spell. There'd been no rain for weeks, maybe more than a month, and so the unpaved roads in New York City were like dust bowls, sending up tufts of powdery dirt with every footfall set upon them. Even the cobblestone streets were covered in a constant layer of the stuff as it blew in on the wind and tagged along on the city's denizens' shoes and clothes.

Now three hundred longhorns trampled along these avenues, their hard hooves digging into the crusty earth, sending opaque, rust-colored clouds floating into the air. The drovers wrapped bandannas and old cloths around their mouths and noses just to be able to breathe; even the steers chuffed and snorted to clear their stinging nostrils.

But none of this deterred the spectators. It almost made Tom laugh as he rode on in front of the herd. The farther into the city they got, the more people were waiting for them, or just coming out of their homes, shops, and high-rise buildings, having heard of the ruckus through the telegraph system or a particularly fast and gossipy neighbor. Young, old, infirm, all variety of people lined the streets and even cheered as the men and the longhorns came into view. The steers didn't much like the noise, or the random hands that reached out from the crowds to touch their horns or slap their rumps. They slowed their gait at times and dipped their heads, butting one another's backsides, eager to get away.

Charro, on the other hand, reveled in it. He took off his wide-brimmed sombrero and waved it in the air, a big grin showing all of his uneven, yellowed teeth. His hair stood on end from all the grease; it had been several days since they'd bathed, and the man emitted a rank odor. This was not a condemnation; Tom was no sweet-smelling flower himself, and a certain level of grime was expected on a cattle drive. He just imagined that if the onlookers had been a little closer, they might not have been so enthused.

As it was, though, they loved it; they loved the spectacle of the drive, and they loved Charro's good-natured theatrics. He waved his hat, and they pointed at him, applauded, and raised their hands in greeting.

"A Mexican!" Tom heard one young man say as they passed, and Charro did his grandstanding. This almost made him laugh too until he realized that this far north, there was a good possibility some folks had never seen anyone who looked like him. Nor had they seen a real live Indian, so when their eyes fell on Ahote next, their mouths went agape, and their cheering ceased. A few even took steps backward, as if they were afraid he would attack.

What was it, Tom wondered, that made them so excited about one man but seemingly scared of the other? Yes, everyone knew of the Indian territories; they had heard about the raids and the scalpings, the terror the indigenous people seemed intent to inflict on anyone who was white.

But they did not know *this* Indian. Ahote was one of the gentlest and most insightful men Tom had ever met, and he certainly had a way with the herd. Whenever the longhorns appeared upset, when the crowd was too much, all it took was a word from Ahote's mouth or bringing his horse in their direction to get them focused again and move them along in a calmer state. Over the course of the drive, whenever they'd had any sort of issue at all—with feeding, illness, or weight gains and losses—Ahote could solve it. How anyone could dismiss him on sight was beyond belief.

Tom rode at the front of the herd, Ahote to his left, Charro to his right, each bewildered—despite Charro's comical flourishes—by all the attention.

"Hieee, Señor Tom. How much longer until we get to the market?" Charro asked during a break from his routine. "I'm not sure how much more of this I can take."

Tom smirked as he peered around the streets, looking for some sort of landmark. "I think the concern, really, is how much more they can take of you."

His eyes landed on a sign—"Smith's Emporium"—affixed

to a storefront on the left. *Ah, yes.* Mr. Drew had told him to look for it.

"It looks like we've made it to Third Avenue, gentlemen," he announced to his partners, "which means we have twenty-four more blocks to go. It shouldn't be too long now."

"This is good to hear," Ahote said—the first words he had uttered since they had set foot in New York.

Nobody knew exactly when the Bull's Head market had come into being; it seemed like it had always been around, as if it had just sprung up from the ground exactly where it was needed. The earliest records of it showed it was in operation in 1755, and at that point it was located just east of Collect Pond, off of Boston Post Road—a crossroads of tanneries and slaughterhouses, livestock yards, and stables. Back then, the market was a tavern, really, more of a gathering place for farmers, drovers, and merchants, where they could incidentally sell some of their wares if they wished.

The next few decades saw it become more organized and focused on the cattle trade. The owner put up pens adjoining the main building, and farmers from the area could bring their steers to put them up for sale. All business transactions were completed right there inside the tavern over a hot meal, some warm beer, and a serving of all the local news and gossip. But it wasn't entirely about work; there were dog fights in the yard too, and a never-ending crack loo game wherein sellers could lose their money. Aside from the farmers, travelers would come and go, sharing tales of other lands, as would country gentlemen in their deerskin britches and Castor hats, just returning from time abroad.

A hundred years later, the market was much the same, only in a new location. As Tom and his crew made their approach down Third Avenue, he saw the large main building and its flanking corrals, which had been emptied out, he knew, pending his herd's arrival.

"You're going to bring us good money with those steers," Daniel Drew had told him in a letter back when Tom was in Illinois. "So I have no problem telling the regulars they'll have to wait for a day."

Daniel was waiting outside for them, or at least that was who Tom assumed it to be. The man was older and stocky, with a square face and a beard that ran along the underside of his jaw. His face was stern, befitting the businessman Tom knew him to be; Daniel had been a financier and a ship and railroad developer long before he'd gotten into the cattle trade.

"Mr. Candy, what a pleasure to meet you," the man said as Tom dismounted. "And right on time."

Tom slipped off his thick leather glove, and the two men shook hands.

"I'm as surprised as you are. I really thought we'd hit more delays than we did," Tom said with a smile, then he let out a breath and raised his head to look around. Behind him, his drovers led the steers into the pens, Charro and Ahote supervising, one on each side.

"And the herd?" Drew asked, his voice audibly expectant.

Tom looked back at him and nodded. "It's good. It's good,"

he repeated as if to assure himself. "We lost some on the way here, but that was expected. Illnesses and all—it always happens. Then a few more didn't make it past the winter."

He stopped for a moment, another pang hitting his chest at the thought. *Winter. Death.* An image of Shawn filled his mind—what the young lad would have looked like here, running around the place shouting with glee because they'd finally made it.

He cleared his throat. "But, ah, that was expected too. I was able to sell some to an old friend of mine in Chicago, Philip Armour, to lighten our load, as it were, and, well, here we are."

"Yes," Daniel remarked, returning Tom's earlier smile. "Here we are."

The two men watched the herd move for a while, a sea of rich brown and white brindle steers, their horns clacking against one another. Those that had gone in the pen first were already lined up at the troughs, getting their fill of water. Others headed for the bales of hay Daniel's hands were tossing over the pen's side fences for them. Tom felt his body relax, knowing that his journey was through. He wondered if the cattle felt the same.

"Well, let's go inside and talk, shall we?" Drew asked, and so they did. Though Tom would be making deals directly with anyone who wanted to buy his steers, the owner of the Bull's Head had some advice for him on pricing, who to sell to, and who to avoid.

"I hate to naysay my regulars," he admitted, his voice low, leaning across his desk toward Tom. "But business is business, right? We all have to watch out for our bottom lines."

Once all the longhorns were corralled, the men were taken to their rooms, where they could rest for a while and, finally, take the baths they needed. They ate dinner with Drew in the tavern's dining room—a special late-night meal prepared just for them; according to the owner, mealtimes were chaotic there, with people actually climbing over one another to find empty seats. Room was at a premium, it seemed.

"Or maybe it's just that our food is so good," Drew said with a low, rolling laugh, then he reached up to wipe a bit of grease from his lips. "It really is a terrible problem to have."

The sales would not take place for two days, so the steers and the men would have time to recuperate. Tom looked forward to the rest, perhaps spending the next day entirely by himself; not that he disliked his companions, but he felt a little solitude was good for the soul once in a while. He could catch up on sleep, read a book, take meals in his room, and update the diary he'd been keeping about the drive. He'd tried all along to write something every few days, just notes on the weather, the cattle, and the experience in general. *Who knew?* he'd thought more than once with a fair amount of amusement. Maybe he would write a book someday.

Regardless, that was not at all how his day turned out. He awoke with the sun, famished despite the large dinner of—what else?—beef steak he had devoured last night. He went down to the dining room to find that Daniel's account had been completely accurate: every seat was filled, and a waiting line ran down either wall. He propped himself against a windowsill on the right-hand queue and prepared to wait.

"Hello, good morning," he offered the next man in line as

he turned his gaze on Tom. The man nodded back and looked away—but then snapped his head right back.

"Are you—" he began, then put a hand up to his almost gaping mouth. "Are you Tom Candy?"

Tom lowered his eyebrows at the man. How on Earth would he know? "Yes, I am," he replied as he stood up straight. If there was going to be a confrontation of some sort—or, God forbid, a fight—he didn't want to get caught unprepared.

The man hesitated for a moment, but then a big smile spread across his face. "Oh, man, can I shake your hand, mister?" He stuck his out heartily, Tom less so. But the man didn't notice his reluctance. He grabbed Tom's hand and shook it so hard, he practically lifted him up and down.

"Wow, comin' all the way here," the man went on, still shaking, "with that big herd o' cattle? All the way from Texas?" He dropped Tom's hand but now gripped his shoulder in what he might have thought was a friendly way, but it sent shooting pains down Tom's already achy back.

"That's just the greatest thing I ever heard," the man went on, his voice growing in pitch and volume with every word. "Congratulations. I can't believe you done it."

Tom smiled tightly and tried to keep his composure. There was no need to be rude to the man, who was just expressing his admiration for what, Tom knew, was a rather unusual feat.

So, just let him, Tom thought. *Don't rain on the man's parade.*

"Well, thank you," he said, bowing his head briefly. "I do appreciate your kind words. It was a long road, but—"

Tom paused. An idea had suddenly passed over the man's face.

"I know," he said, shaking a finger at Tom. "I know. I'm gonna buy you breakfast!"

"Oh, no," Tom immediately protested. "No, I—"

"No, no, it's the least I could do for an important man such as yourself. In fact..." He looked out over the room, at the dozens of occupied tables, the dozens more men who waited. "Uh-uh. No. You shouldn't have to wait. You." He turned to a man seated near them, slurping down a spoonful of runny eggs. "Get up."

The eating man, understandably, did not reply.

"I said, '*Get up*,'" Tom's benefactor threatened, looming large over the table. He was a tall man, thick necked, with thighs like tree trunks. If he had told Tom to move, Tom certainly would have listened.

But the man at the table didn't care. He moved on to a piece of bread that looked and smelled as if it had just been baked. Tom's stomach growled.

"Listen," the man went on, reaching down to grab the lapel of the diner's coat. "Do you know who this is?"

The man looked at him with tired eyes. "No," he said, sounding just as exhausted as he looked. "I have no idea who you are. So just—"

"Not *me*," Tom's friend replied, then jerked this thumb over his shoulder. "*Him*."

The diner peered around the large man and set his gaze on Tom for what felt like a full minute. Then he simply sat back.

"No," he said. "Can't say I do."

"That, my friend, is *Tom Candy*." The man said his name as if it were a precious secret.

Finally—*finally*—the man at the table showed some reaction. He blinked up at the other man, then looked again at Tom and blinked at him too. Once, twice.

"Well, why didn't you say so?" He dislodged the larger man's fist from his coat and stood up from his chair. "Mr. Candy. Please." He backed up and held out a hand, indicating Tom should take his chair.

"Oh, no," Tom said again. "No, I couldn't."

"Please. I insist. It would be my honor."

Tom looked from one man to the other. Both of them watched him and waited, looking as if the balance of the world hung on his answer. Beyond them, he now saw, the rest of the folks had stopped eating and seemed to be awaiting his reply as well.

"Tom Candy," he heard someone whisper, then someone else, then another, until his name had spread the entire length of the room.

"Well." He cleared his throat and took a step forward. "Well. Don't mind if I do."

TWENTY

A Long-Awaited Invitation

1904, Moweaqua, Illinois

Now that Tom Candy stood in front of him, John had no idea what to say. He'd been practicing for this moment for months—how he would introduce himself, the questions he would ask, and the answers he would demand to know. And up until ten seconds earlier, he'd been firm in his convictions. He had a right to know, he'd told himself, just how Tom fit into his father's life and what, if anything, he knew about Edwin Stanton's death.

But all reasoning had left his head. He simply gaped at the man, fixed on that blue eye that froze him to the spot where he stood.

"I…I…" He tried to say his name but drew a blank. Inside the doorway, the old man huffed, then John again heard a creaking noise. The door was closing on him.

"Wait!" he said, though it came out more like a cry. He berated himself for the desperation he heard in his own voice but then put it aside. This was his chance—possibly his only chance—to find out what he needed to know. It called for some urgency, he thought.

"John Stanton!" he said loudly, and the door stopped. The old man peered out at him again. "John Stanton," he repeated. "That's my name. And I really need to speak with you."

The blue eye once again roved over him, up and down, taking in everything from his shoes to his hat, then finally settling on his face. The old man squinted. "I knew a Stanton once. He was the…" He trailed off, as did his gaze, wandering over the floorboards of the porch on which John stood. Then it snapped up to his face again. "The secretary of war. Under President Lincoln."

He stopped again and just looked at John, awaiting verification of this memory.

"Yes," John said quickly. "Edwin Stanton was my father. And I—"

The door suddenly swung wide, and John jumped back in surprise. The old man moved fully into the threshold, seeming to take up the entire space despite his somewhat diminutive frame. In fact, his slight stature was a shock to John; he supposed he'd built Tom Candy up into such a figure in his mind, he'd expected the man to be ten feet tall. Or maybe—

"You *are* Tom Candy, yes?" he asked, just to be sure.

"I am," the man replied with a single nod of his head. "And

I did know your father. Not well—I wouldn't say we were friends. More like business associates. But we met a few times in that capacity, and he was very cordial and very fair. I always admired the work that he did as well." He went quiet for a moment, his brow lowered in thought. "It was a shame," he added, "how it ended up for your father. To have his reputation tarnished like that."

John cleared his throat. "Yes. Yes, well. That's much of the reason why I'm here, you see."

"How did you find me?" Tom asked, ignoring what John had said, or perhaps not caring for what he had to say.

The question made him laugh nervously. "Well, I, uh…" He tried to think of the best way to put it. "I did a bit of sleuthing—I'm a newspaper reporter, you see."

Tom Candy visibly bristled. He took a step back. "Is that so? Well, you'd best be on your way, then. Whoever sent you here should have told you that I don't do interviews anymore."

"No, wait!" John stepped forward. He was almost into the house. "I'm not here as a journalist. I'm here of my own accord." He stopped, closed his eyes, and brought a hand up to his forehead. This wasn't going at all how he wanted. Unsure of what approach might work, he decided simply to go with the truth.

He opened his eyes and looked at Tom. "I don't work for a newspaper. Not anymore. I just want to know what happened to my father. I thought maybe you could help me figure it out."

Tom looked at him, the same long, hard stare he'd been giving John since he'd opened the door. "And why would I know anything about it?"

John sighed, any feelings of hope he had deflating miserably.

This conversation was getting worse and worse every time he opened his mouth. "I don't know," he admitted. "It's just that I've done so much research, and time and time again, your name has shown up. I don't know what the connection is, but I thought—"

"Research into what?" Tom asked.

John blinked at him. He didn't know? "Into how my father was framed," he said, turning his head a little, looking at Tom from the corners of his eyes. Was this some sort of test? Or a game?

"Framed for what?" Tom asked, his expression guileless. He really didn't know.

"For the murder of Abraham Lincoln," John said, his voice firm, his chin held high.

Tom paused. Then he nodded. "You'd better come in," he said, then moved aside to make room for John to pass.

TWENTY-ONE

The Plot Revealed

1865, Washington City

Since the start of the war, Washington City, it was said, had become one of the most heavily defended districts in the world. Whereas in the beginning there had been only Fort Washington, twelve miles away, within the first four years of the war, Maj. Gen. McClellan, commander of the Department of the Potomac, had dug thirty-seven miles of trenches around the Capitol and put an enclosed fort on every one of the sixty-eight hills surrounding it. In the valleys between lay ninety-three batteries of field artillery, fifteen hundred field and siege guns, and twenty miles' worth of rifle pits, all of them facing south.

Unassailable. The word ran over and over through Edwin Stanton's head as he walked across the Potomac River's Long Bridge—the old one, not the new one still being constructed about a hundred feet downriver. He kept his hands folded together behind his back and his gait at a slow stroll. Union soldiers, a pair every fifty feet or so to protect the bridge against Confederate invasion, snapped to stiff-backed attention each time he approached, and he put them back at ease with a loose salute and a nod. From halfway out across the river, he could look back and see all the fortifications, these additions that effectively protected the city, and a swell of pride rose in his chest, followed quickly by the usual anxiety he felt whenever he had a meeting scheduled.

"It's all right. Let him through," Stanton said, waving his hand at a couple of soldiers who had stopped a young man coming toward him. "He's with me."

Dressed all in black, with a wide-brimmed hat pulled down almost over his eyes, Thomas Birch approached. The two men did not shake hands but simply turned and walked, far apart enough to seem casual but close enough that their conversation could not be heard.

"What news do you bring me?" Edwin asked, eager to get this over with. He appreciated the journalist's time and effort, and doubly so the information he provided. At times, Edwin felt as though he might not have been able to govern the war as effectively as he'd done without some of young Mr. Birch's intelligence: dates when Southern troops would deploy, which of the Union outposts most needed supplies, how civilians in different areas were faring with battles raging in their own backyards. All of it concerned Edwin, right down to the last detail.

"Your enemies still abound," Birch reported, handing over a folded-up piece of paper. Edwin opened it. "Down with Abolition!" the headline at the top proclaimed in large, black handwriting. Beneath it was a treatise on just what a traitor to the nation he and his "devils" in Washington were for their weak-minded views on doing away with slavery.

Stanton raised his eyebrows. "This isn't news," he muttered, folding the paper up and handing it right back. "I've been reading that offal for years."

Next to him, Birch slowed his pace a bit, giving an icy look Edwin had seen before. The younger man was moody and intense, too much so for Stanton's liking most of the time. Birch seemed to enjoy the cloak-and-dagger aspect of their relationship; he also appeared to gain a good deal of self-aggrandizement from it. He literally puffed up, like a male pigeon trying to show he was the king of the flock, and he did not like when Edwin shot down his royal offerings.

"Then perhaps you'll be more *interested* in this," Birch said and walked over toward the side of the bridge, equidistant between two sets of the armed, watching guards. He leaned his forearms on the railing and looked out over the water. The sky was gray and the river below churning.

Edwin stood in the middle of the walkway for a moment and then reluctantly followed suit. He did not face outward but leaned his back against a post holding up the beams that crisscrossed the top of the bridge.

"Go on," he said, his sourness coming through clearly in

his voice. Another thing he knew about Birch was that he liked to hear Edwin ask for help.

All part of the game, he reminded himself, watching the journalist, waiting for a reply.

Birch bowed his head and leaned it in close. "I have it on good faith that there is a plot underway to assassinate the president." Then he pursed his lips and moved away again, glaring at Edwin.

The secretary of war sighed. "When *isn't* there a plot to kill Lincoln going around?" he asked. "I'm pretty sure I heard at least three last month. Especially right now…We're at a crucial moment in the war—"

He stopped as Birch began shaking his head vigorously. "No, no, no. This one is different. This one has dates, times, locations. There are names attached. I've checked them out. It all adds up."

"Who?" Edwin asked quickly. "Who's going to do this? Give me the names."

Birch stood up straight. He looked from side to side and then slipped another paper from his coat pocket. He passed it to Stanton, palm facing down. "It's all written down there. Don't look at it here!" he hissed as Edwin started to unfold this paper as well. "Don't look at it here," Birch repeated, lowering his voice and looking over his shoulder once more. "Take it somewhere private, read it, *memorize* it, and then burn the paper. We cannot leave a trail on this—nothing to implicate either you or me."

Edwin's brows lowered. The paper felt hot in his hands. He had an urge to toss it over the railing of the Long Bridge, to watch it sail down into the waters below, to be done with it and Birch all at once. For just a fleeting moment, he pictured himself back in Boston, at his private practice, not having to deal with any of this: the war, the starving troops, the corrupt generals, the sometimes daily threats against the president's life—and sometimes his own.

Instead, he clamped his fingers around the page, wrinkling it, keeping it from blowing away in the low but steady wind. "I will," he said through clenched teeth, his voice low.

"Good, Edwin. Good," Birch replied, his tone soft and soothing, as if he were talking to a child. Then he took a step forward and put his hand on Stanton's forearm, his fingers closing around it tightly. "You *have* to stop this. Promise me you'll do everything in your power to stop it."

"Sure, I—I'll—" Edwin stammered, stepping backward and away from Birch's touch. They'd never had any physical contact; whenever they met it was as strangers sitting near each other in a pub or two men out for a walk in the same park. Hidden. Clandestine. This bridge was lined with soldiers, yes, but they were low-ranked enlisted men who wouldn't care who the secretary of war talked to. And Birch had been so insistent on this exact location.

Still, it was out of line to grab him. Stanton straightened up and cleared his throat. He held the paper up and shook it at the journalist as he spoke, punctuating his words.

"I will do what I can, Mr. Birch. I will look into the matter. I can't promise you anything, of course, but if you say it's credible, I will take you at your word. You have not steered me wrong before. I—"

He stopped short. Behind Birch, a horse and wagon was barreling down the center of the bridge, rattling the wooden-slat floorboards. Supplies, most likely, for the nearby forts.

"I must go," Edwin said, and then quickly turned and walked back toward the shore. Behind him, Birch turned the other way and skulked off, head down, the brim of his hat bending in the wind.

TWENTY-TWO

A Hero's Welcome

1854, New York City

The accolades continued throughout the day. Tom did in fact eat his lunch in his room, wishing to avoid another scene like the one that had happened at breakfast. He met with Charro, Ahote, and the hands in the afternoon; since there were so many longhorns, they would all be helping out at the sale the next day, and Tom wanted to make sure they all knew what to do.

"No one talks you down more than twenty-five cents, you hear me?" he said, eyeing the others, especially the hands. They were young men, experienced in droving but green to the cattle trading business and eager to learn. Still, Tom thought, one whiff of their inexperience and a buyer was bound to try to take advantage.

That evening, much to Tom's regret, Daniel Drew had arranged for a reception of sorts for him and his men—a gathering of his colleagues and peers, plus some journalists, and even a photographer to commemorate the occasion. Tom much rather would have spent the time sleeping or, if that weren't possible, walking around the city.

"You'll have plenty of time for both when the sale is done," he told himself as he headed down the stairs of the tavern to the dining room. "Just go in, smile, and get this over with."

"Tom! Tom! Over here."

"Mr. Candy, just a minute of your time."

"I've already paid for a drink for you, Mr. Candy. Whatever you want, just go on over and tell the bartender."

The crowd of guests swallowed him up as he walked into the dining room, all of them, it seemed, wanting to talk to him at one time.

"Fine, fine, thank you," he said, trying to make his way through to a clear spot, though he wasn't even sure there was one. Finally, a hand reached through the sea of arms and shoulders, gripped his wrist, and pulled him out.

"All right, all right," Drew bellowed, a cigar clenched between his teeth. He still held on to Tom, just in case another wave hit. "All of you, disperse! Give the man some room to breathe."

"Thank you, Daniel," Tom said, straightening out his jacket and tie. "I don't want to seem ungrateful, but that…that was a little much for me."

"Understood, son," said Drew, slapping Tom on the back and turning him around. He pointed, indicating a large, round table in the back, where all of Tom's men sat. "I believe they saved you a seat. Why don't you go on over?"

"Will do," Tom replied. "And thanks again."

As he headed back into the throng occupying the middle of the room, Ahote spotted him and held up a hand. Tom waved back, then held up a finger, indicating he would be there momentarily. If he were going to make it through this, he knew, he would need a good, stiff drink. And besides, apparently someone had already bought him one. Couldn't let it go to waste.

"Yes, one whiskey, please. Double," he told the bartender some minutes later, when he'd managed to get to the bar. Might as well get twice the amount so he wouldn't have to get in there again. As he waited, he looked around as much as possible, which was really only to his sides. On his left, a man with his hat on and his back turned gabbed to another gentleman about how his fiancée had fallen off a horse. The man seemed to think this was much funnier than it probably actually was, Tom surmised, and then looked the other way.

On his right was a young man, gaunt and serious, wearing a dark, double-breasted suit. His wavy hair needed trimming, as did his full mustache, which hung down over his top lip, hiding what Tom suspected was a permanent scowl.

"How do you do?" Tom asked anyway. He was nothing if not polite.

The man nodded at him once, his dark eyes not blinking as he stared at Tom.

Tom turned back; the bartender had slid his glass across to him. "On the house, Mr. Candy," the man said, and Tom thanked him.

"You're Tom Candy," the young man to his right said—a grim sort of statement, not a question.

"Yes, I am," Tom said, turning to leave. "It was nice to meet you."

"I'm from the *New-York Tribune*," the man said.

Tom stopped, letting out a quick sigh. Though he wasn't in the mood for it at all, he knew that speaking with a journalist would only increase the turnout at his cattle sale the following day. If the *Tribune*, one of the city's biggest papers, ran a story in their morning edition…

"Yes," Tom said again, turning back. He set his glass on the bar and held out his hand to shake. "Tom Candy. And you are?"

"T. Burton Blackwood," the journalist said, shaking Tom's hand slowly and lightly, barely moving his lips. "May I ask you a few questions about your…*operation?*"

"Of course." Tom smiled, offsetting the other man's gloom, which threatened to swallow him whole.

"All right," Blackwood said, reaching to an inside pocket of his coat. He pulled out a small notepad and the stub of a pencil, which he licked before applying to the paper. "Now, that's Candy. C-A-N-D—"

"Y," Tom finished, and then reached over for his drink. He had a feeling this would take a while. "Like the sweets. What sort of questions can I answer for you?"

He smiled, but Blackwood merely lowered his brow. "You're not from around here, are you?"

Tom laughed a little. "Well, no. What gave me away?" he asked, exaggerating his English accent.

"How many cattle did you have when you started out?" Blackwood went on, seemingly unfazed by the joke. "And how many did you have when you arrived?"

His delivery was deadpan and off-putting. Tom wished he had kept walking.

"Well, I had—"

A young woman came out of the pressing crowd and grabbed onto Blackwood, cutting off Tom's answer.

"Oh!" she said. She was young and fresh looking, pale skin and flushed, pink cheeks, dark hair parted in the middle and tied up in a neat bun at the back of her neck. She wore a dress made of a shiny, emerald-green material that almost matched the color of her eyes.

"I'm so sorry," she went on breathlessly.

"It's no problem at all, miss," Tom replied quickly, before he could stop himself. "I'm Tom. And you are…?"

"Elizabeth," she said, boldly holding out her hand for him to shake. He did so, holding her fingers lightly, her palm turned toward the floor. "Elizabeth Mason. And it is a *pleasure* to meet *you*, Tom."

She glanced at Blackwood, who still appeared jostled from her bumping into him. With one hand on his shoulder, she patted the lapel of his suit. "I've just been driving Woody here *crazy* asking about you since he found out Greeley was sending him to interview you."

"I'm sorry," Tom said, shaking his head. "Greeley?"

"The editor-in-chief of the *Tribune*," Blackwood muttered,

looking down at his notepad. "Now, about the number of steers...?"

"Oh, give me a minute, Woody!" the woman said to him, slapping his shoulder lightly. "You know how much I've been wanting to meet this man. Now just let me talk to him, won't you?"

Tom didn't mean to, but he smiled at her. After dealing with the journalist for only a minute, she was a breath of fresh air.

"Please," he said. "Ask me anything you want."

"If you'll excuse me," Blackwood said suddenly and, without looking at the other two, took his leave of them.

Elizabeth watched him go, the look on her face falling by the second.

"Sorry," Tom said. "Was it something I did? I didn't mean to—"

"Psh," Elizabeth said, waving a hand at him. "Pay him no mind. Woody's always been a moody one. Ever since I knew him in college, he was always moping around about one thing or another."

"Oh, so you were students together," Tom said, standing up a little straighter. He had wanted to ask what they were to one another—sister and brother? Fiancés?—but hadn't gotten the chance.

"Yes, at Miami University in Oxford, Ohio. I just graduated in May."

"Congratulations," Tom said. "That's wonderful."

She closed her eyes and bowed her head, a lovely gesture. "Thank you." She looked back at him. "Woody graduated last year, though. And then he came out here to write for the *Tri-bune*. Which surprised me..." She got a faraway look on her face, as if pondering the fact, then snapped back to attention. "He was just never much of a writer. But he's very ambitious, so I suppose it's a stepping-stone for him. You know, so he can move on to bigger and better things. Woody is destined for greatness, I'm sure of it. He's so smart. I think he'll go into politics, myself."

"Politics, eh?" Tom asked, imagining the man's sour face behind the lectern at an election rally.

"Yes, or maybe business," Elizabeth went on. "He's always said he wants to be wealthy." She shrugged. "I tell him he should go into banking, like my father."

"Oh, that's a good living?" Tom asked. He didn't have any real interest in banks—he didn't use one himself—but did not want the conversation with her to end.

Elizabeth laughed. "I suppose it is. I don't know. I don't think about money very much."

Then the answer is yes, Tom thought with a bit of a smirk. Only those who had a good deal of money could survive without thinking about it.

"Well, maybe he should just marry you, then," he joked. "Take the easy route."

At that, Elizabeth let out what could only be called a guffaw. "Me? And Woody? *Married*? Oh, no, Mr. Candy. No, no, no. We're just—well, we're very different."

"Yet you're friends?"

She shrugged again. "Woody has a bit of the wounded puppy in him. Makes one just want to scoop him up and take care of him. That's why I'm here in the first place—he sent me a letter at school saying how lonely this big city can be, so I decided to come out and visit him for a while after graduation. I'm heading back home to Chicago at the end of the week, actually."

"So you didn't come just for the cattle drive?" Tom asked, smiling again.

"No, but it is a happy coincidence, isn't it?" She smiled too, and the pair were quiet for a moment just looking at each other. "I am sorry I intruded on your interview, though."

Now Tom waved a hand at her. "There'll be other chances. I'm glad to have met you."

She blushed. "As am I to have met you."

Over her shoulder, Tom saw Ahote and the other men looking over the crowd trying to find where Tom was. Finally spotting him, Charro waved him over once more.

"Elizabeth, listen, I have to go see my hands and my men from the drive," Tom said, turning to pick up his long-forgotten drink. "But I would love to talk to you. Do you know if Blackwood is coming to report on the cattle sale tomorrow? If so, maybe you could accompany him, and we could have another chance."

She glanced over toward the direction in which Blackwood had stormed off. "I don't know about him," she said, then looked back at Tom with a small smile. "But I'll be there. If that's all right with you."

"That would be more than all right, miss," he said, then with a nod of his head he went over to join the men. Suddenly, he couldn't wait for tomorrow to come.

TWENTY-THREE

The Missing Link Is Found

1904, Moweaqua, Illinois

"No business at the table, son," Tom Candy said, gripping a fork in one hand and a knife in the other, hunched over his lunch plate. Across from him at the small, blond-wood maple table sat his wife, Elizabeth, a woman of the same petite stature as Tom. Her dark hair, shot through with streaks of silver, was pulled to the nape of her neck in a bun, and she wore an apron over her light-colored dress, both of which were spattered with flour and grease.

"Sorry," John muttered, bowing his head and focusing on his food. He sat at the side of the table, halfway between the two, enduring the long silence that had descended upon them as soon as they'd sat down. Tom, John surmised from the looks he kept tossing over at Elizabeth, was none too pleased that she had invited John to eat with them.

"Well, the food is ready," she had said when they had come upon her in the hallway, right after Tom had let John in. Her voice wavered with age but was still loud and firm, the kind of tone that could put a rugged old cowman in his place. "I can't tell him to wait in the parlor while we eat, can I?"

Begrudgingly, Tom had agreed but he'd eyed John as well as he'd taken his seat, and then that silence had set in, the only sounds the clanking of their silver utensils against the porcelain plates. Finally, Elizabeth had asked what had brought John to visit their home.

"Well, Mrs. Candy, I came to speak to Mr. Candy about my father, who—"

That was as far as he had gotten before Tom cut him off. Now John stabbed a forkful of green beans and shoved them in his mouth, looking from Tom to Elizabeth and back again as he chewed slowly.

"All right," Elizabeth replied, remaining smiling and sweet, even toward her seemingly ornery husband. "You two can discuss it later. Is it all right to ask where you're from?"

She laughed lightly, glancing at Tom, who nodded at her, a little smile playing across his lips too, as if she had gotten the best of him.

The shorthand of marriage, John thought, and wondered if someday he would find that for himself. He was nearing forty, but this business with his father had occupied him for so long, the thought of a wife and a family rarely crossed his mind. Only when he saw it in action did it tug at him a little bit.

"I'm originally from Boston, ma'am," he began, setting down his fork and wiping his lips with the linen napkin from his lap, then continued on with the rest of his story: moved to New York City for an opportunity to write for the *Tribune*, his decision to leave for what he referred to as personal reasons, and all the places he had seen on his travels so far.

"That is interesting," she said, and John detected the hint of an old Midwest accent in her voice. She picked up her glass of lemonade and looked at Tom over the top of it. "You've been to a lot of those places too, way back when. Haven't you?"

Tom put down his fork, brought his elbows to the table, and folded his hands in front of his mouth. He looked at his wife over the top of them. The two had a showdown of sorts, with John still sitting in the middle, pretending it wasn't happening.

"You'll have to excuse my husband," Elizabeth said, standing up and taking her empty plate. "He woke up on the wrong side of the bed this morning, I think."

She smiled at John and laid a hand on his shoulder briefly as she left the room. In a moment, he heard the sound of her setting down the plate in the washbasin in the kitchen.

"So," John said, looking at Tom with a smile. He got no response, just a slight shift of Tom's eyes from his wife's empty chair over toward him.

Then finally Tom pushed back his chair. "Let's go for a walk."

John got up and followed the older man through his house. There were many rooms—the dining room where they ate, the kitchen, a parlor, a library—and he passed through or by each of them in turn. Finally, they came to a set of doors that led out to the expansive back lawn dotted with the purple, blue, and yellow wildflowers John had seen from the road. Tom led him over that too, not paying too much attention to the blossoms as he went, crushing some underfoot here and there. Soon they met up with the gravel path that led from the road down into the compound. The breeze picked up a little as they followed the path, and John could smell the distinctive aroma of the cattle pens. It reminded him of the streets of New York.

"How long have you had this place?" he asked, once again attempting to win Tom over with some polite chatter. John hadn't expected the old man to be so cross. He wondered if Tom were always like this or if his presence had put him in such a foul mood.

Tom appeared to be in thought for a moment. "Let's see," he muttered, seemingly to himself. "Married Elizabeth in 1856…Caroline was born in 1868…So we bought this five thousand acre parcel, and I guess we started the main house about 1880." He stopped and leaned against a gate to one of the heavily reinforced breeding pens. He looked at John and actually smiled.

"It's a funny story," he said, his faint English accent mixed with a Midwest drawl from all his years in America. "Would you like to hear it?"

John smiled as well, standing before him with his arms crossed. "I certainly would."

Tom settled back against the fence and thought for another moment. "That was the year," he began, "that I took my daughter to her first cattle auction. I had only recently stopped driving and settled here to become a cattle buyer between Denver, Abilene, and Chicago. My breeding business was new, but I was still selling a carload of steers every two weeks to a shoe and boot manufacturer from Massachusetts. So I had plenty of money coming in. But I needed more for prize breeding bulls. That was why I went to the auction, to try to sell off some of my better Hereford stock for higher prices."

He paused and looked around, and John followed suit. He saw some movement inside the building attached to the pen, the silhouettes of men and bulls moving around one another.

"Caroline was just twelve then," Tom went on. "But she'd always been interested in what I did for a living—not just the animals, as you'd expect, but in the business part of it. She always asked me how much I paid per head, how much I sold them for, what kind of profits I made. Quite inquisitive questions for a child."

John nodded, still looking over Tom's shoulder and across the pen. Now he saw another form in the corral: a small woman dressed in cowhand's gear, her blond hair tied up on top of her head in a bun. She came into view in the doorway, where she leaned her shoulder against the frame.

"When we went out to the auction," Tom continued, "she brought all the money she had saved up over several years—two hundred and ten dollars, I believe. That was all the allowances we had given her, all payments she had earned from doing small jobs...Elizabeth and I always tried to teach our children about responsibility, about putting in a hard day's work and earning your pay at the end of the day."

He turned and looked now, to see what John was so intently

gazing at. Seeing the woman in the doorway, he raised a hand, and she returned the gesture. Even from afar, John could see the bright smile that lit up her face.

"She wanted to buy a red shorthorn heifer," Tom said, turning back to John. "And I could not dissuade her no matter what I said. Nor could I persuade her to sell the animal once she had it in her possession. She had a couple of offers that would have given her a nice profit, but instead she took what remained of her savings and bought—can you guess?"

"What?" John snapped his attention back to Tom. "Sorry. What was the question?"

Tom sighed and then he looked over his shoulder again. He raised his hand once more and this time waved the woman over. Without hesitation she stood up and began to walk across the lot.

"If you're going to stare at her," Tom said to John, "there might as well be a formal introduction. But let me continue my story. Caroline had bought the heifer, then she managed to strike a bargain to buy herself a yearling bull, too. Now she had a pair. And that was how she got herself started in the shorthorn business."

"Dad," the woman said as she approached. On the other side of the fence, she brought her boot up to rest on one of the slats and lay her forearms across the top. Then she looked at John and smiled. "I didn't know we were having guests or I would have made myself presentable."

Tom grinned. "Caroline," he said, turning from her to John. "Meet John Stanton. He just dropped by to talk to me about—uh, about my New York cattle drive."

Caroline laughed lightly. "You mean that's still news?"

Tom smirked. "John, this is Caroline—my daughter and the proprietor of Homestead Cattle."

"It's a pleasure to meet you," Caroline said, holding out a hand for John to shake. He leaned in and took it, feeling bewildered by this woman's bold behavior and strangely thrilled by the touch of her hand.

"The pleasure is mine," he said, pulling away again. He nodded at their surroundings. "You have an impressive setup here."

"Oh, thank you. But my father is the one who takes care of the buildings and ranch lands with the main herd. Or his men do, at least. I'm just responsible for the breeding animals and the sales. And the money," she added with another laugh.

"Yes," Tom jumped in. "I was just telling Mr. Stanton about your first auction."

Now she laughed louder, clapping her hands before her once. "Oh, yes! What an experience. I knew from that day on that there was no choice but for me to follow in my father's footsteps."

"And you've done a fine job," Tom said, standing up straight once more. "Now, if you'll excuse us, my dear, I'm going to show our guest around a little."

"Of course," said Caroline, again jutting out her hand. "Mr. Stanton."

"John, please," he said without thinking, this time grabbing her hand eagerly. "Miss Candy."

She smiled at him. "Caroline. And I do hope we meet again."

"Likewise," John said, but Tom was already looking impatient, standing a little farther down the road with his hands balled into fists at his waist. "Another time."

He turned and walked quickly away, looking back only once to see Caroline still standing at the fence, smiling warmly in his direction. Seeing his glance, she waved at him, and he gave her a surreptitious wave back.

"If you're ready to go on," Tom said when John finally reached him. The warmth that had come into his tone when his daughter had appeared was now gone.

"Yes. Yes, sir," John said, and the pair walked on, following the gravel path, this time more slowly.

Tom clasped his hands behind his back. "So tell me exactly what it is you want to know from me."

"All right." John cleared his throat as he quickly tried to gather his thoughts. Where should he start? At the beginning of his father's story, going back to before John was born? With his own quest to uncover what had happened to his father and, hopefully, clear his name?

"My father's first wife," he began, choosing the former route, "died at an early age along with their young son. Then my uncle hanged himself—all within the same year. Suffering so many losses in so short a time changed my father, people have said. His usual hearty good humor was replaced by a brusque and sometimes even rude intensity."

Tom reflected on this. "That sounds like the Edwin Stanton I knew. We only met a couple of times, but he struck me in both instances as an intelligent man who was, shall we say, lacking in social niceties."

John nodded. "From all accounts, that's an apt description. Now, after all this tragedy in his life, my father moved to Pittsburgh, where he met and married my mother, Ellen Hutchison. He also dedicated his life to the law and became a ferocious litigator but then left that in 1860 for public service—to be the attorney general in James Buchanan's administration."

"Buchanan…He must've been a lame duck by then."

"Yes, very much so, and he was letting the Union drift toward certain calamity because of it. My father couldn't take it. He resigned after only a year and returned to his practice, but the year after that, Lincoln came into office and made it his mission to clean house, shall we say. One of his first acts was ousting the current secretary of war, Simon Cameron, whose corruption and ineffectiveness had filtered down through the ranks. Lincoln asked my father to take Cameron's place, and though he'd never considered such a position, my father felt he could do a great deal of good for the country this way, and he accepted. He proved to be a strong and effective cabinet officer, instituting practices to rid the War Department of the waste and corruption that had been the norm for so long."

"That had to have been hard work," Tom said as they approached another large pen. He stopped and leaned again against the fence, almost sitting on the middle slat, putting his hands on his knees and leaning over. "Which explains why he was always so dour."

John joined him this time, perching next to him on the rail of the fence. "I'm sure it affected him greatly. And I know his anticorruption campaign ruffled a lot of feathers—even Lincoln's at times. The two clashed, and in private my father had some not-so-positive opinions about the man and his policies. But I know that in the end, the president respected my father and recognized his ability. I know this because even with so many calling for him to remove my father from office, he steadfastly refused. In fact, Lincoln once called him 'the rock on the beach of our national ocean against which the breakers dash and roar, dash and roar without ceasing.' He said that without Edwin Stanton, he would be destroyed."

Tom looked at him and grinned. "That's quite poetic for a president."

John laughed. "Indeed. And high praise, especially given their tumultuous relationship. Which did get better, by the way. After the Union army won the battle of Antietam, my father overwhelmingly supported the president in all that he did. He even became a Republican and adopted Lincoln's views and goals as his own. After the president's death, my father was quoted as saying, 'There lies the most perfect ruler of men the world has ever seen.'"

"Mmm," Tom said, looking as though he were deep in thought. "I met him too once," he said, his voice sounding just as far away. "Very briefly, in a tavern. But there was something about that man, something obviously good and right. I'm inclined—"

"Wait." John turned his body toward Tom. "What did you just say?"

Tom blinked at him. "I met Lincoln in a tavern once. Many, many years ago. Long before he'd probably even thought of being president. I don't see what—"

"That has to be the connection," John muttered, turning

back, rubbing his chin as he thought. "You met Lincoln…My father was the secretary of war under Lincoln…"

Tom laughed a little. "Yes, there seems to be a bit of overlap there. But John, don't read too much into it. I had nothing to do with Lincoln and his presidency. I helped your father out by driving some cattle to the army outposts to feed his men. That was the extent of it. I never even laid eyes on Lincoln when he was in Washington. Don't get me wrong." He held a hand out, palm toward John. "Having heard the story you just told me, I believe more than ever that your father has been judged unfairly by history. How could he have orchestrated the assassination of someone he so clearly admired and respected? What would be the sense in that?"

A silence fell between them, heavy and thick like the rays of hazy sunlight that burst intermittently through the clouds, illuminating random spots on the ground below. John felt a welt forming in his throat, a sob he tried as hard as he could to keep from breaking free. After spending so many years turning his father's story over and over in his mind, and then over and over again, he'd become almost numb to the facts of it. But to hear another man, a stranger, say the words out loud gave them a gravity he had not expected. Hearing Tom talk about the assassination, knowing that even he—this person who barely knew his father and seemed so far removed from it all—had heard the rumors…it was enough to bring John to his knees.

Tom looked at him, watching him for a while without saying anything. "I'm so sorry for what happened to your father," he finally said in a gentle tone. "But I'm sorry, John. I just don't see the connection between him and me."

John let out a sigh that was more like a moan of frustration. He ran a hand through his hair and stood up. "That damn missing link!" he said, pacing in front of Tom. "I keep running into it time and time again, yet I have no idea what it is. And if you don't know, either..."

He made another noise, this time more like a growl. He stopped pacing and put his hands on his waist inside his jacket. The afternoon had grown warm, and the intensity of this situation wasn't making it any better. His brow began to sweat.

Tom stood up as well. He put a hand gently on John's back and guided him down the gravel path once more. With their movement a cooling breeze hit John's face. He took a deep breath.

"I am sorry," he said, keeping his voice even. "It's just so frustrating. I hope you understand."

"Of course I do. Of course," Tom said, his hand still on John's back as they walked. "And I want to help you, John. I sincerely do. But I have no idea who could have—" He stopped for a moment and squinted at John. "Where did you say you worked again? What paper was it?"

"The *New-York Tribune*." He shook his head. "Why?"

Tom patted him on the back heartily. "John, my boy, let's go back to the house and sit for a spell. My old bones are tired, and we have some talking to do."

With that, he set off on the path again, heading back toward the compound house. John just watched him go for a moment. "Talking about what?" he finally asked.

Tom, already about a hundred feet away, stopped and turned. He raised a hand over his eyes to shield them from the blazing sun. "About your missing link," he said. "It's not Lincoln."

Then he turned back around and kept walking home. John ran to catch up with him.

TWENTY-FOUR

The Trail Driver Enters High Society

1854, Chicago

Tom Candy had become a celebrity. Who would've thought a simple cattle drive, as he humbly referred to it whenever a journalist asked, and many of them did, would have brought such acclaim? Hundreds of bidders showed up for the sale, and Tom got mostly the high prices Daniel Drew had advised him to ask. Normally, they wouldn't have paid up to eighty dollars a head, but this was a spectacle. This was history in the making. Just to say they bought a steer from Tom Candy's Texas herd, they were willing to pay a premium price.

Once he'd sold them all off and divvied up the money between himself and his men, the group of them disbanded, and he was left with a couple of pockets full of cash but no direction on where to go next. People still offered to buy him drinks and meals wherever he went; some even asked him to work as a drover or tending the cattle at their ranches. He respectfully declined all offers; he didn't know what he wanted to do, but he knew he needed some time off. A few months, maybe, and then he would see about getting back on the road—or wherever else fate decided to take him at that time.

"Chicago," Elizabeth Mason said to him as they sat across from one another at the Bull's Head tavern. She looked so lovely that evening, her hair pulled back tightly as usual, her dress a deep, shiny blue like the ocean on a clear day. He could just sit there and look at her all night, and had done so for a couple of hours already. Now, their dinner long done, he simply listened to her talk, which she could do non-stop. Fortunately, he adored the sound of her voice, and—

"Tom," she said, and he sat up straight, realizing he hadn't heard most of what she'd said.

"Yes," he replied and then cleared his throat. "Yes, Elizabeth?" He picked up his after-dinner drink, a dram of whiskey, and took a sip.

She laughed lightly. "I was saying that I'm leaving for Chicago tomorrow, as you know. My visit to New York is through, or so says the train ticket I've been keeping in my suitcase for three weeks. I bought it as soon as I got here so I wouldn't have to worry about it when I left."

"That was smart of you," Tom replied with a smile, hoping it wouldn't betray how crestfallen he truly felt over the thought of her leaving. In the week they'd been acquainted, he'd known from the beginning that this time would come, but he'd been able to put it to the back of his mind. Now that it loomed, it was more difficult for him to remain in denial. "And what time does your train depart?"

"First thing in the morning," she replied, her voice soft. "That will take me as far as Pittsburgh, then a change of trains will get me into Chicago by midnight." She brought an elbow up onto the table and rested her chin on her hand, her lips pushed out in a bit of a pout. It seemed she was dejected, too. "And all by myself the entire way. How boring."

"Mmm." Tom took another sip of the biting whiskey, hoping it would fortify him. He looked down at the almost empty cup, folding his hands on the table around it. "Well, Elizabeth…" He inched his chair in closer to the table, fidgeting around as his mind searched for the right words to say. "About that…"

She smirked behind the edge of her fingers, which covered half of her mouth. "Spit it out, Tom. Don't be shy."

Tom smiled too, curling his fingers around his drink. "Well, I was thinking…" He paused again and took a drink. He had never had a problem with words, and he'd practiced this bit anyway before he'd come to meet her tonight, just in case. Why was it so difficult now to say what he wanted to?

"Tom, do you want to come to Chicago with me?"

He let out his breath in a big puff, expelling a short and nervous laugh with it. "Well, I, uh—"

"That is what you were going to say, isn't it?" Elizabeth took her elbow off the table, folded her hands in her lap, and watched him expectantly, fluttering her eyelashes in mock innocence.

He smiled and lowered his gaze. "Yes, Elizabeth. That is what I was going to say." He looked up at her quickly then. "But only for your safety, of course."

She smirked again. "Of course. Of course," she said.

"Right. One never knows what could happen to a young, beautiful woman traveling by herself over such a great distance."

She looked at him for a moment, seemingly stuck on his description of her. Then she cleared her throat. "Of course," she repeated and let a silence fall between them. They looked at each other across the table, both grinning like cats that had just shared a fine canary dinner.

Tom had heard a saying once that money attracts money, and the more time he spent with Elizabeth, the more he saw that it was true. Though she never acted privileged or haughty in any way, she came from quite a wealthy background and ran in some elite social circles. As the daughter of a Chicago banker, she had never wanted for a thing in her life, yet she had no airs about her, no sense of entitlement or the off-putting, superior attitude Tom sometimes encountered among the *nouveaux riches*.

What she did have, Tom knew, was a bold and brazen personality. This he had seen the moment they had met back in New York. While other women relegated themselves to kitchens and parlors, Elizabeth was in the drawing rooms and even the taverns with the men, arguing about politics and talking business. Whenever she dragged Tom out to a party or a dinner or a get-together—and she did so often—her laugh was the loudest in the room, her smile the brightest, and the line of people wanting to talk to her undoubtedly the longest. Much of the time, Tom would simply stand by her side, smiling and nodding politely but unable to follow any conversations, his attention too wrapped up in Elizabeth, just like everyone else's.

"Isn't that right, Tom?" she had asked him at one such event, the direct address pulling him out of his stupor. It had to have been near midnight already, and he'd had a few drinks; he could've fallen asleep on his feet.

He looked at her, eyes half closed. "I'm sorry?"

Elizabeth had laughed and laid a gloved hand lightly on his cheek; it took all his strength not to lean into her touch, to lose himself again to daydreaming about this girl while she rambled on to someone else. In the month he had been in Chicago so far, she had become his night and day, the sun and moon and stars—his entire world, blocking out anything around her from his vision. Elizabeth was larger than life, and Tom was content just to bask in her glow.

However, that wasn't always possible. Though he'd thought he'd left all that fame folderol behind in New York, word of his cattle drive from Texas had reached Chicago before he had, and as soon as anyone learned his name, a barrage of congratulations and questions invariably ensued. It took the focus off of Elizabeth momentarily, but she never seemed to begrudge him that. She just looked at him with as much awe as everyone else did, and she listened to his stories with rapt attention, as if she hadn't heard them a hundred times before.

"Oh, tell them about the buffalo stampede," she urged him one time at a very fancy gala she had taken him to. It was a benefit for a society to help orphaned children, and many of the city's wealthiest—including Elizabeth's father—were in attendance. Even Will Cody was there to greet some of the children who attended. At one point, Tom found himself in the middle of a crowd of local businessmen and politicians, all of them staring at him expectantly.

"Well, yes, all right," said Tom, hoping this one-man show would end soon. "It was just dawn, and when I awoke, my traveling companion was nowhere to be seen…."

An hour later, he was telling the same story to a different crowd. This one consisted of people from out of town—Western Illinois and Missouri, mostly. It seemed news of Tom's feat had made it out their way as well and even to Texas, even to California, from all reports. He'd had no idea word could travel so far and so quickly, or that anyone would be so interested in what he had done. Mostly everyone wanted to know what his next feat would be: Another cattle drive? Maybe to Chicago this time? Or north to Montana territory? Or maybe from farther away?

But Tom had no such plans. For the time being, he had enough money to live on and some extra to save, so he was content just to spend as much time as he could with Elizabeth and not worry about getting back to work for a while. This was odd for him, this desire to rest; he'd never been one to sit on his laurels and wait for the next thing to come. But he'd never been in love either, and as he was finding, it changed everything.

TWENTY-FIVE

A Midnight Raid

1904, Moweaqua, Illinois

"Dear, do you remember that one party? The one with Phineas and Monty, where everybody was talking about Lincoln?"

Tom just looked at his wife, his old, blue eyes looking tired from the long day. He and John had spent the better part of it in Tom's study, hashing and rehashing all the details each of them knew about John's father's situation. Halfway through, Elizabeth had come in with afternoon tea—one of the traditions Tom had carried over from his youth in England—and, of course, joined in the conversation.

"Which one?" Tom asked. "And who's Monty?"

Elizabeth laughed as she poured John a second cup of tea. The young man sat on a chaise lounge, legs stretched out and hands folded on top of his head as he stared out the nearby bay window. When Elizabeth held out the delicate cup and saucer to him, he brought his focus slowly back to the room, thanking her with a distant smile.

"Montgomery Ward," she said to Tom, who nodded in recognition of the name. "You remember him. He was a young man at the time, just came out from Michigan and was working for Field Palmer and Leiter, the big dry-goods house...." She turned to John as she spoke and kept her voice gentle. Now that she knew what the young man's visit was all about, she felt quite a bit of sympathy for him. Poor dear, lost his father in such a horrible way and now grasping at straws to try to make some sense of it. "You'd know him as the founder of Montgomery Ward and Company, of course. Everyone has bought something from their mail-order catalogs at some time."

John nodded as well. "Yes, my mother bought much of her cooking goods and fabric for sewing through them when she was older and couldn't get to the shops. I didn't realize you two were friends with him."

"Yes, Tom has traveled in some rather interesting social circles," Elizabeth replied, smiling at her husband. "He became so famous after his cattle drive to New York, everyone wanted to get to know him. We met so many people in the years after that—"

"You know Will Cody?" Tom interrupted, looking at John.

"Buffalo Bill?" he replied with a laugh. "Don't tell me—"

Tom nodded solemnly. "We're still friends, though we

haven't seen him as much since he stopped touring with that Wild West show of his. In fact, we named our son after Will," he added wistfully. "Who else, Elizabeth?"

His wife thought for a moment. "Oh, well, of course there was Phillip Armour—I understand you met his family."

"Yes," John replied. "I know Phillip was a good friend of yours. His widow and his son were very respectful of and concerned with your privacy when I spoke with them, as was your friend, Charlie Goodnight."

Tom nodded, the faintest smile crossing his lips. "They've all been good to us through the years." He looked back at Elizabeth. "I have another name for you: John Clay."

Elizabeth clapped her hands together once. "Oh, John! I haven't thought about him in ages. And who was the other one? Alexander Swan, right?"

Tom nodded and was about to speak, but John cut him off. "Founder of the Swan Land and Cattle Company—a million-acre ranch, in Wyoming if I remember correctly."

"Yes, very good," Tom replied. "And of course a very important place for us drovers in the day. John Clay was his general manager. Managed some other powerful ranches after that one too. You'd know him if you were in the cattle trade, son. John Clay is our highest authority—and our *de facto* historian. I've always told him he could write a book with all he knows."

"And Swan?" John asked.

Tom sighed. "Afraid he's in poor health. Ended up in a sanatorium over in Ogden, Utah—sort of went out of his head after his ranch failed in the big blizzard of '86."

"So sorry to hear that; he was on the list of possible contacts the Armour's gave me," John replied, then took a sip of his tea in the ensuing silence.

"Well, back to our discussion," Elizabeth said at last. "John, we were at a party in Chicago, and Phineas—oh, you would know him by his stage name, P. T. Barnum."

John swung his feet onto the floor and sat up straight, teacup and saucer in hand. "The circus fellow? You're friends with him, too?"

The old man was putting a scone, freshly baked by Elizabeth, onto a plate for himself. "Sure. We didn't get to see him too often, what with his traveling show, but when he was in town, he always made time for us to get together."

"And that was how we all ended up at the party," Elizabeth interjected. "It was one of my father's—he was a banker and was always holding these soirées and whatnot for clients of his. Tom and I went to so many—"

Her husband snorted. "It felt like a job after a while," he said, raising an eyebrow at John. "Got to the point where I was going out on cattle drives just to get out of going to the parties."

"*Tom*," Elizabeth said, but she was laughing. They exchanged mischievous looks, and then she turned back to John. "Well, this must have been more than thirty years ago, in Chicago. It was right after Lincoln had been killed. Monty and Phineas and Tom and I were all talking, and there were some others there too—oh, I think it was Potter Palmer and some other local businessmen, and even a politician or two, powerful people in the city. And the general consensus was that the man that was blamed—what was his name?"

She snapped her fingers a couple of times and looked up

toward the ceiling. Finally, she thrust out a finger. "Booth. John Wilkes Booth. No one thought that he really did it all by himself."

John finished his sip of tea and swallowed, perversely enjoying the scald of the liquid as it made its way down his throat. Perhaps Elizabeth had been expecting some riotous reaction from him, but this was nothing he hadn't heard or thought himself a hundred times before. "And who did they put the blame on?" he asked, just to be polite.

Elizabeth set her teacup down on the small table next to the settee on which she sat. "Well, that's the thing. There wasn't one person to pin it all on, they thought. The entire group was convinced there had been a conglomerate of men who were unhappy with Lincoln's abolitionist views, and they conspired to kill him. Then, of course, there was a cover-up."

"A conglomerate." That one *was* new to John. He too had always thought Booth had not acted alone, but he'd never considered there might be a multitude behind Lincoln's death, an anonymous group who had plotted, schemed, and, he was sorry to admit, succeeded in killing the president without leaving a speck of evidence that they existed. Could these have been the same people who had thrown his father to the wolves after the fact? Who had spread just enough rumors and misinformation about him to lead the public to believe he was the mastermind behind the slaying—that he had actually given Booth his marching orders?

"Yes." Elizabeth shrugged. "I'm not sure that will help you at all, John, but I thought it was worth mentioning. I remembered it just now, when Tom said something about Woody. He was at that party too, don't you remember, dear? He was in Chicago doing a story, and—"

"T. Burton Blackwood was at that party?" John asked, setting his teacup and saucer down noisily. He leaned his elbows on his knees and looked from Elizabeth to Tom and back. "Did he join in this conversation about Lincoln?"

"Oh, now, let me think." Elizabeth gazed out the bay window, at the sunset just dipping beyond the cattle pens. "You know, I don't remember him being involved, but good old Woody." She laughed. "He had a way of just *knowing* things. I suppose it was his nature as a journalist. You're probably the same way, John."

He nodded absently, rubbing his chin with his fingers as he thought about his former boss. Blackwood had never done John any favors in any sense of the word, but he had a keen eye for news, John would give him that. And he did always seem to know everything that was going on way before the other city editors did. Blackwood knew people; that was what everybody always said. Perhaps that was how—

He looked up at Elizabeth. "How did you know Blackwood?"

"Oh, we went to college together," she replied. "He was a dour young fellow, but he followed me around like a lost puppy until I befriended him. Unfortunately, he was interested in more of a relationship than I was."

Tom, sunken down in his wingback chair, crumbs from his scone littering the front of his shirt, let out a laugh. "That was only because of your daddy's money," he said, then held a hand up to his wife. "No offense, dear. It's nothing to do with you. Blackwood has just always loved money and power more than anything else on this Earth. And he has no use for anyone who can't give him one of the two. You know this is true."

Elizabeth sighed and looked from Tom to John. "It is. It's true. He confided in me once that it was why he'd moved from Chicago to New York. He'd write for the *Tribune* for a while, he said, and then he'd push out Greeley, the editor-in-chief, and take his place. From there, he figured, he could do anything. Business, politics—that sort of position, in Woody's mind, would open up all doors to him. I suppose marrying me, if I had agreed to it, would have been a quicker route to the life he wanted."

"So would killing the president," Tom muttered, and the statement dropped like a ten-ton weight in the middle of the room. The other two just looked at him, mouths agape.

"Tom, you can't mean that," Elizabeth said at last.

He sat up straighter in his chair, adjusting his old, frail body as if trying to make himself look more assertive. "I'm not saying he did it," he replied. "Just that I've always believed he knows something about it." He turned to John. "This is what I've been trying to tell you, son. It's not Lincoln who tied me and your father together. It's Blackwood."

The name hung in the air. The study was completely still, with only the ticking of the clock above the fireplace to mark the passage of time. John just stared at Tom.

"Well, don't look at me like you don't think it's possible," Tom said at last, holding his hands out in front of him, an exasperated gesture, at the other two. "John, did you ever hear that Blackwood took a leave of absence from the *Tribune*? Took some time off to travel or some such?"

"Oh, uh, yes," John sputtered, trying to regain his voice. "That is what I've heard. He took three years off, maybe four, and when he came back, that was when he ousted Greeley. But that was before my time. Must've been about…oh, forty years ago or more." He shrugged. "No one really talks about it. I just overheard it mentioned in the newsroom once, by one of the older reporters. He didn't say why, though. Why Blackwood left, I mean."

Tom shook his head. "It wasn't that he was *leaving* the *Tribune*," he said, sitting back in his chair. "It was more that he was *going* someplace. Elizabeth, do you remember—"

"The war," she almost whispered, her eyes wide as she stared down at the floor, remembering. Then she looked up at John and Tom. "Woody went to be a war correspondent. He told me, but he said he never told anyone else." She laughed dryly. "I always thought that was so odd. All he wanted was power, and there he was, interviewing the president and the…"

She looked at John and then at her husband. "I just don't know, Tom. Sure, he was there. And there's even the possibility that he did talk to John's father at some point. But we can't know that. We can't know that he—"

"My father had a spy," John blurted out. "He told my mother about it once. Said he had a journalist feeding him information from the front lines." John paused and shook his head. "The whole idea made her uneasy, so my father never talked about it again. She was always afraid for his life, and this journalist was saying…" His eyes grew distant as his mind ironed out the idea. "He said there was a plot against the president's life. That was why my father had told my mother. It really unnerved him because it seemed—" He looked at Elizabeth, then at Tom. "Well, he said it seemed very credible at the time. That is what my mother said."

Elizabeth and Tom glanced at one another, their worry evident on their faces.

"John, still, we can't know that was him," Tom began, but John held up a hand to stop him.

"No. No," John said, another thought just ready to break the surface of his mind. He sat on the edge of the chaise longue, hand still held up, with his palm out in front of him. "The journalist's name was Birch. Thomas Birch, according to my mother." He looked at Elizabeth. "What's the T stand for in T. Burton Blackwood?"

She swallowed hard. "Thomas." Her voice was little more than a rasp.

John snapped his fingers and pointed at her, then turned his attention to Tom. "And a birch tree is known for its white bark. White bark that has shapes like eyes on it, no less. That's why it's called the Watchful Tree."

"White bark…Blackwood." Tom looked at John, smiling wide. "I have also heard the name Birch, on a cattle drive I made for your father, during the War. By George, son, I think you figured it out."

John took his nightclothes out of his bag and laid them on the bed in the Candys' guest room. Elizabeth had taken all the rest of his clothes to launder and was waiting for what he currently had on, so he changed as quickly as he could, and then left his pants, shirt, and jacket outside the bedroom door. Then, with the room all dark, he stood by the window facing the rear of the property. The sky was inky, the full, white moon hanging almost directly overhead. He'd stayed talking with the Candys through dinner, for which Elizabeth had served cold lunch leftovers in the study, and well into the night. John guessed it was at least eleven o'clock now, yet there was still activity in the corrals outside. Men herded the shorthorn bulls into the barns, bringing them in for what would undoubtedly be a chilly night. He could just hear their lowing as they moved along.

"How will I ever sleep tonight?" he muttered to himself. His body felt exhausted, but his mind was nowhere near ready to turn itself off. There was too much new information to think about. There was the revelation about Blackwood and his father, of course. And that Elizabeth used to be Blackwood's friend until Tom got in the middle of them. Blackwood was the reason the two of them had met in the first place. But there was something beyond her as well. Tom Candy had become a celebrity. He was famous, which Blackwood craved, and he had harbored a grudge against Candy for years, it seemed. And all the more so because he believed Tom had stolen his girl from him. As Elizabeth had mentioned, Blackwood had wanted to marry her in the worst way, but she had been smitten with Tom since the first time they had laid eyes on one another. That, coincidentally, had happened when he'd just arrived in New York with his herd from Texas. Blackwood, then working for the *New-York Tribune* as a reporter, had been sent by his editor-in-chief, Horace Greeley, to cover the event.

"Once he saw how Elizabeth and I got along," Tom had told

John, "he was furious. He did the story, but not how Greeley wanted. Blackwood wrote that my drive was just a publicity stunt and didn't even mention me by name. Greeley buried it on page eight of the following day's late edition."

The grudge, it seemed, had continued on for years. The more powerful and wealthy Blackwood had gotten, the more it seemed he was out to get Tom, and the more capable of ruining Tom's life he became. Though there was no concrete evidence, Tom was sure that some incidents over the years were direct results of Blackwood's will: buyers backing out of their agreements to purchase Tom's cattle; strange, lethal illnesses afflicting his herds out of nowhere; and, worst of all, a train derailment that had killed Tom's nineteen-year-old son only a few years earlier—a train that Tom was supposed to be on instead of his son.

"It was ruled an accident," Tom had said, tears welling in his eyes, his emotions as raw as they had been on the day the fatal crash had happened. "But I know that somehow, Blackwood had a hand in it. The coincidence is just too much."

Still, John had trouble believing it. Not that Tom hadn't proven himself trustworthy over the course of their day together. On the contrary, he'd been much more open and frank than John had expected on their first meeting. But to kill the man's son just because of a decades-old grudge over a woman? Could even Blackwood stoop so low?

John grew still. *Of course he could.* Knowing what he now did about his former boss, John had no doubt in his mind that Blackwood's depravity knew no bounds. The things Tom had told him—

Outside, the bulls were in the barns and the hands had

closed up the doors. A few of the men, done with their work, walked toward their nearby quarters. They talked and laughed; John could just barely hear their voices from his perch by the upstairs window.

Among them was Caroline. When John saw her, he instinctively took a step back, hiding himself behind the window's curtain. He was in his nightclothes, after all. Peeking out, he could see she had put on a thick leather coat lined with sheepskin, and half of her hair had tumbled out of its earlier topknot. In the middle of a laugh at something one of the men said, she threw her head back and clasped her hands together in front of her. As she looked ahead again, her eye seemed to catch on John's figure in the window.

He froze. Caroline's steps faltered, but her gaze remained steady, as did her smile. John even saw her raise her hand a little, behind the men so they wouldn't see it, and give him a wave. He lifted his hand and waved back weakly, feeling sure this was in no way appropriate.

Then, as quickly as it had come, the moment was gone. Caroline looked back at her workers, patting one of them on the shoulder as if congratulating him on a job well done. John watched until they were out of sight, then he let out his breath. He hadn't even been aware he'd been holding it.

He moved over to his bed and lay down, feeling his body sink into the mattress. It wasn't the softest thing he'd ever slept on, but it was better than the hard train seats he'd been napping on for the last few months. As soon as he closed his eyes, he felt himself drifting off.

A clatter in back of the house awakened him again. He

opened his eyes. Had Caroline forgotten something at the corrals? It had sounded like the clank of a gate's hasp being opened.

"Never you mind," John told himself and turned over onto his side. There was no reason for him to get up and look. This was Caroline's compound, after all. It wasn't like she would be in some sort of trouble out there.

But then if he got up, he could get one more look at her. Maybe she would see him again too and give him that smile of hers that lit up the night. John stood up quickly and tiptoed to the window, ensconcing himself in the thick fabric of the curtain once more.

It was not Caroline outside.

Instead there was a group of men, four in total, all on horses and toting Winchester lever-action rifles outlined against the gas night-lights. One was kicking at the lock of a gate outside the first corral, ostensibly trying to open it. The other three stood watch, their backs to the leader, the butts of their guns jutted into their laps, rifles pointed at the sky.

An icy feeling crept quickly up John's back. Was this a robbery? They weren't Caroline's men; John had seen all of them while out on his tour of the compound with Tom earlier in the day. These men had not been among them. And why show up at almost midnight, when it seemed all the day's work had just ended?

Without thinking, John turned around and strode toward the door. The clothes he had left outside were gone—Mrs. Candy had picked them up to wash—but he gave that only a moment's thought before heading down the hallway in his nightshirt. Seeing a dim light seeping out from underneath one of the doors, he knocked on it quietly. There was no response.

"Mr. Candy?" he called, rapping on the door a bit louder.

John heard floorboards creaking within the room, and a moment later the door opened. Tom's blue eye peeked out through the crack, just as it had at the front door when John had first arrived.

"Mr. Candy," he repeated, feeling breathless and nervous. "There are four men outside the house, out back by the stalls. They have rifles, and it looks as if they're trying to break in."

The eye looked at him for a moment and then the door closed. John once again heard the wooden floor creak, but the movement was faster this time. Tom reappeared. He opened the door slightly and slipped out.

"Take this," he told John and put an old Smith & Wesson Model 3 in his hand. John's arm dropped unexpectedly with the weight of it. He had never held a gun before, and his first instinct was to give it back. But by the time the thought formed in his head, Tom was heading down the stairs, also in his nightclothes, a Springfield M-1903 bolt-action rifle clutched tightly in one hand. John caught up with him just when he reached the back door.

"On three," Tom said, his hand on the doorknob. "One... Two..."

He swung the door wide, so hard it hit the inside wall, and then stormed out the door, rifle at the ready. He slammed a shell into the chamber and released the safety. The sound got the rustlers' attention. They all turned at once to look.

"Tom!" John said in a loud whisper, peering out the door from inside. "This isn't safe. Come back—"

One loud shot broke the silence of the night, followed immediately by another. John raised his head to see past Tom. A cloud of white, the output of a fired gun, hung in the damp night air, enshrouding the men.

"Get back, get back!" Tom shouted to John as he came barreling into the house. He flattened himself against the still-open door and waved frantically at John until he did the same against the wall on the other side of the doorway. Outside, another gunshot sounded, and John heard the sound of glass breaking. A window just behind him crashed in shards to the floor.

"Get down," Tom said, and John crouched. Tom took a deep breath, swung himself into the doorway, let off a few rounds with the rifle as more shots were fired by the riders, and then jumped back to safety. Outside, John heard the whinny of a panicked horse and the unmistakable groaning of an injured man.

It was the opening Tom needed.

"Come on," he said and moved back into the doorway. "We shook them up. Now let's run them off."

A volley of gunfire ensued that seemed to John to last an eternity. From his vantage point inside the house, he couldn't see much of what was going on, and the ever-growing white cloud of acrid gun smoke between the parties didn't help. He stuck his hand out the doorway from time to time and squeezed off a shot, unsure if he was even aiming in the right direction.

Finally, all noises ceased. Then from the mist, John heard

the crunch of the horses' hooves on the gravel road. One, two, three, four. He counted them as they passed, crouching low and riding hard in single file.

Tom leaned against the doorframe and let his body slide down until he sat on the floor. He looked older and more tired than John had seen him yet.

"Are you hurt?" John asked, and Tom opened his mouth to speak but never had a chance to reply. All at once the household and backyard erupted—Elizabeth running in to weep and fuss over Tom, Caroline and her men hurrying to make sure the breeder bulls were safe. John sat silently in the middle of it, the Smith & Wesson still clutched in his hand. When he realized it was there, he dropped it on the floor and kicked it away like a flea-ridden dog. He wanted nothing to do with it. Just the thought of having fired it—of potentially having shot one of the men outside—turned his stomach.

"Don't look so scared, son," Tom wheezed as Elizabeth and a couple of the men hoisted him up onto a chair. "You did well."

John nodded and tried to smile, but all he managed was a grimace. He'd never shot a gun before. He hoped he'd never have to do it again.

"If they weren't after the shorthorns, then what did they want?" John asked. He sat at the kitchen table, hands curled around a mug of steaming tea.

Tom, sitting opposite, winced as his wife dabbed iodine onto an ugly furrow on his forearm, the remnant of a bullet's graze. His face didn't look any better when she blew on the cut to make the tincture dry.

"Think about it, John," he said, his voice clipped. "They came in right after the barns were closed up for the night. They made so much noise, it got you out of bed. And by the way, thanks for that. Thank you for alerting me."

John nodded, drinking his tea.

"If they were true rustlers," Tom went on, holding out his arm as Elizabeth began to wrap it up in cotton gauze, "they would have come in the middle of the night, when everyone was sound asleep. They wouldn't have made so much noise. Good thieves are stealthy, John, not clumsy, as these men appeared to be."

John sat back, leaving his cup on the table. He ran a hand over his hair. "So they wanted to get your attention." He thought for a moment, and then looked straight at Tom. "You don't think they came here to...to hurt you, do you?"

Elizabeth clipped off the cloth on Tom's arm and tied the ends in a knot. She gathered her supplies, kissed him on the top of his head, and went to put them away.

"Well, it's either me or you, John," Tom said in a low tone, bringing his injured arm to rest on the table. "Or perhaps both of us. They thought they could draw us out by messing with the fence, and then..."

He let the sentence trail off, but John knew where he was going with it. If the gunmen hadn't been so inept, they would have shot Tom on sight as soon as he'd walked out the door. They were both lucky that Tom had been able to fire first, spooking their skittish horses.

"But why?" John asked. Out of the window behind Tom, he could see the men once again securing the barns for the night. He stretched a little, looking for Caroline, but turned back to Tom when he didn't see her. "Why would they want to hurt us?"

"Because somebody put them up to it, of course," Tom said right away and then took a drink of his own tea. He reached for the sugar dish Elizabeth had left on the table, picked up a lump, and dropped it in his drink.

"Blackwood," John said. "You think Blackwood's behind it."

Tom glanced up at him and then looked back at the tea as he stirred it. "Son, Blackwood had no compunction about trying to frame your father for the assassination of the president. Is it so hard to believe he'd want to kill us both now that you've found your missing link?"

TWENTY-SIX

A Lurking Threat

1864, Washington City and Missouri

They say no great feat can be replicated once it's done, but Tom Candy aimed to prove that adage wrong. Or, at least, that was what he was being asked to do. Through word of mouth, his name had been passed on to someone in the government—an Edwin Stanton, the telegram said, supposedly the Secretary of War—and now this person wanted to see him posthaste.

"What do you think?" Tom asked his wife as she finished looking over the message, leaning against the sideboard in their kitchen, her belly just starting to protrude with their first child.

She looked up at him. "I think that when the secretary of war summons you, you'd better do as he says."

So he packed a bag and hopped a train for Washington City. The least he could do, he figured, was go and hear what this Stanton fellow had to say.

"I want you to drive a herd of cattle for me." The secretary's gruff voice filled the small office in which they sat, he behind a desk, Tom on the other side. He thought that for such an important man, a larger room would have been in order.

"I'm sorry?" Tom replied. "You want me to do what, now?"

Stanton leaned forward in his chair, folding his hands before him on top of the desk. He squinted a little at Tom. "I've been told you are the best. Did you or did you not drive an entire herd of longhorns from Texas to New York?"

Tom's face grew warm. "Well, yes, I did, but—"

"And do you think you could do it again?"

Tom just looked at the man. Could he do the drive again? Surely, in a heartbeat. It wasn't like he hadn't thought about it before, hadn't revisited the route a thousand times in his mind. Sometimes when he was out on the trails, he remembered something he had done on the big drive, a mistake he would go back and correct if he could.

But that didn't mean it was supposed to be. He had a life now; he had a wife, and soon they would be a family. He did all right with his short drives from Springfield to Chicago, where he kept Armour and a couple of other butchers in meat. And he was beginning to buy cattle in Kansas and ship them by rail to Chicago markets. It was a regular routine by then—a job he could depend on and not have to think too much about.

Though it did, he had to admit, get a little bit boring at times.

"What do you have in mind?" he asked, seeing no harm in at least hearing what the secretary proposed.

"My men need food," Stanton said, getting right to the heart of the matter. "My soldiers in the field, on the front lines. They've exhausted most of the local supplies, and the Confederates have cut off our trade routes through many of the border states. The only way around is through the Indian territory between Texas and Missouri, and no drover I've met yet has been willing to take that risk."

"But you think I will," Tom said with a nod of his head.

The secretary shrugged and nearly smiled, but not quite. "You've done the impossible before, Mr. Candy."

That was true. The question was could he bring himself to do it again?

Reflecting on it later as he watched his riders circling the large herd, talking in low, soothing tones to bed them down for the night, Tom realized there had been no question. He was meant to be out on the trail, and there was no way he would have said no to the secretary of war. Not because of who the man was; as far as politicians went, Edwin Stanton seemed like one of the decent ones, but Tom had no particular love for men of his ilk. Even if the president himself had asked, he wouldn't have put any additional weight on the matter. As a matter of fact, Lincoln himself had added his vote of confidence in Tom Candy, saying he was indeed the man to bring beef cattle north to feed the Union troops—much to Edwin Stanton's surprise.

What matters is right there, Tom thought, still gazing at the immense herd, which numbered just under ten thousand head. *Just get them to their destination.* The difference now was that if they ran into fences or blockades again, his sizable army escort, trailing two miles behind, would tear them down, or he would just stampede the unstoppable herd right through it. He grimly remembered what one of the old ranchers had said: "If'n they git in yer way, son, jus' go callin' Texas style."

Tom stoked the fire he'd lit within a circle of rocks on the ground and dropped himself down in front of it, holding his palms out to collect its warmth against the cold night air. They'd been on the trail for what—two months now? He reached over to his pack and pulled out a small, leather-bound tally book with a pencil stub stuck in between the pages. He licked its lead point and scratched out another hash mark in the book, where he kept count of the days and his notes on the drive. Only twenty more until they'd be expected back in Illinois, well north of the front battle lines.

"No sense in running those cattle *all* the way up," Stanton had told him. "Just get 'em to a northern state, and we'll take care of dispersing them from there by rail."

He had taken the northern route through to Abilene, Kansas, and so this second drive was already a little easier than the first. Add in the cadre of horses and even wagons Stanton had provided, and Tom felt as if he were traveling as a dignitary.

"Sir, the main herd is mostly bedded down," reported one of his drovers—a young Union soldier named Ethan McCall, who was serving as a temporary cowboy. The other riders not on night herd came in to the "chuck" wagon—the name Tom had given the ingenious cook wagon, after his new young friend Charles Goodnight, who had designed it—for coffee and to settle down beside the fire.

"Thank you," Tom replied. "Let's all turn in, then. It's been a long day."

There was a chorus of grunts in agreement as the men rolled out their canvas bedrolls and retrieved blankets from the supply wagons, Tom included. He drifted off to sleep to the sound of the crackling fire.

In the morning, Tom cradled in both hands a chipped, blue-enameled tin cup, full of steaming black coffee, sipping carefully as he watched the cowboys ride out to relieve tired night riders and roust out the steers to ready them for the trail. With a herd this size, it took some time to move out, and the hands went on ahead in intermittent pairs, getting the trail-weary animals moving at a good pace. Tom would finish his coffee, and then ride out to catch up. The horse wrangler had saddled him a fresh mount from the large remuda, and reintied him to the nearby willows.

He threw a little dirt on the fire, which had long since gone out, but the burning embers remained. When he was sure it posed no threat, he rolled up his blankets into his bedroll canvas, tied it to the back of the saddle, and then mounted his horse to set out in a northeasterly direction. The drag was still within sight; it would take him only minutes to reach the upwind left flank if he rode at a gallop. He picked up the reins in both hands, ready to give spurs to his horse…and then a thought struck him.

My tally book. Had he packed it? He checked his saddle-bags and the pockets of his coat, but found nothing. He even got down from the horse and unrolled the blankets he had so recently stowed. The volume was nowhere to be found.

Quickly, he remounted his horse and grabbed the reins to wheel the animal around. They headed back toward the camp-site at a clip, Tom already worried about the lost time and the lost book. He had to catch up to the herd. If the point got too far ahead—

"Whoa," he said, drawing the word out as he drew back hard on the reins. The horse skidded and slid to a stop, and then raised its head and reared for a moment up onto its hind legs. "Whoa," Tom said again, patting the alarmed animal's neck as it lowered its forelegs back to the ground. He tugged the reins to the right, spurring the horse over into the seclu-sion of a thick stand of trees.

In the nearby clearing stood a circle of men—four in all, each with a new Henry repeating rifle and wearing a sidearm, a matching number of steeds behind them. One of the men kicked at the ashes of the fire Tom had smothered. Another one held Tom's small, leather-bound book in his hands and was flipping through it.

"Damn," Tom muttered, his mind racing. Who were these men? Where had they come from so quickly after he had left? And what did they want with his tally book? All four of them seemed to be interested in its contents. The one who turned the pages would stop every now and again and read aloud or point to something, and the other three would nod their heads.

As Tom hid and watched this search, he remembered the Army captain escorting the herd say that nine hundred .44-caliber, lever-action repeating rifles—just like the ones these four men were carrying—had been stolen from a Union supply post by confederate spies. These brass-frame rifles carried sixteen rounds in their breech loaders and could fire at a rate of twenty-eight rounds a minute. The muzzleloader-armed Confederates who had to face this deadly sixteen shooter called it "that damned Yankee rifle they load on Sunday and shoot all week." So Tom knew that these four men had to be associated somehow with the Confederate covert war effort, a group of deadly spies and assassins. He suddenly realized that these four men, armed with the new Henry repeating rifles, could hold off the entire Army detachment trailing the herd.

Finally, the man holding the tally book found the telegraph from Stanton, which Tom had folded up and kept in the back of the book. The man unfolded it carefully and read it aloud to the other three.

"Well, that's him, then," the reader said as he stuffed the letter back into the book, crumpling it in the process. He looked around at the surrounding landscape. "But he ain't here no more."

The other men grunted and grumbled. The leader, as it seemed he was, held his hands up, one of them still holding the book.

"Now, now. Let's not get all dismayed. At least we have this." He shook the book at them. "This time we've got our proof, and ain't nothin' ol' sourpuss Birch can say about it. Besides, we gotta be careful here, what will all those soldier boys jus' down the back trail. Now we're sure it's him, we'll have to find a better time an' place to do our job."

Tom gritted his teeth. "Birch," he muttered, but the name was not familiar to him. What could he possibly want? What did Tom have that was worth his life? Surely these men had been sent here to collect more than his tally book. He watched as the man shoved it into his pocket, then the quartet mounted up and rode off in the opposite direction. Only when they were out of sight did Tom dare to leave the cover of the trees and escape.

TWENTY-SEVEN

A Matter of Life or Death

1904, Moweaqua and Chicago

John Stanton could not pack his bag quickly enough. Though there was no train service in the middle of the night, by the time he reached the station it would be dawn, and he would take whatever line was heading out of town first.

"Are you sure this is the best idea?" Elizabeth asked him, standing in the doorway of his room. Tom stood just inside it, both of them in their dressing gowns, Tom's arms crossed over his chest.

"Yes," John said firmly. "And I think you two should do the same now that I've stupidly led them to your doorstep."

"Don't blame yourself." Tom sighed. "And where are we

going to go? This is our home, John. We're not leaving it, no matter who thinks they can rustle us out."

John stopped, a damp, folded shirt in his hands. Elizabeth had indeed done his washing, but he wasn't about to wait around until it dried. "Tom, aren't you in the least bit scared?"

The old man let out a dry laugh. "Scared? No. Blackwood's men have been after me for years. I couldn't always prove it was them, but…" He shrugged. "You learn to recognize your enemies in this world, John. Every man has them. But you can't let them see you're frightened."

John latched the top of his bag roughly and picked it up from the bed. "I don't plan to show them anything," he said, turning and crossing the room. He stopped in front of the desk in the corner, where he'd spread out some of his notes and writings. He bent over and picked up his other bag from the floor, then began carefully putting the papers in it. "And I certainly don't plan to stay in one place and be a sitting duck." He looked up at Elizabeth and Tom. "No offense to you both."

"None taken," Tom said absently. "Listen, John—"

"Please, don't," John interjected, pausing to stand up straight and hold out a hand to the old man. "Don't try to convince me to stay. Don't tell me things will be all right." He looked away for a moment, out to the stables, where everything seemed to have settled down. A couple of the men stood outside their quarters, rolling cigarettes from a shared Bull Durham tobacco sack, but otherwise the yard was dead.

"I will forever be grateful to you both for all you've done for me," John went on, his voice low. "Thanks to you, I finally have some answers about what happened to my father." He looked back at the couple. "That information is more valuable to me than life itself."

He went back to putting the papers in his bag.

"And what will you do with that information?" Elizabeth asked gently.

John paused again but did not look at them; his eyes were far away as he thought. Finally, he looked up. "I'll do what I know best," he said, his tone firm and resolute. "I'll expose Blackwood for the coward he is, and I'll do it right there in his own medium."

The older couple exchanged glances.

"John, do you mean to say you're going to publish what we've discussed?" Tom asked.

"Yes, that is what I intend. I have friends at both the Chicago *Tribune* and the *Tribune* in New York, and I can—"

"Hold on," Tom interrupted. "Can we just talk about this for a minute? I never meant—"

But John wouldn't let him finish. He slammed his hand down on the desk, the force of it sending a shuffle of papers to the floor. "Don't you want some sort of vindication? For all the years he's tormented you? For all he's taken from you?"

These words hung in the air between them, heavy and thick. The corners of Elizabeth's mouth turned down as she lowered her gaze to the floor. Tom's eyes, on the other hand, were suddenly full of fire.

"I would like nothing more than to see him burn!" he shouted, taking a step closer to John. "After all he's done to us, to my family…" He stepped back again, letting out a moan. "But I'm just not so sure this is the way to do it. We don't have any hard proof, John. It's all just hearsay, just some pieces we've been able to put together, and the puzzle is incomplete."

John shook his head. "Not in my mind, it's not. Our collective evidence is damning, as far as I'm concerned. Blackwood is devious, for sure, but he's not as smart as he thinks he is. And once the word is out there—once I put the idea into people's minds—"

"Aren't you afraid of him coming after you?" Elizabeth asked, looking up at John. "Like he's done to us? You know now how he can be toward people who—" She looked over at Tom. "Well, people who he thinks have somehow done him wrong."

John considered it for a moment but then shook his head once more. "If he comes after me, so be it. His enmity will be a small price to pay for clearing my father's name and exposing the torture Blackwood has put you both through."

Tom and Elizabeth watched as he finished putting the papers in his bag, then he picked it up and crossed the room once more, this time stopping right in front of Tom. He held out the bag to the older man.

"I need you to keep this for me," John said. "For safekeeping. In case anything happens to me. It's all my research, and I've added in some notes about what we have discussed. It's all there."

Tom looked at him for a moment, and then reached out and took the bag by the handle. It was heavy and pulled his arm abruptly down toward the floor.

"Will do," he told John, then he looked at Elizabeth, who nodded once. "I know just the place we can hide it for you… until you see fit to come back and get it."

When the train pulled into the Chicago station, it was just after high noon, and John was starved. He hadn't eaten since the Candys' tea time the previous afternoon, and his stomach rumbled as he jumped down onto the platform with his bag of clothes in tow. It felt extremely odd to be traveling without his briefcase full of notes, without its familiar weight to slow him down. But he knew it was in good hands. Wherever Tom's hiding place was, John was sure it was secure.

On the streets, the lunchtime crowd was out in droves. John made his way for a block or two and then ducked into a nearby automat—brand new, by the looks of it—for a sandwich, which he ate as he continued to walk. By the time he reached the *Tribune* offices all the way across town, he figured, George Hollings would have returned from his midday break. John couldn't wait to talk to his old friend about his findings and see how George could help him in his quest to take Blackwood down.

But at the office, he found no one there. Not George, not even his secretary who usually sat right outside his door. The nearby newsroom was quiet, too—everyone out on assignment, most likely. John remembered those days with a rueful grin.

"Well, I'll come back later," he said, though no one was there to hear it, and he searched around the secretary's desk for a pencil and paper. He'd leave a note for George, letting him know he was in town and that he needed to speak to him urgently. He leaned over and licked the pencil's lead, then lowered it down to write.

But he stopped as he heard the click of a gun cocking behind his head.

"Put down the pencil," a voice said. "And stand up slowly."

John did exactly as he was told, holding his hands up at his sides to show he wasn't armed. "Whatever you want," he said, "I can—"

"Turn around. Slowly."

Again he followed the man's orders, and when he turned he saw that the perpetrator was not alone. Behind him stood another three men, all bringing their handguns out of the holsters concealed under their broadcloth coats. All muzzles were now trained on John.

"What is it you…" he began to ask, but he let the question trail off as he got a glimpse into George's office, through the doorway in between the cohorts. Everything from the desk was on the floor: lamps, papers, binders, and pens. Every drawer was pulled out, and books had been pulled randomly from the shelves. They too lay on the floor, their spines broken and their pages torn.

"Where's George?" John asked quickly, his concern for himself suddenly gone. "What have you done with him?"

The gunman, however, did not reply. He simply stood there, pistol at the ready as he peered into John's face. He tilted his head left and then right, as if trying to get a better look.

"What's your name?" he finally asked, so close that John got a whiff of the character's atrocious breath.

He coughed. "Stanton. John Stanton."

The gunman sneered and looked back at his hangers-on. "Well, would you look at that," he said with a laugh. "We got two for the price of one."

"Look, where is—" John began again, but the gunman turned back with a downright evil snarl on his face, silencing him.

The man poked the nose of the gun into John's chest. "Give me the papers."

John just looked at him, his heart thumping so hard he felt it all over his body. "Wh-what papers?"

He pushed the gun harder. John could feel the cold metal gun barrel through his shirt.

"The papers," the man repeated. "All that stuff you wrote about Bir—"

"Boss!" one of the other men cried, and the leader whipped his head around, throwing him a venomous look. The younger man cowered. "Sorry, I just thought you might not want to, you know, name any names."

The main gunman glared at his crony for a while, sending him a silent message that he should keep his mouth shut the next time. Then he turned back to John.

"So, hand them over."

John cleared his throat as Tom's words rang out in his head: *You can't let them see you're frightened.* He straightened up and raised his chin.

"I do not know what you are talking about," he said, his delivery forced and clipped.

The man bore down with the gun again. "I said. Hand. Them. Over."

John took in a quick breath, hoping it didn't sound too much like a terrified gasp. "I don't have any papers," he said quickly. "All I have is that bag." He nodded toward it on the secretary's chair. "You're welcome to search it if you want."

The man glanced down at it, and then nodded to the nearest of the other gunmen, who stepped forward and unlatched the bag. He dug through, ripping out the contents and throwing them onto the floor. When the bag was empty, he looked up and shook his head.

"There ain't no papers in there, boss," he said, sounding just as perplexed as his expression looked. "So what do we do now? You said Birch told us to get the papers and then shoot 'im. If we can't find the papers, are we still supposed to finish him off?"

The main gunman closed his eyes and shook his head. "Why don't you just tell him all our names while you're at it?" he said to his underling, his voice rising with each word so that he was shouting by the end. Then he turned his attention back to John.

"I don't know what kind of game you're playing," the gunman said, "but like that idjit over there said, we do have our orders. So if you're not gonna turn them over..."

He gave his pistol one last shove, and it inched in between two of John's ribs. He winced in pain but gritted his teeth to keep from crying out.

"I...I can get them," he uttered. "I can get the papers. If you'll just let me—"

"All right. Thanks for lunch. Talk to you later!"

All heads snapped toward the sound of the voice in the hallway. John turned to look as well as he could with the gunman's weapon still pushed into his chest. Out of the corner of his eye, he saw shadows of people coming their way.

The gunman had seen them, too. "This ain't over," he told

John in a low, menacing voice, then, holstering his gun, he turned and motioned to his gang. Silently they slipped out of the office, scurrying down the hall in the opposite direction of the shadows.

"Hey, who are you?" the voice said, growing closer and closer until it reached the office door. There was a pause as the person looked around at the utter chaos the men had left behind. "What...My God, what's going on here?"

Still facing the back of the office, John let out a long breath. "George," he said as he turned around, relieved to find his old friend was unharmed.

"John," George said, his tone of voice expressing his disbelief. "What on Earth happened here? Are you all right? Who were those men?"

John Stanton knew then with no uncertainty that he had to deal out a blow of his own before they somehow stopped him.

TWENTY-EIGHT

A Great Man Falls

1865, Washington City

Edwin Stanton sat in his office, silently gazing out the window to the street outside. Spring had barely arrived and with it the requisite return to life, the joy that warmer weather always seemed to bring. Flower shoots sprang from the ground, and the beginnings of leaves coated the trees. Despite the war, which had seemed to consume everything in its wake, Mother Nature continued on as she always did—a fact that Edwin had found reassuring in all the years the battle had raged on.

This year, though, he had a different reason to celebrate the season. It had been only five days since General Lee had surrendered his massive army at the courthouse in Appomattox, Virginia, and he wasn't yet used to the idea that the war might actually be considered over. No truce had been worked out yet, no treaties signed, but the fact that Lee had given up the fight…just the thought of it brought a powerful surge to Edwin's chest, a feeling that he could jump up from his seat, throw open the window, and shout out to the heavens, "It's over! It's done at last!"

But he had to reserve his glee for a later time because nothing, in essence, had changed just yet. Washington City was still all but locked down, with only one point of egress— the Navy Yard Bridge leading into Maryland. One way in, one way out. The streets and shops and pubs were still congested with soldiers and journalists and politicians, elbowing and eyeing each other as they stood side by side. The city was a prison, it seemed, and the inmates were getting restless. Even Edwin felt stifled and tired most of the time, not just physically but mentally and emotionally as well.

And then there was *this*. He glanced over at the paper on his desk, the one Birch had given him. It had been folded and refolded, put into pockets and hidden in books in the weeks Edwin had possession of it. Now it lay open, the ink on it smudged and already beginning to fade.

"James Dunwoody Bulloch—financier," it said at the top of the list, then went on to name at least a dozen other men, all of whom Birch said had a hand in this so-called conspiracy, this latest plot to assassinate the president. Edwin knew Bulloch, or knew of him. A Confederate secret service agent based out of Liverpool, England, of all places, he was responsible for the blockade runners and commerce raiders that had kept hard currency flowing into the South. He'd served in the U.S. Navy for fifteen years and had become one of the war's most dangerous men, as far as Stanton was concerned. That he might be involved in this matter at hand now would not be very surprising. But he was out of Stanton's reach.

The rest of the names on the paper—some he recognized, some he didn't. Some had descriptions of their involvement—transportation, weaponry, and so on—and some were just names. He'd put those he could identify under surveillance. Was Birch unsure of those solitary names? The informant had given Edwin little explanation, just handed him the paper and told him to read it later. He'd also told Edwin to burn it after reading, but he had not been able to bring himself to do it. This was evidence, some tangible proof should any of it come to pass. It seemed too important to destroy.

After the list of names came another array, this of places where the deed might take place. The Capitol Building, the White House, while in a carriage between the two—the choices were vague and few, not enough to give the president any real warning. Edwin had mentioned it to him, of course; the man had a right to know when his life was allegedly in danger. And Stanton had increased Lincoln's secret service detail. Whereas he usually had a personal guard, sometimes two if the occasion called for it, he now had a dozen men skulking in the shadows, watching out for anything that seemed off. In general, the president was not impressed; he took this threat as he had all the others: in stride and as a necessary evil of his time in office.

Other than the extra security precautions, Edwin had not

advised the president to alter his routine in any way. Lincoln had been looking forward to taking the night off, and he continued on with that plan. He would have dinner out with Mary, his wife, and then head out to see a play. In fact right now, Edwin thought, checking his watch, he was probably just in his usual box at Ford's Theater, standing up to stretch his long legs during the intermission. Perhaps he—

The door to Stanton's office burst open. He turned with a jolt, shocked by the sudden clamor and excitement of it. Nothing like that ever happened in this quiet, administrative wing.

"Sir," cried a young man, breathless and red-cheeked, his curly hair flopping around atop his head. Edwin had seen him around the building before—he was an aide of some sort, though he wasn't quite sure to whom. "Sir, there's been an accident."

Edwin leaned forward on his desk, glancing at that paper again. "What sort of accident?" he asked, not sure he really wanted to hear the answer. "Who was involved?"

The young man blew out a quick, loud breath. Were those tears Edwin saw forming in his eyes?

"It's the president, sir," he said, and a strange heat poured into Edwin's gut. "And I misspoke. It wasn't an accident. Someone has shot him."

Everything seemed to be moving so quickly. Though the event had happened several hours ago, people still rushed in and out of the room—women with bandages and buckets of water, the president's staff members looking for information. Was he all right? Could they do anything to help?

"You can help by staying away!" Edwin barked at them, then turned back to Lincoln, who lay flat on the bed with no pillows and no blanket. Around him, the white sheets were splattered crimson, with an ever-growing pool of red beneath his head. Lincoln's eyes were rolled up in his head, his breathing shallow and faint.

"Hold on, Abraham," Edwin muttered, clutching the president's arm but getting no response. He looked up to the surgeon, a young army doctor who had happened to be on leave and attending the play when Lincoln had fallen in the theater. From what Stanton had been able to piece together, it seemed the culprit had somehow made it into the president's box seat, shot him point blank in the head, and then escaped by jumping down onto the stage and running out. The doctor had rushed to aid Lincoln and, finding him unresponsive, had him transported to this house across the street.

The surgeon caught his glance and shook his head. No further diagnosis needed to be given.

"Where is Parker?" Edwin shouted, looking around the room, his fury renewed. "Where was he when this happened?" He had stationed the man specifically at the door of Lincoln's theater box to guard the president for the duration of the play.

"Sir." It was the young aide again, the one who had gone to alert Stanton of this travesty. "Mr. Parker never showed up for duty this evening."

Stanton let out a low growl, a guttural noise originating in the depths of his despair. What had Parker been thinking? Edwin had given him strict orders not to leave Lincoln's side. "Find him," he said, turning his attention back to the president. Lincoln's body jerked slightly as the surgeon stuck tweezers in the entry wound behind his left ear, removing a blood clot to alleviate pressure. The bullet remained in his head, the doctor believed, lodged just above his right eye.

"Go and find him," Edwin said again to the young aide, turning his head halfway back. "Wherever he is, root him out and bring him here!"

The boy did not return that night, and truth be told, in time Edwin forgot about Parker. He would deal with the man—and deal with him harshly—when the time came. At the moment, there were only two things that really mattered: tending to the president and making sure the coward who had committed this crime was caught.

"What news?" he asked John Hay, Lincoln's secretary, who had been helping to organize the manhunt.

"He escaped on horseback, that much we know," Hay replied, referring to a paper full of scribbled notes he held in his hand. "And he made it across the Navy Yard Bridge. The sentries on duty let two riders pass without challenge."

Edwin shook his head. Was no one paying attention in this city anymore?

"I want Washington secured," he told Hay, his voice booming. "Nobody goes in or out from now on, until I say. I want military guards on all points, at all ports, whether they are open or closed. And get a hold of Lafayette Baker. Send him a telegram and tell him he is needed here immediately."

"Baker?" Hay questioned for verification.

"You heard me," Stanton shot back, well aware that his choice might not be a popular one. Lafayette Baker had enjoyed an illustrious career as a Union infiltrator during the war and had done so well Stanton had recruited him to be the head of the Union Intelligence Service and the National Detective Police, his undercover, antisubversive spy organization. Given his background, it was not surprising that over the years, Baker was accused of everything from treason to corruption, and he eventually had been caught tapping telegraphs coming into Stanton's office, for which Stanton demoted him.

Still, Baker was the smartest and most wily investigator Edwin had ever known. If anyone could head up this investigation and bring the perpetrator to justice, it would most certainly be he.

"I'll get right on it," John Hay replied, then with a nod of his head left the room. Edwin turned back to the president's bed.

"How is he doing?" he asked the doctor—a new one who had come in to relieve the army surgeon.

This one too simply shook his head. "I believe he's comfortable enough." He looked down at Lincoln's nearly still form. "But it's only a matter of time."

Edwin dropped down on his chair again, the one he'd kept stationed at the bedside for the last several hours. Again, he put his hand on the president's arm but gently now, the urgency in his actions completely gone. He sat like this for some time, for hours that passed like minutes, until finally the inevitable came. He began to hear the death rattle in the president's chest, the sign that his lungs were filling up with fluid.

He got up and went to the door. "Come in, come in," he whispered to the others in the hall, the assistants and cabinet members who had come to help or simply to stand vigil for their leader. They all looked at one another for a moment, unsure of what to make of his sudden passivity, since he'd been barking orders at them for most of the night so far.

"Please," he said, then waved his hands at them, beckoning them in quietly and quickly. They filed in and made a circle around the bed, standing two and three deep.

"Let us pray," Stanton said and was the first to drop down on his knees. Everyone else followed suit. He folded his hands together and pressed them hard against his forehead then led the group in a slow, emotional recitation of the Lord's Prayer and Psalm 23.

When he looked up again, after the last amen, the president was gone. Lincoln's chest no longer rose and fell; the rattling had been silenced. The doctor leaned over him and closed his eyes.

"There lies the most perfect ruler of men the world has ever known," Edwin said, his voice breaking on every word. "Now he belongs to the ages."

All men of greatness are misunderstood at one point or another in their lives. Edwin, though he never would have called himself a great man, tried to remind himself of this: that with Lincoln gone, and with so much responsibility for the civil government falling on his shoulders, he was bound to make an enemy or two. This was perfectly fine with him. Edwin had never been known as a people pleaser, as someone who cared about the opinions of others. Some said he had been too quick to institute martial law in Washington City once the war had begun; others held that he was responsible for the president's death, as it was his personally-appointed guards who had abandoned their posts, leaving Lincoln vulnerable.

Perhaps they were right about that. It wasn't as if the thought hadn't occurred to Stanton himself. What if he had sent another guard? Or put more than one on the detail? Would things have gone differently? Could he really have stopped that train once it was in motion?

Regardless, he had a job to do, and he would do it no matter who objected and no matter what the general public—and, often, his own peers in the government—thought of him.

As soon as Lafayette Baker had arrived, he had sent men into Maryland to pursue Lincoln's assassin, who Stanton now knew as John Wilkes Booth, an actor and, it seemed, a coconspirator in a greater plot. Just as Birch had intimated there would be, there had been many hands on the trigger that sent the bullet into Lincoln's head. Within two days, Baker had arrested four and had the names of two more, Booth included. A week after that, the gunman had been shot himself during an apprehension attempt.

Baker had searched the man's body and found a diary, which he'd turned over to Stanton. In it were pages and pages of information, laying everything bare. He sat with it in his office for days, just reading over everything: the names of the coconspirators, their roles in the plot, and notes on every conceivable angle to carrying it out.

And then there was his name. Over and over, on page after

page. Outlines of his meetings with Birch, including dates and locations. Notes on the information Birch had fed him.

Was it all a setup? he wondered, laying down the diary on his desk and staring absently through the warped windowpane. He thought back to his first meeting with Birch at that tavern, about how the younger man had come up to him so confidently, so sure that he would take the bait. And he had, hadn't he? He'd fallen for it hook, line, and sinker, always believing his informant was on his side, never once considering that maybe Birch had been playing for another team. In his fervor to rout corruption from the military's ranks, had Stanton put everything else—and everyone else—in harm's way?

This wasn't the first time the thought had occurred to Edwin. In fact, it had been plaguing him of late—so much that he'd set Baker on the case, directing him to go to New York and find out the truth about Birch. Did he work for the *Tribune*? Had Greeley really sent him on his alleged assignment to cover the war? Turned out he did, and he had. Baker found nothing untoward, nothing that pointed to Birch—real name Blackwood—being some sort of criminal, someone who could and would orchestrate a plot to kill the president. He was an upstanding, even respected reporter just following his editor's directions. Did those directions include volunteering to pass surreptitious information to the secretary of war? Baker found no evidence either way, and of course Greeley wouldn't say. Even if he had, what would Edwin have done with it? Now that this diary had come to light, there was no way to point a finger at Birch without also pointing it at himself.

He thought too about the criticisms and outright condemnations that had been leveled at him since the time of the president's death. Lincoln's bodyguard, who had not shown up that night, was one of Stanton's men—specifically appointed by him, to be exact. Edwin had also personally appointed the troops at the Navy Yard Bridge who had not followed orders, allowing Booth and his coconspirator to pass right through. Only the secretary of war had the kind of power it would take to allow this travesty to occur—while the city was under martial law, no less. That was what people were saying: that he had not just the authority, but the will to have cleared the way for the assassination and the damnable coward's escape.

None of it was true, of course. And, Edwin thought, there was no sense in beating himself up for it now. What was done had been done. There would be no going back.

Still there was the diary to consider. What if someone found out about it? What if Baker talked? The book had Edwin's name all over it, and who would believe that was merely a coincidence?

After one last long look at the journal, he reached over quickly and picked it up again, then turned to the first page with his name on it. He hesitated for only a moment before grasping it and tearing it out. Then he found the next, and the next, until there was a pile of eighteen pages stacked on top of his desk. He looked at them, repelled by the sight. As soon as he got home, he would burn them in an ashcan. Not because he had anything to hide but because, as he learned over again every single day, if he gave people an inch, they would take a yard. All his detractors needed was to learn that he had ties with a member of the conspiracy, and his life as he knew it would be over. And, more important, he would be in no position to bear on his own shoulders Abraham's burden of holding the Union together, which was his greatest priority.

TWENTY-NINE

The Scandal Is Revealed

1904, New York City

"Bill," John said, looking over his shoulder, back down the street in front of 154 Printing House Square. It was two in the morning, and scant few other souls were out—just a carriage driver here and there, most of them snoozing in between fares. "Can you hurry, please? I don't want anyone to see us here."

"Yes, yes," Bill replied as he picked through a series of keys hanging from a wide, metal ring. "Sorry, John. I'm just nervous, and it's making me—oh, there it is!" He held up one long, silver skeleton key that gleamed in the light of the gas streetlamp.

"Excellent," John said, trying to hurry his friend along without sounding too rude or pushy about it. Bill was, after all, doing him an enormous favor. "Let's get inside, then."

Bill smiled as he fit the key into the door's lock and turned it, then he cringed as he pushed the door open and it let out a low, moaning creak.

"Sorry, sorry," he whispered as they entered the building through the direct entrance to the printing room. "Been meaning to put some grease on that. Just haven't gotten around to it yet."

"It's fine," John replied, crossing his arms and looking up and down the darkened room to make sure they were alone. Although if anyone were there, he wouldn't be able to see them anyway.

"Let me just—" Bill said, then leaned over and eased on a gas lamp mounted on the wall. Then he turned back and pushed the door closed. The noise it made now echoed through the space.

"There." Bill turned to John with another weary smile on his face. In the lamplight, he looked tired and rightfully so—he had left this place only two hours earlier, having finished the layout of the early edition, and would have to be back in only four more. "Come on. This way."

He put a hand on John's shoulder and guided him across the back of the room, lighting another lamp here and there as they made their way. In the small pools of light the lamps cast, John could see the outlines of the massive machines that turned out the morning and evening editions of the *New-York Tribune* on a daily basis.

"I couldn't leave everything set up, unfortunately," Bill said, leading John over to a row of tables where, he knew from past visits here, the printers laid out each page of the newspaper to be printed. Bill bent over, looking along the shelves below the tables. "But it shouldn't be too difficult to find the one we—there it is!"

He knelt down and slid out a template for one of the news-paper pages, all laid out with the metal-letter slugs he had made earlier in the day on his Linotype machine. He put it on the table and ran a hand over it. "Page four," he said, then turned to John with a wink. "Just as we agreed. No one ever looks past page three before we go to print."

John nodded. They had discussed this the previous eve-ning, when he had first gotten into town. He'd gone straight to call on Bill, to ask for his help with this scheme. John had an article he needed to print, but nobody could know about it until the edition was released. Bill had been confounded—at least until John shared with him what the article was about. Then his former coworker was eager to help.

"We always do a test run," he'd explained to John, keeping his voice hushed as though they were in his own living room. "And someone will look at the first page to make sure it's all in line. Sometimes, depending upon who does the check, he'll open it up and look at pages two and three as well." He'd shaken his head then. "But no one—no one—ever looks at page four. We simply don't have the time. It's get it off the press, check it quick, and get those machines running again. Can't miss a deadline with Blackwood, right?"

John had laughed at the time, though he'd found no humor in the joke. Not given what he was about to undertake.

"Thank you, Bill," he said now, watching as the other man

took a section of slugs out of the template. "Are you…are you sure you want to do this?"

Bill stopped and looked at him. "I told you last night, John, anything to help my friend. And if it manages to bring Blackwood down in the process, well, then I'd say this was time well spent."

John nodded as Bill went back to his task, taking out the rows of metal letters, laying them on the table one by one. "But you know you could lose your job over this." He hadn't mentioned that part of it yet; he'd been avoiding it, actually. But he couldn't go through with this with the thought weighing on his conscience.

Bill, done with the slugs, wiped his hands on his already ink-stained pants as he looked at John. "*Could* lose my job? Oh, I most certainly will. But John, it would be an honor to be axed for such a noble cause."

Then he let out an uproarious laugh, so bold that John put his fingers to his lips, gesturing to him to be quiet.

"Shh, right," Bill said, his nervous laughter abating, then put a hand on John's shoulder and guided him over to the row of Linotypes. He stopped in front of his usual machine—the one he sat in front of day in and day out, laying out each story for the newspaper letter by letter—and sat down. He gestured toward the chair at the next machine. John pulled it over and took a seat.

"Well." Bill ran a hand over the keys of his machine, dusting them off. "Are we ready to begin?"

John did not hesitate. He reached into his coat's inside pocket and took out a sheaf of papers folded into thirds. He opened them, sat up straight in his chair, and cleared his throat. Then, very slowly, so Bill would not miss a single syllable, he began to read aloud.

SECRETARY OF WAR STANTON CLEARED IN LINCOLN ASSASSINATION

Tribune Editor-in-Chief Instead Implicated in Multiple Conspiracies

New York, NY, September 5—In a shocking turn of events, John Stanton, son of the late Secretary of War Edwin Stanton and formerly a reporter for the New-York Tribune, has come forth with evidence that his father had no involvement in the assassination of President Abraham Lincoln, as has been popularly believed. Instead, he has found, there was a vast network of individuals who conspired at the time to kill the president and frame the elder Mr. Stanton for their heinous deed—including but not limited to T. Burton Blackwood, the editor-in-chief of this very newspaper.

It is well known that during the Civil War, Secretary Stanton utilized every measure he could to rout out corruption in the military. Among these methods was his ongoing use of spies who were able to infiltrate the army's ranks and report back to Stanton on any improprieties they learned of or witnessed. One such spy was a young journalist who went by the name of Thomas Birch and claimed to be from the New-York Tribune. According to Mr. Tom Candy, a cattle driver who knew both parties, Thomas Birch was actually T. Burton Blackwood acting under an assumed name.

Through his position as a clandestine operative for the secretary of war, Blackwood, as Birch, fed Edwin Stanton hints about the assassination prior to its happening, in an attempt to implicate Stanton and draw attention away from the real culprits. After Lincoln's death, he continued to spread misinformation about Stanton's involvement, claiming that he had called off his own guards to give the assassin, John Wilkes Booth, access to the president. In reality, the guards were, unbeknownst to Secretary Stanton, pawns of the conspiracy, and that was why they had disobeyed his orders, having received other false orders to stay away from their posts on the night Lincoln was killed.

The presidential assassination was not the only conspiracy of which Blackwood was a part. In addition, he has gone after the aforementioned Tom Candy, who is known for his historic Texas-to-New York cattle drive in 1854. When Tom wed Mr. Blackwood's friend and unrequited love interest, Elizabeth Mason, in 1856, Blackwood swore a secret vendetta against Candy, and still to this day sends men to stalk Candy and make attempts on his life. Once Mr. Candy and the younger Mr. Stanton met, Blackwood sent his thugs after them both. Tom Candy also believes that Blackwood was behind a train derailment that killed Candy's nineteen-year-old son, William.

Blackwood had read enough.

He dropped the newspaper, open to page four, down on the top of his desk, then took off his glasses and tossed them in the same direction. They landed on Stanton's article, the lenses magnifying the words *multiple conspiracies*.

"Stanton will pay for this," he muttered, propping his elbows on the edge of the desk and running his fingers through his thinning, salt-and-pepper hair. "And whoever helped him." His voice rose as he spoke until he shouted, "All of them will pay for this!"

Out in the newsroom, the reporters all glanced over toward his office. They were gathered around each other's desks and leaning against the walls, all of them reading that infernal article. They eyed him with outright contempt—a jury convicting him before he had even been allowed a trial.

He went back to muttering to himself. "Stanton…never should have hired him…knew he'd be trouble from the start."

He sat back and closed his eyes. But instead of peace all he found were a myriad of pictures floating through his mind: that eager look on Edwin Stanton's face whenever Blackwood showed up to give him information, the lustrous sheen of Elizabeth's dark hair when she was a young woman, the sparkle in her eyes when she had looked at Tom Candy for the first time, when Blackwood had introduced the two.

A low growl emitted from his throat, and he let it come, let it grow until it was a full-fledged roar and he was standing behind his desk, arms outstretched, fists clenched in rage. In the newsroom, one by one the reporters began to slink away, putting on their coats and hats as they scurried from the office like a pack of mice.

"Go ahead and run!" Blackwood shouted after them. He didn't need them anyway. He was T. Burton Blackwood, the most powerful man in journalism. He could replace them all on a moment's notice. Why, he could pick up the phone on his desk and in an hour—

He sat back down, eyes falling on the article once more.

Who am I fooling? he thought. Certainly it wasn't himself. No matter how vehemently he could deny all that John Stanton had written about him, no matter how loudly he could say it was untrue, there was that old saying—once the bell has rung, you can't unring it. The early edition had already hit the streets. It was only a matter of time before his phone started ringing and the questions poured in. Before the tide of public opinion not only turned against him but swallowed him whole.

No longer would he be T. Burton Blackwood, editor-in-chief of the *New-York Tribune*, one of the most respected men in the nation. Now he would be nothing but a former war spy, a conspirator in the plot to assassinate Abraham Lincoln. All his power, all his money, all the years he had spent building his personal empire, and none of it meant a thing anymore.

He groaned, his gaze cast down on the article.

"John Stanton," he read aloud. "Tom Candy. Edwin Stanton."

And then again he closed his eyes. He knew deep down these men were finally getting their revenge and their vindication…and he was ruined.

Everything somehow seemed brighter to John. Sitting outside at a sidewalk café in New York City, the streets had never looked so alive to him, so full of life and promise. The people's faces as they passed looked more animated than usual, the sound of their chatter and laughter like music to his ears. The sun, warm and comforting, shone down on his shoulders, which felt as if they had been relieved of a very great weight.

"The truth shall set you free," he said, then glanced over at Bill, who sat on the other side of the small table, taking a sip from a tall glass of iced tea laced with fresh mint leaves.

"If that's the case," he said, setting down the drink, "then you are the freest man on Earth, my friend." He paused. "And so am I, I suppose, quite literally!" He let out a loud, sharp laugh, and John joined him, though a pang of guilt hit his chest.

"I'm sorry about your job," he said. "I—"

But Bill waved away the thought. "I volunteered to help

you, remember? I could have said no. And I resigned simply because I was going to be fired anyway. I wanted to leave on *my* terms, not Blackwood's."

John nodded. He understood that sense of pride, of standing up for what was right. "Well, I know you didn't have to do any of it, so thank you. Anyway, with the firestorm we've created here and in Washington, I dare say you'll come out a hero for what you've done."

Bill raised his eyebrows and drew down the corners of his mouth. "A hero, huh? I like the sound of that."

The two fell into a silence again, John watching the people go by once more, Bill reading the afternoon edition of a rival's paper. It had been only two days since their article had hit the streets in the *Tribune*, but its impact had been substantial. There'd been a call for a congressional inquiry into the conspiracy surrounding President Lincoln's death, and Blackwood was in hiding. There were rumors he might end up leaving the country.

"So what will you do now?" John asked, turning back to his friend.

Bill sat back in his seat and folded his hands behind his head. "Well, I've contacted our old friend George Hollings, and he's made me a very generous offer to join him out in Chicago."

Now it was John's turn to look surprised. "Oh, really? Well, I never thought I'd see the day Bill Winston agreed to leave New York City."

Bill nodded. "I surprised myself as well. I do love this place…" He looked around them for a moment. "But I do think it's time for a change." He took another drink of his iced tea, folded up his paper, and laid it on the table. "And what are *your* plans now that your long quest for justice is over?"

John grinned. He felt his cheeks get hot. "Well, let's just say that I have something in mind."

"Oh, Mother." Caroline put down the stack of heavy, white ceramic dinner plates with a clatter on the kitchen table. "Don't be so pessimistic."

At the stove, Elizabeth stirred the boiling water in a large pot, a mix of potatoes and carrots bobbing around inside. "All I'm saying is that something like that changes a person." She looked over her shoulder at her daughter. "John Stanton is a very nice young man. But there's a sadness about him after all he's been through. Couldn't you see it in his eyes?"

Caroline, leaning against the table, gazed out the window, her thoughts now miles away. "His eyes," she said, remembering how green John's were, the right one with a small fleck of brown.

"Caroline," Elizabeth said, drawing her back to the kitchen. "Caroline, I just don't want you to get caught up in waiting for something that's not going to happen."

"What's going to happen?" Tom asked as he entered the room, leaning on a cane as he walked. All the excitement of the last several days had left his old body feeling weak and tired.

Elizabeth put a lid on the pot and turned around, wiping her hands on her apron as she spoke. "Caroline was talking about how excited she'll be when John comes back to retrieve his papers." She eyed her daughter. "Says she wants to hear *all* about his story, from beginning to end."

Tom eased himself down into a chair. "And what's wrong with that?" He looked at his wife for a moment. "I'd rather say I'm looking forward to seeing the young fellow again myself."

Elizabeth shook her head. "You're just as bad as she is." She turned around again and headed to a cupboard to retrieve a bowl. "John Stanton is not coming back. You two mark my words. He is a young man still, and he has a life to get on with. Now he's done what he set out to do, perhaps he'll have a chance to—oh, I don't know. Meet a nice young lady and settle down at last."

As Elizabeth ladled the vegetables from the pot into a bowl, Caroline and her father looked at one another. Tom reached out, squeezed his daughter's hand, and winked at her. She smiled.

"He'll come back," she said. "You wait and—"

A knock on the front door cut her off. The three of them in the kitchen looked around at one another.

"Well?" Tom asked at last. "Who's going to answer it? Because it's certainly not me. I can't seem to move faster than a turtle today, what with…"

His voice receded as Caroline drifted into the hallway, the only sound in her ears her thumping heart. The foyer was dark, only a few beams of late afternoon light coming in through the high window above the door.

"Yes?" she said from inside the door. "Who is it?"

At first, there was no response. Only silence, and then the thump of what might have been a suitcase setting down on the wooden planks of the porch.

"Hello?" she called a bit louder, and someone outside cleared his throat.

"Caroline?" The response was muffled, the tone of voice unsure. But it gave her a funny, fluttery feeling in her chest. She hesitated only a moment before standing back and throwing the door the entire way open.

"John," she replied and stepped forward, right into his arms.